Hiddensee

Also by Gregory Maguire

Hiddensee

A Tale of the Once and Future Nutcracker

Gregory Maguire

WILLIAM MORROW
An Imprint of HarperCollins*Publishers*

HarperCollins
PUBLISHERS
Since 1817

FIRST EDITION

DESIGNED BY WILLIAM RUOTO

Library of Congress Cataloging-in-Publication Data has been applied for.

ISBN 978-0-06-268438-7 (hardcover)
ISBN 978-0-06-283711-0 (B&N Black Friday edition)
ISBN 978-0-06-283709-7 (B&N exclusive edition)
ISBN 978-0-06-283708-0 (B&N exclusive signed edition)
ISBN 978-0-06-283710-3 (BAM signed edition)

17 18 19 20 21   LSC   10 9 8 7 6 5 4 3 2 1

For Barbara Harrison

In honor of her love for Greece, our homeland

I will remind the reader that the perplexities into which the poor old gods fell at the time of the final triumph of Christendom . . . offer striking analogies to former sorrowful events in their god-lives; for they found themselves. . . . compelled to flee ignominiously and conceal themselves under various disguises on earth. . . . several, whose shrines had been confiscated, became wood-choppers and day-laborers in Germany.

—Heinrich Heine, "Gods in Exile"

For some reason, we know not what, his childhood . . . lodged in him whole and entire. He could not disperse it. And therefore, as he grew older, this impediment at the center of his being, this hard block of pure childhood, starved the mature man of nourishment. . . . But since childhood remained in him entire, he could do what no one else has ever been able to do—he could return to that world; he could recreate it, so that we too become children again.

—Virginia Woolf, "Lewis Carroll," in *The Moment and Other Essays*

Most of the ancient groves are gone, sacred to Kuan Yin
And Artemis, sacred to the gods and goddesses
In every picture book the child is apt to read.

—Robert Hass, "State of the Planet"

do you know what it's like to live
someplace that loves you back?

—Danez Smith, "summer, somewhere"

Contents

Part One

A Household Tale

I.

Once there was a boy who lived in a cabin in the deep woods with no one for company but an old woman and an old man.

In the goat shed one day, the old woman said, "Watch and you'll see where life comes from."

The boy looked where she was pointing. With an expression of disgust and boredom, a cat pulsed a sac from between her hind legs. The mother cat chewed the silvery slipcase, unwrapping her kitten. It twitched and lay there, as exhausted as if it had swum its way to shore. "Was I so damp and furry when I arrived?" asked the boy. He was still very young.

"I've told you a dozen times. You're a foundling, Dirk. You didn't grow inside me. We collected you in a basket."

"What kind of basket?" This was the only question he could think of.

She ignored that. "In those days, you could hardly go into the woods for mushrooms or acorns without tripping over some abandoned brat. A nuisance, to be sure."

"Don't put folly in the boy's head," said the old man.

The boy had gone back to watching the mother cat. She licked the transparent webbing into ribbons. Another kitten emerged from her. A third. They stretched and settled. One of them turned its head toward Dirk. Its eyes were closed. "Hello," said Dirk. "Where did you come from?" He was still young enough, back then, to expect it would answer.

The kitten opened its mouth, but the old man said, "Come away and give them some privacy. It's cruel to scare them so early in their lives."

So Dirk never learned what the kitten had been about to reply.

The old woman. Here's what she was like. Her face was scored with lines from working outside in all weathers. She wore dull clothes in colors that had forgotten to be colorful. It didn't matter, she hadn't much to celebrate by way of looks. Her nervous eyes were bulbous, her lips dry and inclined to pursing. When she hitched up her skirts to wash her calves once a month, however, her lower legs and ankles were smooth and pretty. Dirk always found this confounding. "One day you'll be too old to watch me wash myself," she said. "Towel."

Was she loving or was she harsh? Dirk didn't know. A child who lives in a hut in the forest can't answer such a question. She was as she was, the way the wild boar is a wild boar, or the butterfly a butterfly. She thinned her ale with spring water. She cooked almost enough for supper every night. Quite often her bread refused to rise. Her family ate it anyway, and gave thanks—a thanks both rueful and brief.

"If we lived nearer the village, you could send me for baked bread," Dirk told her.

"You're too young. When you're older, Papi will show you the way. But mind me, if you ever set out on your own, you'll get lost. It'll be up to you to find yourself. We won't come looking for you."

But you already found me, he wanted to reply.

"He's not going off," said Papi. "Don't put notions into his head."

"What head is that?" she replied, cuffing Dirk above the ear, but affectionately.

So next, Papi.

He was old, too; he was the old man to her old woman. His pathetic beard was the brown of iced mud. Dirk didn't know if the old man had been born with that hunched shoulder or if the ailment had come from years carrying an axe.

He was a woodcutter. He maintained four cutting stations some distance away in the deep forest, one in each direction from the lonely waldhütte where they lived. Upon a tree at each station he'd hammered a wooden box. Beneath the box he left trimmed logs and stacked kindling. If passersby wanted tinder for their ovens or hearths, they could take what they needed and, in exchange, drop some coins in the box. Sometimes they took more than they paid for. Sometimes the portion they got was a little greener than would be useful. It evened out.

The old man was spare of speech. When he opened his mouth it was often to contradict the old woman. He might have been cross by nature or maybe his lumpy shoulder gave him bother. He didn't like to wring the neck of a barnyard chicken when one was needed for the pot. He made the old woman do that job. But once during a hard winter, when a rogue wolf came prowling, he managed to trap it and kill it with his axe.

The wolf bled to death under the moon. In the morning, the old woman broke off a portion of frozen blood. It was like a cracked brown plate. She brought it home to thicken the evening stew.

"Papi, get out the carving knife if we're to have sausage meat from that hairy old sinner," she said.

"I'd rather drag the carcass to the village and sell it, and buy something already minced and spiced," he replied.

"No one would give a pfennig or a ham bone for that mangy creature. You are a coward still. I'll butcher the beast myself if you won't."

"Let me come with you to the village, Papi," said Dirk.

"No one's going to the village," shouted the old woman. She named the rules. "Nobody here knows where it is." That was a regular lie to make Dirk shut up—they all knew that the old man went for provisions every now and then.

The old woman hung the wolf by its back legs so it could finish bleeding into a bucket. The chickens and the barn cat and the cow didn't seem to mind.

As the dead beast twisted on its truss, sometimes the upside-down head turned toward Dirk, who sat on the milking stool and watched. The eyes had grown filmy and red. Some flies that wintered in the barn crawled upon the wolf's snout, but the corpse eyes didn't blink. What are you seeing behind that calm red death, wondered Dirk. Where are you now that you aren't bothered by the twitching of flies?

Dirk. The old man and the old woman. Birth and death. Birth and death and the woods all around. And questions that never got answered, because they couldn't easily be asked.

2.

You might be expecting to hear something about Dirk himself now. But what is there to say?

He was a boy who was short when he was younger but grew a

little bit each year. He had a hand at the end of each arm, and above his nose, two eyes spaced evenly enough apart not to be upsetting. If he was outside, his hair color changed from dusty wheat in the summer noontimes to red-gold in sunset light. When inside, his hair was more brown, like an old master sketch done in Conté crayon. His incidental smile, if it broke through, was pleasing because it was rare. He smelled like dirty clothes when his clothes were dirty. On bathing day he smelled like raw boy.

He didn't look like the old woman or the old man, not only because he was a foundling, but for that other, obvious reason: When does a boy ever really look like an adult until he gets there?

If he gets there.

The old man taught him his catechism and his letters. The old woman taught him how every soup begins with an onion. The old man showed him how to carve a potato, and said one day he might get a knife of his own that could carve wood, but not today.

In the long, dark winter evenings, while the old man shaped animals and other figures from knots of pine, the old woman told Dirk stories.

This made the old man impatient. "It's a sin to tell a lie," he said.

"Another sin to deny the truth," she replied.

The stories involved princesses and disguises, castles and enchantments, third sons out to make their way in the world, ancient witches, cunning magicians, animal patrons and guides. Almost all of the stories started with the death of a mother in childbirth. "Is that how my mother died?" he asked the old woman one night.

The old man went out of the waldhütte and slammed the door, even though frost was in the air.

"No one knows his own story, and that's the way of it, unless you make it up yourself," she said at last. "Now, that girl in the red cape; there's a wolf coming along. Just like the one we made sausage out of. Listen to what happens next."

He listened.

And all this was in 1808, or so, in Bavaria.

3.

When Dirk had grown about as tall as a broom handle, he awoke one night to the sound of muttering below. He rolled on his pallet of straw in the loft and put his ear to a crack in the boards. The old man was fighting with the old woman. Dirk picked out a few words—"necessary"—"feeble"—"scarcity." Whispering can disguise the shape of syllables, but not of mood. Dirk heard fear, and blaming.

It reminded him of something. But of what did he have experience but this hut in the shrouded forest, these two elderly keepers? Only the occasional Bible story that Papi read slowly by firelight. Elijah in disguise, Isaac and Abraham. Or the tales that the old woman told, of the goose that laid the golden eggs, of the twelve brothers turned into swans. The stepmother who stewed her children and served them to her husband for supper.

A thin catalog by which to reference human charity and suffering.

The old woman's sniveling gave way at last to an aching silence. None of the old man's heavy snoring, which meant he was lying awake uncomforted, staring into the dark.

In the morning, the old man said, "Dirk, today I will take you into the forest and teach you to fell a tree. It is time . . ."

He did not say what it was time for.

Dirk had always wanted to go with the old man and learn his skill. The old woman had always forbidden it. Today she turned to the iron pot over the hearth and said nothing, neither blessing the day's plan nor prohibiting it.

Before they left, she wrapped bread and cheese in a muslin and pressed it into Dirk's hands. "Mind your way forward and find your way back," she said to them once they were over the threshold and through the gate. Did her voice quaver because her little foundling was growing up? Dirk glanced back. She was not there waving. The door was shut.

4.

They walked in silence for what seemed like half the morning. For a while the branches of pines were low with wet. It was a day in autumn. One of those bridging days between brightness and gloom, though which direction it was headed—which direction Dirk was headed, gloom or brightness—was unclear.

He followed the old man, keeping his eyes on the axe head swaying behind the old man's shoulder.

The boy was still wondering of what the argument last night reminded him.

Once, according to rumor, Napoleon's armies had come nearby. On their way to the Battle of Ulm, perhaps. Or the French emperor was said personally to be driving his men forward to Russia. The old man and the woman were unclear on the specifics, but they fretted how best to stay out of the way. To the boy's regret, no stray infantry battalion came anywhere near them. No runaway soldier, not even a lost bugle boy. Still the old man and the old woman had argued about danger. Fearing conscription, the old man had huddled close to home. The axe, holidaying in the shed, had grown a cobweb beard.

Or perhaps Dirk was only remembering the old woman's stories. In her repertoire, starving parents abandoned their children in the woods with shocking frequency.

Dirk didn't want to be sold to an army or left alone in the woods. He didn't know if the old man would think of such things. Perhaps last night's discussion had only been about whether Dirk was old enough to swing an axe. He was still young. But not as young as he had been.

They came to an upland stand of trees, very dark and dense though a canopy of yellow foliage crowned their heads. From stout trunks, muscled limbs split into elbows, forearms, and fingers. No sound of bird chatter here, or the chitter of insects, either. Not even the tidal sweep of wind in leaves.

"If we are here, we are here," said the old man. "Now I will show you a blow so great you won't soon forget it. Stand there, and don't move."

Dirk did as he was bid.

The old man unshouldered the axe. He held it in front of himself with two hands. "Here is how you hold the axe. Imagine the handle is divided into three equal portions, like three sausages the same size. Place your right hand here, and turn it so. Your left hand otherwise. Do you see? How well you hold the axe determines your swing and the force of your blow. You can do a lot of damage with a good blow."

Dirk tried to understand.

The old man said, "First we clear the lower limbs. This helps us to see higher, and determine the best direction for the tree to drop. This tree here, it is not so old. A young but sturdy specimen. We will start with this."

With swift strikes and loud, the old man trimmed the lowest branches. Soon all that was left below was a pole of a trunk, bleeding sap. Above, a heaviness of leaves still clouded the sky, though some had been shaken off under the assault.

The old man wiped sweat off his forehead. His eyes were wide. More to himself than to the boy, he said, "A cruel truth: Life demands death."

"Now will you show me how?"

"There's making and there's killing. I never brought down a tree but that I snapped a small limb of it to carve into a figure. You kill and you make. What will I make of you?"

The boy took a step back. "But it's my turn now."

"I can't," said the old man, "I must." He turned all around in a circle, as if the boy might be gone when the old man faced forward again. Dirk waited.

"Papi, let me try."

"Where's the harm there? The moment is now or it comes in a moment, almost the same thing." He handed the axe to Dirk. "I need to catch my breath and my nerve. You might as well have a hand at it."

They exchanged places. Dirk picked up the axe. He knew how heavy it was, because he'd often shifted it around the woodshed. Still, he'd never hoisted it chest-height before. He staggered under its weight.

"Don't imagine you'll slay the tree in one stroke," said the old man. "The first strike is just to make a mark. Swing at an angle from shoulder-height to waist. Gravity will add force to how you land the blow. Keep your grip firm at impact or you'll lose control. You'll have calluses in two minutes, but then, they won't trouble you for long."

He stood, that old man, one hand in the pocket of his jerkin, fingering his beads, the other raking his beard in a contemplative gesture.

Dirk tried to fashion his stance as the old man had stood. Left foot forward, right leg back and braced. The wood held its breath.

Making or killing. What an argument to have.

He swung. The axe head wavered in a half-circle around Dirk, but it picked up speed. As it came near to burying itself in the tree trunk—or to glancing off it, more likely—something twitched at the roots of the tree. As if the tree were flinching. It was a mouse with six baby mice along her flanks.

The mother mouse looked up at Dirk. The baby mice all tucked their heads under her legs and belly. As Dirk veered, the axe head wobbled, and the whole tool flew out of his grasp. The axe drove itself in the old man's leg just below the knee.

5.

An unholy aria of muffled wailing and laughing from the old man. Dirk could hardly make out the words. "You bloody moron, and who can blame you," the old man said, as far as Dirk could tell. "Oh, owww, a pox on you." The axe fell out of his leg to the ground. Beneath the torn legging, a flap of hairy shin turned slick with blood. "Your scarf, boy, before I bleed to death."

Dirk handed over the muffler. Wincing and cursing, the old man tightened a tourniquet just below the knee. "Did you mean to kill me?"

Dirk couldn't speak. The blood was luscious until it matted the cloth, then it turned the color of dirt. "I'll kill that axe," the boy finally said.

"Help me up."

But the old man couldn't stand. He collapsed with a cry of pain. "The bone may be fractured. Find me"—a wordless moan—"find me something to use as a crutch. A staff, Dirk, a cane."

"I'll hold you up."

"You'll falter. Look for something to the height of my underarm—something up to your chin would be the right height."

Dirk scrambled. The undergrowth supplied only spindly wands, too supple to provide support. "There's nothing near."

"If you can fell me, you can bring down the damn tree. It's time to do it. Take your old friend the axe." The old man was beginning to fade from loss of blood. "Finish off the tree I chose, then trim a straight limb from it."

The old man closed his eyes and opened them again. "Aim for the center of the trunk. First stroke, chop straight in, next, downward from above. Let the chips fly. You're making a gap in the tree so it will fall on itself, of its own weight." His eyes closed again.

Dirk went to work with an energy born of terror. He was sorry to have hurt the old man, but he was more concerned with not being abandoned in the woods.

He hoped the mouse and her babies were safe somewhere else.

After a time he turned to ask Papi how he was doing. The old man had slipped sideways. Only a fainting spell, wished the boy, and not the final sleep.

Perhaps what was needed wasn't a crutch but a sledge of some sort, so the boy could pull the old man along slithery dry needles toward—

But Dirk had no idea how to get back.

For the first time, he struck the tree with the axe with anger. He didn't want to be hanged for murder.

He struck it a second time. He had nowhere to go for help. He'd never met another living soul but the old woman and the old man.

The chips flew. The trunk of the tree groaned. A mouth opened wider and wider, eating the blade each time the blade rode home. The living wood was pale, even ghostly white, the color of the skin of Schneewittchen, the girl who ran away to live with the seven little men, as the old woman had told it. The wedge-shaped scraps that flew away among the shavings were like smiles scared from the tree and discarded on the ground.

Disturbed by the commotion, a small brown bird came down and landed on the breast of the old man. Papi didn't brush it away, which filled the boy with a greater sense of dread than before.

He struck the tree. Again, again.

The bird hopped along the old man's chest and made a comment or two. Dirk let the axe fall still for a moment and listened. "Are you giving me counsel?" he asked the bird.

The bird flew up. Dirk thought the airy rush of her wings sounded like an army of birds. Or an army of angels, bearing the old man's soul away to heaven. It was no such army, but the falling tree, which had had enough, and crashed upon the boy, killing him.

6.

It wasn't that he was falling—was he falling?—so much as that the trees rose up against him. Pale branches ripped into him. Blood rose to the surface of his skin in buttons. He pumped with his feet the way he once had done when jumping into a pond deeper than reckoned. His thighs met swirling arms of long-needled conifer. As if the trees were circling on their stems, crowding in to slow his descent. Finally he was heels-down on somewhere. Underneath the dead leaves and dry needles, the ground writhed. The offended roots of these trees.

He didn't take in that he was dead. He just didn't want to be crushed. He struggled against the forest, lunging forward in small steps, tipping down a slope. Sap stung his eyes. The trees seemed to be shifting out of the way to either side. Making a path, an only path. He was naked. His skin seethed. Now one of his eyes was glued closed. Sap or blood.

At last the slope leveled and he landed on his knees, his face in the soil. The trees lashed at his buttocks and his spine and the back of his neck. The top side of each stroke was punishing and the return, apology.

"You've come so far and you're going to crumble like morning cake?"

He rubbed his eyes and straightened up. A small brown bird perched on a branch above him. A bird can only look at a boy one eye at a time, and her eye was cold and temperamental. Her beak was shut.

"You've come for a crutch, you'll need to work for it," continued the voice, not a bird's voice. The boy looked down.

A dark knob on the ground, hardly larger than a walnut, stirred and rotated. The top of it had the face of a homunculus. Ironstone, petrified oak, char of primordial ooze—the boy had no idea of what it was made. Gnarly head hunched over knees drawn up to bearded chin. Squatting old creature with a cranium like a brussels sprout. "What are you waiting for? Is it ever the wrong time to act?"

"I don't know what to do." So, yes, his voice still worked. The boy was relieved.

"Take a grip of me, and I'll befriend you."

"You'd best think twice about helping him out," said the bird to the boy. Her voice was pure and high, but thick, like sweet golden honey.

"Don't listen to Fräulein Thrush. Such a busybody. Always sticking her beak where it's not wanted. Now you've got here, help me out."

The boy swiveled. The thrush had no more to say, but she rolled her head skyward and let loose with a melodic curse.

The trees began to pull back. While their branches still thrashed, they no longer beat him. The boy was able to lean nearer and look at the knobby figure squatting among dead leaves and needles. If the boy could find the nerve to touch the mouse-size gnome, the creature would fit in his palm.

"You help me and I'll help you," said the gnome. "Foundlings united. Where's the harm in a plain exchange like that?" His small face floated a little toward the scalp of his skull. The boy wondered what was wrong with his petitioner. His arms were fused around his knees. His spine had no give. Only his expression was alive, or so it seemed to the boy. "Why are you waiting?"

"I've never met anyone like you before," said the boy.

"Consider this your unlucky day," warbled the thrush, hopping from branch to branch.

"I'm a citizen of this land, enough said," insisted the gnome. "Treat me no different from the way you treat anyone else. Manners, child."

"I don't have manners," the boy explained. "We live in the forest between hither and yon, and no one else lives near us to be mannerly with."

"So you'll be wanting to set out for the great town," said the thrush. "Some call it the Temple of First Desires."

"More like the Mausoleum of Holy Disappointments," said the

gnome. "You don't want to go there. But to business. You were a soldier hunting a stout limb to use for a crutch, is that so?"

"Hardly a soldier!"

"A vandal, no less," said the thrush. "You murdered our sister with that axe."

"What's done is done," snapped the gnome-thing to the bird. "Though it beggars belief, another immortal dame is fallen. Boy, I will help you carve from her corpse a branch suitable for your uses. All you need do is release me from the soil where I am planted, and I promise to help you. Grab me as you would a handle, and pull."

As the boy's hand prepared to close around the figure, the thrush shrilled, "Go away! Don't dig him out! He is a schemer, he is not your friend. It's his fault we are in such a fix."

Though a talking bird might be rare, a gnome was rarer still. The boy closed both hands around the gnome and began to tug. The thrush darted and battered, trying to flush the boy away. But having begun to worry the creature loose, the boy wouldn't stop. The gnome grunted in pain or some private exertion of his own. Before too long, the boy fell backward on his rump. Clots of soil rained down upon his face and chest.

"Aha!" cried the gnome. "Free at last, Fräulein. We shall see what is what."

"We will never get back now, but be homeless forever," wailed the thrush.

The boy brushed dirt from his mouth. He studied the excavated object. The gnome proved to be the handle of a short, sharp knife. The squatting figure was like a bitter, glaring vegetable, and the knife below him a single denticle.

"Enough of your moans and premonitions," said the gnome to the thrush. To the boy: "Beyond lies Dame Ash, whom you murdered. I shall help you carve a cane or a crutch from what is left of her. When I have paid you for my liberty, you will put me down and let me go."

The thrush said to the gnome, "Haven't you done enough damage?"

The gnome told the boy how to select a limb, how to flex it to produce maximum stress before slicing into it. Though the excavated knife-blade was short, it was hard and sharp. It made quick work of the job. The boy felt that the gnome himself was pushing upon the blade to force it through the pure wood.

"You've begun your afterlife with another act of malice," said the thrush from behind him. Her voice was now low and it hummed with feeling. The boy turned. The thrush was nowhere to be seen. Instead, the bird's voice issued from a soberly handsome woman. She wore a wreath of woodland laurel. Bracelets of ivy adorned the sleeves of her shift. One hand was lifted to her brow, as if fending off the sight of the hacked branch.

"What you have done," she said.

"I could do nothing else," said the boy. "The old man is a wood-cutter. It is all I know."

"I won't give you comfort," she said. "You murdered our sister and carved up her corpse. I won't allow you passage in our realm. Off, back," said the princess, the queen, the thrush-goddess, whoever she was. She threw her hands out, dismissing the boy.

"So we agree on one thing," said the gnome to her. "Let him go. Yes, loosened at last, I can now trouble you at my pleasure. It's been too many centuries of stasis for me to uncoil all at once, but uncoil I will."

"Scoundrel. I shall be ready," she said to the gnome. To the boy, she added, "Though it troubles me, I send you back. Exiled. You've earned no place among us."

"Now set me down," growled the gnome to the boy, "and our transaction is completed."

The boy put the knife between his teeth as he picked up the severed limb of the maiden tree.

"Not my concern," cried the queen to the gnome. "That's what comes of trusting the innocent. They're as malign as everyone else. Save yourself, if you can."

She raised her hands, and a chorus of birdsong rose all around them. A maelstrom in the air, of summergreen leaves and pine needles and bits of bark and twig. With both his hands on the newly trimmed staff, the boy closed his one capable eye. It felt as if the forest were retreating, and the Queen of the Thrushes with it. The gnome on the head of the blade swore fiercely, but the boy didn't open his jaws.

7.

The sound of speaking voices brought the boy around. The surprise wasn't so much that he was alive again but that the voice wasn't the old man's voice. The old woman was talking to a visitor—the first they'd ever had.

Dirk tried and failed to raise himself on his elbows. He wasn't in his loft but laid out upon the bearskin in the nook that the old woman sometimes called her changing room. The cloth that hung in the doorway blocked Dirk's view of the main room.

He was so surprised at the novelty of a guest to the waldhütte that he lay his head back down and just listened.

"You are very good at telling these tales," said the visitor. He had a kindly tone, the sort that seemed to welcome further comment. "They come out of you so naturally. Do you have children or grandchildren to tell stories to?"

"Not a one," said the old woman. "It's just me and the old man here, and always was. I wouldn't have a child about here. I couldn't stand the bother."

"Your command of the old folk tale is impressive, given you've no youngster to sit agog at your feet." (Dirk held his breath.) "Tell me another."

"Come back tomorrow," replied the old woman. "I have mending to do, and hog fat to render, and I can't sit in the sunny hours amusing you with tales of the forest. Are you able to find your way here again?"

"Stories have their own pull," said the guest. Dirk now thought of the visitor as a young man, or younger anyway than the old man. Dirk sorely wanted to see a stranger. Something in the old woman's tone of voice, however, made him hold his tongue.

"Until the next time, Frau . . . Fräulein . . . ?"

She didn't supply a name. The door clicked open and clacked shut.

Dirk felt the fur of the bear irritate the back of his neck. He wanted to roll around and collect the bearskin all about him and hide in it. Become a bear, and lumber away. He couldn't yet move, though. He might be able to speak if he tried, but he didn't try.

"So he's gone," said the old man, coming in. "I hid out in the lee of the shed until I saw him leave. What did he want?"

"Not what you think," said the old woman.

"Did he ask about Dirk?"

"He wanted stories. He wrote down what I said and then read it back to me. I told him one of the hoary old tales. He couldn't wait to go back to the village and tell his brother. He'll be back tomorrow." She began to cry.

Usually at a moment like this, Dirk would have felt a rise of warmth toward her, but this time he could not.

"Why did you bring the boy back?" she managed at last to say.

"I thought it would be better to sling him in the hog pen than to leave his body in the wood where hunting dogs might find it. The hog has to eat, too."

Dirk thought perhaps he wasn't actually alive, but only halfway, somehow.

"And you with that wound in your leg!"

"As near as I could make out, the boy had cut a useful crutch for me before the tree fell. Once I woke to see his prone form by the fallen tree, well, what was I to do? Better to butcher him here than to have someone stumble across his corpse and start asking questions. We have the only waldhütte in this district. We would be the first to suspect."

"You can't do a blessed thing right." The old woman began to berate the old man with a tongue more foul than the boy had ever heard her use.

As much to silence her as for any other reason, Dirk cried out, "Where have I been?"

The silence in the room was like a heavy ghost pressing all the air down to the rude floorboards.

"And now the saints have deserted us," hissed the old woman. She meant it as a whisper but Dirk's ears were alert with panic. "The boy *is* alive. You ought to have buried him there when he was too far gone to suffer. And so it all starts again. How shall we manage now?"

"He made me a crutch," said the old man. "What else was I to do?"

"Where have I been, and where have I come back to?" called Dirk.

The cloth in the doorway whipped aside. "Hush you and your mouth," said the old woman. "You'll wake the dead."

"He woke himself," said the old man, at least a little kindly. "How are you feeling?" He peered over the old woman's angled elbows. He was leaning on a crutch.

"Why would you lie to that man about me?" asked Dirk.

"You've had a bad spell, you're making up stories in your bruised head," the old woman said. "You don't understand."

He managed to sit up. He pulled the bearskin with him and clutched it around his sides like a blanket. "What happened to me? Where is the Queen of the Thrushes? Where is the fierce little knife-man?"

"You've been told too many stories," said the old man, "and that's the truth in a nutshell."

"From what I hear, you were dead," said the old woman. "I have known it to happen once or twice before. A maiden from Arnhelt was struck by lightning and crumpled to the ground, and the smell was bitumen and sulfur. She had no pulse when they reached her. Her face went that color of plums too far gone for jam. Then some-how, she came back."

"Back from where?" Dirk managed to say.

"From death. But she was never the same. She had been an accomplished young woman, daughter of a wool merchant. The banns for her marriage had been called. After the lightning hit her, though, she wouldn't marry. She took up the flute and played till—well, the end. Rarely spoke to a soul, or smiled. That's a bad eye you've earned; be glad for what you won't need to see."

"Don't scare the lad," said the old man.

"He's witnessed enough to be scared already, I can't make it worse." She clapped her hands suddenly, but the boy didn't start.

To the old man: "Do you see what I mean? And now what are we going to do?"

They went outside to talk beyond the far side of the woodshed, for privacy. The dark was falling, though whether this was the dark of the same day or some other day, Dirk didn't know.

He looked down. He wasn't naked anymore, but dressed in his same clothes, his only clothes. Cut-downs from the old man.

The old man and the old woman had meant to lose him at best, to kill him perhaps. If he'd truly come back from death, they must be terrified.

He hated them. He also didn't want to terrify them anymore.

He didn't know why he was such trouble to them, but he couldn't wait around to find out.

So he made the effort to pull himself up. He dragged the bearskin with him, turning it around so the black fur was on the outside. He stumped to the table in the middle of the main room. There was a knife with a carved head lying there next to a red, red apple. He left the apple but picked up the knife and wrapped it in a scrap of leather for safekeeping.

The old woman wouldn't care—she'd wanted him gone anyway. But the old man might follow him. The boy took the crutch so as to slow the old man down should he consider pursuit. Then the boy climbed out the window. He left his life, but in a more conventional way than before. He was still a boy, but he was no longer a child.

A Posthumous Education

8.

At this point it would be false to say the world sang to Dirk in his new freedom. It may have been singing, but not to him; or he was deaf, unschooled in such melodies. He tramped along, aware of his bruises and aches, unaware of shafts of Rheingold light, birdsong, malodorous water cabbage, rococo flourishes of ivy along the boughs of ancient oaks.

A bit of a dolt, that is to say.

The farther he got from the waldhütte, the more indistinct it grew in his mind. As if he'd never lived there. Peculiar, especially since he had never lived anywhere else.

The light was rational and the shadow romantic, and he could sense a purring tension, but he had no words, no references by which to articulate it. And no one to tell it to.

The one thing he did notice was the water. It seemed every time he crested a slope and walked or slid down the other side, he found a stream at the bottom.

You can't be so surprised; where else is mountain water to go? It doesn't just stand upright on the tops of ridges, picking its nose, said the figure on the knife in his hand.

Of course, knives don't talk. Dirk suspected he was imagining things out of worry. Nonetheless, to be polite, he asked the knife which way he should go.

If what you want is to live among your kind, then follow the next substantial stream, said the knife. It will end in a lake or a river. People tend to gather on those shores. They will provide interest and possibly supper. But if what you want is to be unencumbered by human sorrow, keep to the forest. True, the forest is full of appetites on four legs. You might easily satisfy one of them before you know it. Your bearskin cloak will conceal you only so long. But you will be free until the forest catches up with you. And I'll be free when you let me go. I've waited this long, I suppose I can hold my temper until then.

The hours passed. The light shifted. Everything nearby looked the same, but the depths of the forest were growing blacker. When Dirk approached a newly fallen tree that spanned a river, a little brown bird emerged from the greyed, papery leaves that still clung to its branches. You'll have to cross eventually, said the bird.

Birds don't talk, he said, trying his foot on the muddy roots to see how stable the tree might be.

Of course we don't, not to humans, said the bird, cheerily enough. You're probably just lonely. Still, watch your step. Keep to the trunk and take your time.

Oh, she added, when Dirk was about halfway across, you might drop that knife in the river if you wanted. It will do you no good, and water is efficient at rusting mettlesome items.

Beware advice you haven't asked for, snarled the knife-head.

Both of you, be quiet, said Dirk. I must concentrate or I'll end up washing my clothes with me in them. I'm still learning the one-eye skill.

Coming off the tree involved a run through tangled branches. His feet got wet in the far shallows. The bearskin dropped in the water, and there it stayed. Sodden, it was too heavy to lug along.

The knife and the bird fell silent. Beyond the bank, a clearing. Dirk scaled the slope to see what he might see. A wooden fence and a small stone house. A woman hunched on a bench in the westering sun. She was winding a ball of yarn. She didn't look at the sun or at the yarn. Her eyes seemed to be settled upon something invisible in the yard, halfway between her lap and the gate.

She was an old woman, but not the old woman that Dirk had left behind. Perhaps older. Dirk had no practice at making distinctions.

The brown bird, who had fluttered about Dirk as he lumbered along, hid herself in the hood of an oak tree. She sang sweetly as the light and the shadows both lengthened. She commented on her own song as she sang it.

> From far enough away, the piccolo is like a bird.
> Far enough away, the bird a piccolo.
> From long enough ago, the sharpest joy you ever heard
> Cuts like a knife, if long enough ago.
> So childhood gets stronger as we age
> And haunts and taunts the venerable sage,
> Till childhood itself from wherever it had seemed to go
> Returns, and takes up note by note and word by word
> The word we heard when bird was piccolo.

The leathery old woman shuddered, though the air seemed warm to Dirk, and the breeze refreshing. She cried out. A man came through the door and settled a bonnet upon her head, tying the strings under her chin. He wasn't old the way she was. Though older than Dirk.

"What's ailing you, Mutter?"

She flapped a hand in dismissal, and didn't look at him. He went away and came back with a shawl. She pulled it over her shoulders with a kind of angry greed.

"Sunset can make the sweetest fig taste a little tart." The man sat on the doorsill and pulled a long pipe out of a vest pocket. Crouching in the shadows, Dirk examined this enterprise of family. "Having one of your days, then?"

"Achh." She spit on the ground. "God's blood in a thimble."

From the cottage came the smells of plenty—warm bread and sizzling meat, perhaps a joint of venison. Carrots in honey. Dirk's mouth went so wet he wanted to spit, too, but wiped it out on his wrist, so to keep silent and watch how other people talked. He heard chairs scraping on wooden floorboards, so he knew someone was inside, working on supper.

Then, inside, a woman sang something nonsensical, and a child went laughing at it. The words were indistinct, but the exotic performance crowded out the bird's song from Dirk's mind. Such lightheartedness sounded dangerous if not insane.

The man struck a safety match upon the stone and lit his pipe. "Do you know who I am today?"

"Saint Jerome the scholar," replied the elderly woman after a time. An effort at being canny.

"Hardly that! You always said I had noodle pudding in my skull."

She crossed herself, apologizing for her mistake perhaps.

"Try again," he said. "Bring yourself home, Mutter. Who am I?"

She turned the ball of yarn in her lap but didn't look down at it. Perhaps her sight was gone. "You are the king who has a virgin daughter to marry off."

"That's a good one. You've walked sideways into one of your own stories that you used to tell me when I was a lad! But really, I'm the great king of nothing, Mutter, and I don't have a virgin daughter but a virgin son, whose sausage hasn't yet filled its casing. Come now. Do you really not know who I am?"

"A pest, with all your nonsense!" In a rage, she swatted at him and nearly fell off the bench. He paid her no mind.

"Who are you then? Do you remember that?"

"You tell me, if you know so much," she snapped.

"You're old Dame Mitzelhaupf. Agathe Mitzelhaupf. You have lived your whole life in this parish. Your husband was Gustav—do you remember Gustav? He was good to you and built you this house. Here you raised me and my sisters, till they all went off to get married."

"Good riddance to them," she said; and, "But I never had daughters. Too expensive."

"And now you live here with your son, Hans. That's me. And my wife, that's Berthe. And our boy, your beloved little Torsten."

"Ah, Torsten." She sat up, as if this was the only part of her life she could identify. "Where is he?"

"Helping his mother lay the table. But it is time for him to bring the cow from the pasture. Torsten!" called Hans. "Come at once!"

A young boy appeared, smaller than Dirk. "Here is Torsten," said Hans. It was the first child Dirk had ever seen. "Torsten, your grandmother has been vague in her mind again. Give her a kiss."

"Come, child." Imperiously she pointed to her withered cheek. Little Torsten planted a kiss there and backed off.

"Now to your chore. The cow is just beyond, in the pasture, wanting to come home. Go open the gate." Hans pointed. Dirk turned his head. A cow was indeed regarding the domestic scene, chewing through the drama of it.

As Torsten scampered down the track that led to the pasture, Dirk retreated into the woods and followed him. Torsten in light and Dirk in dark.

Hans had been curiously jocular. The grandmother had seemed regal and difficult. But Torsten was only a boy in lederhosen, with plump pink knees and soft flyaway hair. Dirk found him easy to follow.

As Torsten fussed with the rope that tied the gate, Dirk squatted down among the ferns. When he found a smooth stone the size of a robin's egg, he threw it at the boy to get his attention.

At the impact, the boy whipped around. It seemed to Dirk that Torsten was staring straight at him. "Who's there?" he cried.

Another stone to speak with. Dirk threw it.

The boy fled, leaving the gate wide open. The cow followed through without complaint.

Again Dirk paced beside the boy's path, keeping deep enough in the cover of woods that he couldn't be seen. By the time Torsten was in his father's arms, the little lad was weeping. Blood made a prettiness on his cheek.

"Did you fall?" asked the father.

"What's wrong with the child?" asked the grandmother.

"Something in the woods!" cried Torsten. "I was struck five times with stones! I turned and looked."

"What was there?" asked the grandmother. "What did you see?"

"I saw a gnome, a little schwarzkopf, staring at me with an evil grin!"

"Nonsense," said his father. "There is no such goblin in these woods, Torsten."

"Don't be so sure," said the grandmother. "Torsten knows what he knows."

"It was a hateful creature, small enough, but fierce and ugly, and it had a hunch on its back and a sack to carry me away in!"

"Stay away from black-caps, stay out of the woods," said Agathe Mitzelhaupf.

"Don't talk foolishness to him," said Hans crossly.

"I know what I know," said Agathe. "I've heard that gnome calling to me from time to time, but my knees are too much like soft cheese to go clock him on the head as he deserves."

"Supper on the table," called a woman from inside. Berthe, probably.

"You heard no goblin black-cap, Mutter." Hans lifted his mother to a standing position. "It's wicked to mix up your old tales with the truth. All you could hear from the woods was a little evening birdsong. Torsten, wash your face and your hands. Mutter, mind the step or you'll go off to the devil before he's ready to receive you."

"Angels will carry me to Paradise, where I intend to make a lot of trouble." But she was laughing a little now. Whatever crisis she had been suffering was over.

Dirk stood and watched the door close. The aroma of supper drifted out the open window.

The bird was silent. Indeed, she was nowhere to be seen. Dirk looked at the carved handle on the knife. Its crouching gnarled figure grinned with protuberant eyes at him. It looked as if it had a little woven cap upon its bulbous head, fitted as neatly as the cap of an acorn upon its kernel.

9.

At darktime, Dirk spread out some lengths of burlap on a heap of hay in a stall next to the cow. He lay down. It was too cold, but there was nothing else to use as a blanket. He shouldn't have abandoned the drowned bearskin. In a cubby with a tin lining he found a sack of milled flour. It was sewn shut. With some effort he hauled it to the hay. He lay down beside it as if it were a person who could keep him warm, and he spread the burlap over both of them. He thought about that little boy, Torsten. He would have liked to have a friend, or a younger brother, if only in his dreams. However, he wasn't in the practice of having dreams.

A barn mouse, several in fact, climbed the hill of the sack while he slept. Hardly believing their good fortune, they gnawed through the threads. They had a better supper than he did.

10.

He woke before dawn. His shoes in one hand and the staff in the other, he slipped out the side door of the barn. He was intending to tiptoe on the grass, get going and get gone, when he was stopped by a sound from the house.

The father, that Hans, stood in the open door of the kitchen. He was dressed in a long greasy shirt. His legs and feet were bare. He had his pipe in his hand. He had been about to knock it against the doorsill to clear it out. Enjoy a draft of cherry tobacco before the day's work began.

Dirk and Hans, they stared at one another without speaking.

If Hans would just pick Dirk up the way he had done little Torsten, that would be fine indeed. Dirk was, after all, younger in mood and mind than perhaps he was in years, having been raised an isolate.

The father shifted his foot and kept working at his pipe, but his eyes were trained on Dirk, who stood like a rabbit ready to dash.

"Our Torsten said it was a little dark dwarf with a black cap," murmured Hans, loud enough for Dirk to hear. "Are you he? Do you darken as the day gets longer? Or are you the dwarf's counterpart, to bring some sort of a blessing? You're welcome here, if you promise to do no harm."

They talk sometimes of *l'heure bleue*, that segment of evening when the sun has fallen below the horizon but the vegetable world is still visible. Also more intense, as a consoling purple rises beneath every grieving leaf. Pre-dawn has a counterpart. A sort of light is cast from the world itself, before the sun gets to its job. It is beige and yellow, or amber like an ale.

Dirk stood in *l'heure bronze*, and waited. If his heart trembled, his eye remained unblinking.

Hans stooped to put down the pipe on the doorstep. When he stood up again, to comfort the waifling, the boy was gone. Without a sound.

As Dirk moved through the newborn world, clouds of fine meal puffed from his clothes, rendering him more solid, less an apparent ghost-child than he must have seemed in the barnyard.

II.

Dirk continued downstream. The world breathed and steamed. Wherever the little river slowed to widen and to shallow, sheers of wisp arose, dissolving into loose columns.

If you want to keep my company, go back to the forest, advised the gnome-knife. See those stones ahead where the river narrows into a rapids? You can cross back to the wildness there. I can't follow you into the human world.

The boy is made for his own kind, not for ours, said the thrush.

A rushing river means a mill. A mill means a settlement. He is of no use to us. Leave him to his destiny.

And me to mine. You have no agency here, Fräulein. He may not be our salvation, but send him to the human wolves? A kugel-head like him? The world would carve him up. Whereas *I'd* rather do the honors.

Dirk interrupted them. "Hush."

The brown thrush whisked about him in the air as if she could bully him forward. Dirk kept on, but not because of her. He knew a bit more about people now that he was able to add Torsten, Hans, and Großmutter Agathe to his collection. He wanted to learn more. He was too young to be a hermit.

Misty forests leaned in upon the encircling slopes. Before long the cataracts descended around a corner and were tamed into a millpond.

Storehouses and other timbered structures were arranged around a well. There, a young woman rotated a crank, lowering a bucket. His sixth new person, not counting the visitor to the waldhütte, whom he hadn't actually seen.

The thrush flew up to the roof of the well but made no comment.

The boy wondered if this was the village that he'd always been prohibited from visiting. Though probably there was more than one village in the world.

Against the chill, the doors were closed and windows shuttered. Roosters marked the hour, cows lowed to be milked, but the village was still sleeping. Only this woman in her apron, keen to her task.

He stood a distance, waiting for her to look up. She had a full, satisfied belly and her russet hair was undone in the back. "Oh, you startled me," she said when she turned to decant a pail of water into one of two pewter pitchers. "Where do you come from, tousle-head?"

He shrugged.

"A changeling child? Did you go to sleep as a piglet and wake up as a boy? They're much the same, in my experience. I've known pigs to take better care of their grooming than you do." She kept working as she spoke. Her manner wasn't unkind. She was young, he thought. Younger than the old man and the old woman. Though old enough to be grown.

He thought about the visitor to the waldhütte, the man who'd been hunting stories. The old woman had said that the curious fellow and his brother were staying in the village. "Have you had guests overnight, two men?" he asked the maiden.

She patted her spreading waistline. "Two men? You're cruel and sinful to suggest such a thing. Wasn't one enough, to get me into such a barrel as this?" She winked at him, a gesture he didn't understand. He tried to wink back, uselessly.

"Bat your ugly eye at me, will you? You're too young, and I've already had a journeyman at my threshold, as you can see. But I must get inside before others are about. The pastor says it's unseemly for a woman in my condition to be out and about, confusing the morals of the young. So I rise early to do my chores, and hide my shame from the daylight and the neighbors. Let me pass."

"I mean, guests in the village overnight," he said. "Two men, two travelers?"

"You're the only traveler we've seen since Lent." She heaved the ewers and balanced one upon each shoulder. Small tongues of water splashed in her wake.

"Don't follow me," she said after a while. "The fools all say I'm a vessel of sin. They'll think you're the imp assigned to punish me. Or that I'm leading you astray."

She reached a house with a set of steps up the side. She climbed the steps. When she got to the top, she put the pitchers on the landing so she could work the latch. Dirk stood below.

"I thought I told you to go. What, do you want a scrap of food? Am I my brother's keeper?"

He thought she meant she would give him something. He came forward a few feet till he stood at the bottom of the steps. She lifted one pitcher of water and dashed it over him. He shrieked and tried to back away, but he wasn't fast enough. "That's why I always take two, one for me and one to share." She cried with laughter. "If you want charity, gnaw like a church mouse at the door of the minister. See if he gives you more understanding than he gives me." Slam, went the door.

12.

He stood shivering for a moment. His mind only a bowl of ice blood. But eventually he realized that if he was to go see the minister, perhaps he should clean up first. He washed at the fountain as well as he could.

13.

A woman with white hair hobbled by. She was picking over a basketful of moldy rolls, and offered him none. But she pointed out the chapel to Dirk. Locked or not, she didn't know. The minister's schedule was none of her concern.

The small building stood opposite the village well. A façade of grey stuccoed plaster, tidy to a fault. A side door was propped open, so Dirk mounted the steps and peered inside.

His eye adjusted to the gloom, but it was hardly worth the effort. The windows weren't visions of the Life of Christ in colors, as the old man in the waldhütte had loved to describe. Instead, panes of watery glass, slightly greened and dotted with imperfections. Between white mullions the overcast Bavarian sky was divided into rectangles of equal size. In vain Dirk looked for statues of the Madonna and Child, something the old man had described with a ferocity of feeling that almost approached anger. No statues. No paintings of Saint Paul knocked on his breeches by lightning, or Saint George and the dragon, or Saint Ursula and her retinue of eleven thousand virgins.

Golgotha; Dirk wanted to see what Golgotha looked like. And Bethlehem, and the castle of Pontius Pilate. And the tomb of Lazarus. And Christ walking on the waves.

And the Garden of Eden. Snakes and apples. Ripeness of possibility. It was a bitter blow, all this severity.

"If you've come for salvation, you've come to the right place," said a man, emerging from a broom closet under a pulpit. He must be the minister. His forehead was big and his chin dissolved into his neck, and his hair had gotten knocked askance on the low doorsill, so he looked like the uprooted head of a scallion.

Dirk said, "Where do you keep the stained glass? I heard there were apostles and martyrs to look at, and a cock crowing by Saint Peter's weeping eyes."

The minister dusted his hands on the front of his Geneva gown. "Ach, seeking the propaganda of Rome? You won't find it here, my boy. Those pictures are made by savage, deluded men. Here, the Heavenly Ghost delivers perfect peace in our hearts without such blasphemous imagery."

"Not in mine." Dirk didn't mean to argue but he was famished.

"You're just stupid and lazy, and besides, the young like to be fooled. How well I remember. I suppose you're hungry as well as dirty? The rules of mercy apply to all, regardless of persuasion. Come along. I have a plate of sweet cakes left from last night's dinner."

That sounded good, so Dirk followed the minister through a passage to a set of rooms in the back. The boy clenched the knife in his pocket just in case, but the minister was beyond reproach. He laid out a small blue plate and poured a glass of milk that was only a little sour. Then he brought forward butter in curls, and pastries with gooseberry jam, and two rounds of ruddy wurst and another of soft yellow cheese. "First we ask God to bless the food, then we eat it," he told the boy.

"I'm not a fool, I know about blessing."

While Dirk gobbled the breakfast, the minister talked about faith. He warned against the visions of the devil. He said Dirk must beware of icons and statues. Those temptations threatened the innocent, all those Catholic paintings of naked martyrs bound for piercing. The minister had a good deal to say, and it lasted the entire meal. When both rounds of sausage, three rolls, some pastries, the milk, and most of the cheese had disappeared into his stomach, Dirk said, "Are you practicing?"

"Practicing what?"

"A sermon? I never heard a sermon before."

"What congregation do you belong to, boy?"

"I don't know."

"Then it's a good thing I'm steering you away from occasions of sin such as Rome in her pagan way promotes. Babylon's fleshpots."

"Where might I see these saints and statues and all that?"

"But haven't I just been warning you against idolatry?"

"I should probably see them first, to know what to avoid."

The minister sighed. "You seem to have one spoiled eye already.

Don't abuse the second. Now about that crutch you carry like a lance over your shoulder. It isn't the right size for you. Yet you burden yourself with it. Why? Is it a weapon?"

It took Dirk a while to think up something to say. "I am probably bringing it to someone who needs it."

"Listen, child. The stories of saints, the landscapes of those Italians and of Rembrandt, you don't need them. They are all a crutch. A distraction. Throw those illustrations away. Throw that pike away. You don't require it and it doesn't fit you anyway. And I won't harm you."

"It's left over from someone else's life, but I might grow up tall enough to need it myself."

The man laughed at that. "My name is Pfarrer Johannes. You may stay here and eat my food every day until you are sure you need no such crutch. If you like. In the meantime, let me stitch you a patch for that bad eye. Can't imagine how you came by that."

This is how Dirk turned into an assistant to Pfarrer Johannes, and how he came to live with him, and every morning to sweep the cold chapel clear of mouse droppings. The thrush never appeared on any windowsill. The knife-head had been struck so dumb by holiness that Dirk forgot it had ever spoken to him.

Once Dirk asked Pfarrer Johannes about the young woman with the big belly, which detail by now Dirk understood to mean "with child." Dirk had never seen the woman again. Pfarrer Johannes hawed and hemmed but finally said, "She went away."

"With the child?"

"Twins. No. I mean she died."

"Oh. Did the twins die?"

"No, I'm afraid not. They became foundlings, more or less."

Oh, thought Dirk. Then: "But what of their father? Couldn't he take care of them?"

"Poor mites, they had no father," explained Pfarrer Johannes, wincing.

"Like Jesus, then."

"Not exactly. Aren't you picking up anything at all while you are here?"

"Crumbs," said Dirk. He was getting bigger.

14.

In the years that Dirk spent with Pfarrer Johannes Albrecht at the village church of Achberg, the old woman and old man with whom Dirk had once lived never came looking for him. Nor did they come to town for any other reason. Dirk asked the minister if he knew those two old people living deep in the forest, not so far off. When the minister asked for their names, Dirk found himself at a loss. The old man had addressed the old woman only as "You old Fräulein," and spoken of her as "the old Fräulein." She had called him only "Papi," and so had Dirk. Though Papi wasn't Dirk's father, of course, except by accident.

So on the subject of their Christian names, Dirk couldn't answer Pfarrer Johannes. The question was dropped.

Dirk swept the floors, washed the clear windows till they shone, took the minister's laundry to the laundress and picked it up again. He wasn't required to attend service, but he loitered in the vestibule, keeping a beaker of water on hand in case Pfarrer Johannes needed to clear his throat between first and second hours of the sermon. And the boy listened a little. Mostly his mind wandered. But it didn't have anywhere special to wander to.

Apparently it was customary for Pfarrer Johannes to take in abandoned children from time to time, for no one seemed surprised to see Dirk answer the door to receive a loaf of bread, a flagon of wine, hoops of sausages in a basket. Gifts for the minister. No one asked Dirk his name, neither did they propose he ought to attend school. They probably assumed he was being educated by the good father.

Perhaps he was and didn't know it. Once, he said to the minister, "Why do you keep me here?"

The man took off his spectacles and began to polish them. "Do you recognize kindness? Do you know it?"

"I know the word."

"Well, no matter. None of us can see the blessed air, but that doesn't stop us from breathing it."

"But why do you keep me here?"

"To practice my sermons on, don't you think?" There was a merry quizzicalness in Pfarrer Johannes's face. Dirk gave up and went on with his chores.

He kept to himself. Of other children—for there were children in the village, of course there were—he knew little except the sound of their voices at play, in the gloaming of long summer days. He liked the sound of their laughter, but only in the sense that it had a musical cadence. Other than that, their calling and shouting in games and play sounded, frankly, stupid.

When his legs felt eager to run and join them at play, he didn't want to. When he wanted to, his legs stayed still.

15.

Came the day, perhaps seven years into Dirk's apprenticeship at the chapel, when a troupe of musicians entered the village near sunset. They had been on their way to sing a High Mass for the local margrave in his palace nearby, but a midday summer thunderstorm had washed out the road. Two horses had slipped into a ravine, breaking any number of legs between them. While replacements were sent for, the musicians required housing for the night.

By now the ecclesiastical situation had become clear to Dirk. Pfarrer Johannes's congregation, small and devout as it was, saw itself beset on all sides. The village provided sanctuary for this outpost of a Swiss-inflected Calvinism. But its faithful had grown thorny and inward-looking from being outnumbered by the vast Roman Catholic population of the kingdom of Bavaria.

That evening, at the tavern, the visiting Catholic choir members and the local Protestant farmers came to some disagreements over scripture. The discussion concerned the Christian souls of animals. The pious butcher lost three teeth. The traveling kapell-meister was cursed to the fifth level of Hell. Worst of all, in the middle of the night a few of the visiting rogues managed to breach the locked doors of Pfarrer Johannes's austere chapel.

When Dirk arrived at the side door to open up the next morning, he discovered the disaster. A bear was wandering about in a state of distress. It had knocked over candlesticks and shat upon the tiles. Maybe under cover of night someone had lured the wild creature into the chapel. Or maybe, once the doors were broken open, some woodland bear feeling the need of repentance had come for salvation. No one could say. Somehow the battered door had closed behind the bear and latched itself. The bear had spent an uneasy dark night of the soul.

After Dirk regained his footing, he circled to the front of the building. He flung open the double doors. The bear lumbered out on all fours, to begin a life of penitence and good works, perhaps, or to take the Protestant Gospel back to the forest.

Its fur coat was still usefully upon its own back. That was something.

Nursing headaches, the choir members left the village about midday, pursued by a congregation of equally muddle-headed locals. No one was bothering with *mea culpa*. It fell to Dirk to mop up the mess.

"This is beyond toleration," said Pfarrer Johannes, bringing one bucket of water after another. "Filthy animals."

"I don't think the bear could help it."

"I wasn't talking about the bear."

Dirk regarded the broken window. The shards of glass were on the floor, so the window must have been smashed from outside. Smears of blood showed that the bear had cut its paw prowling in a circuit around the pews, looking for an exit.

Then: "We all show too little tolerance for those who are not like us."

"Do you think bears have souls?" asked Dirk. This was perhaps his first abstract question.

"It is not what I think." Pfarrer Johannes sounded prim and tired. "It is what God thinks."

Usually Pfarrer Johannes was comfortable being God's spokesperson, but as he seemed taciturn today, Dirk dropped the subject. He concentrated on the task. The sky through the broken mullions, the torn hymnals, the quality of bearish odor even when a bear has been absent for several hours. It all added up to some other question, though whether it was about bears or not, Dirk wasn't sure. Could a bear be christened? If a bear died and lost its skin, could it ever go back and reclaim it so that its cousins in heaven would still recognize it when it arrived?

After an evening meal, Pfarrer Johannes went from house to house and interviewed some of his flock. Then he came home and locked himself in his study and didn't come out till the morning. He intercepted Dirk in the path by the churchyard. Dirk was airing yesterday's cleaning rags on the gravestones.

"Dirk," said Pfarrer Johannes. "I need ecclesiastical advice in this matter. You are to carry my complaint to the Roman Bishop's residence in Meersburg. I will include a letter to introduce you. What is your last name?"

All these years in, and this was the first time the minister had asked. Dirk could only say, "I am a foundling."

The minister turned over the packet of correspondence in his hands. "I can't call you Dirk Foundling," he said. His voice betrayed an unaccustomed tenderness. Perhaps he was ashamed of his lack of curiosity up till now.

"You could baptize me with a new name," suggested the boy.

Pfarrer Johannes wasn't one to joke about matters of faith and good works. He stood in the shadows of the arborvitae. Young children in the nearby school-yard screamed in pleasure, torturing some poor idiot smaller than they were. The clock in the village tower sounded the hour. A brown bird hopped on the edge of a stone urn, and chirped.

"Dirk Drosselmeier," said Pfarrer Johannes Albrecht. Whether this was a christening or not, Dirk didn't know. He had no reason to argue, though. A fellow needed two names, one for affection and the other for civic duty. "Get your things, young Herr Drosselmeier."

"I'll be coming back?" he asked.

"God knows the answer to that question."

Dirk had an extra shirt in his nook. He packed it in a leathern satchel that Pfarrer Johannes gave to him. Into the pack Dirk also put a hunk of bread, some ham, a round of cheese. He remembered his gnome-hasped knife just in time, so he could cut through the cheese's rind.

"How will I find Meersburg?" he asked.

"Come. I shall walk with you to the right road and point you on your way." The minister sighed. "If you see that bear in the woods, tell it I harbor no ill will." Dirk had nothing to say to this. He had learned that Pfarrer Johannes was kind, but he couldn't tell when Pfarrer Johannes was making a joke. The minister went on: "I see, Drosselmeier, you still have your crutch."

"Yes."

"I remember what we said about that when you arrived. I told you to throw away your fanciful stories and your need for vivid paintings and images of the life of Christ and the way of faith. I asked you if that staff was yours, and you said you couldn't yet tell me. Have you learned anything while you were here? Have you out-grown childish things, Drosselmeier? Now you are getting toward being a man? Can you throw your staff away?"

"It fits me nicely now," said Dirk. "It is not too big any longer."

"All in good time, then. Do you realize I will miss you?"

"Not too much," replied Dirk.

The minister shook his head fondly and waited for Dirk to say something more, but the boy had nothing to add. So Pfarrer Johannes kissed the boy and sent him on his way.

Bildungsroman

16.

The worthy minister had pointed out the only road that tended toward Meersburg. A bit of a hike; Dirk would be leaving the Kingdom of Bavaria for the Grand Duchy of Baden. It would take several days, depending on how lucky Dirk was in getting a lift. And in getting accurate directions.

"Lucky?" Dirk had asked.

Pfarrer Johannes had corrected himself. "Blessed."

Luck and grace: an unmatching pair of boots with which to address a long dusty road.

The early summer day was fine. Dirk minded his gait. For a while the path ran between golden meadows and fields. Barns and farmhouses squatted among them, stout with prosperity. The world was at work. An early harvest of hay on that slope, with hired workers stopping to break bread and share ale at noon. A family tending a fenced garden of peas and beans. Dirk asked for no portion. He was happy to anticipate his own bread and cheese.

Before long the road left the arable terrain behind. An airy woods of aspen and larch closed around the boy. He was to follow the road toward Lindau and then ask for directions to Meersburg.

Making his way around the brow of a ridge, Dirk saw the three

arches of a stone bridge spanning a vigorous stream. The path before him diverged. The main route led over the bridge to the far
bank. The second path kept to the side on which Dirk had been
traveling. It dipped underneath the nearer arch, into darkness and
out the other side. Deeper into the forest.

He knew which way he was meant to go, but not which way he
would go. He paused to think about it.

A brown bird came down from some bower and landed upon
the rustic rail of the bridge. She sat there, almost encouragingly,
were he to think about it like a poet. Come, come this way, bright
world ahead, she seemed to want to say, in short bursts of song.

And yet what now is hidden in shadows below may become
more welcome to you in the long run, growled a voice in his pocket.
This is my third and final warning. You can leave the path entirely,
don't you know that? Pick up your bearskin.

How I have grown, thought Dirk to himself; that I can now
hold two contrary thoughts in my head.

All paths lead to the same place, and that place is whatever
comes next.

At this rate, I shall soon be ready for university.

He tried to whistle a response to the songbird in a complemen-
tary key, but he ducked his head and chose the lower path, grinning
at the thought of bridge trolls or billy goats gruff huffing and
stamping beneath, waiting to rake him in.

17.

Another two or three days, or four. Nights in sheds, and once
in the back room of a tavern, among barrels of beer that
made him drunk on the fumes. Along the Wolfsbach River to-

ward Lindau, then down to a great lake, the Obersee section of the Bodensee—or Lake Constance as he also heard it called. He kept northwest along its shores to pretty Friedrichshafen, crinkled, pleated with sharp shadow in the dawn light. Now that the forest had given way to open spaces again, Dirk could better understand the height of the terrain from which he had descended. Though disappeared from view, the mountains rose in his mind like flat friezes of snow and rock. They hinted nothing of the lives lived within their crags and crevices. All the silent fish and unheard birds. The renegade wolf, the rogue king stag, the parliament of bears.

Dirk walked to the edge of the land to see how it managed to lose itself in the water. There, as luck or grace would have it, he was offered passage on a steamboat if he might help an elderly dame and her crippled son manage their valises. And so he made his way to Meersburg handily enough.

18.

Meersburg, seen from across the water. A small walled city in two parts, a lower town near the lake and an upper area bristling with municipal stateliness. A stone jetty reached toward them as they approached from the east. A breakwater of sorts. Boys were fishing there, and men repairing nets. The quay beyond, a staging area for commerce and drama. "Mind your wallet in this crowd," said the old Dame as she departed. But he had no wallet to worry over.

Either Dirk hadn't listened correctly or Pfarrer Johannes himself hadn't understood. According to the dockworkers on the quay, the local Bishop's palace had been appropriated for civic uses a decade or so earlier. True, the Roman Catholic Bishop, whose seat had been relocated to Constance across the lake, had indeed been seen in Meersburg earlier that season. Now, however, he was taking a few weeks as the guest of a wealthy family who repaired annually to their lakeside schloss some distance west of the city walls.

A cheery farmer offered Dirk a ride in a cart heaped with dung. By late afternoon, Dirk had escaped the cloud of flies and made his way to a pair of gates. Beyond the iron fretwork, the house looked like a generous slice of old creamy egg-bread set upon the flashing blue tablecloth of the lake. All the flourishes of iron seemed to Dirk like the alphabet of an unfamiliar script. Its message was clear, though: Stay Away.

Ah, but I have a job to do, said Dirk to the gate, and pulled on a bell-rope.

Dirk had long since realized he was talking to himself in moments like this, so he wasn't surprised that the gate didn't reply.

An underling scurried to work the latch. Dirk was led to a side door, where he was interviewed by an overseer of some sort. Dirk was told: "The good Bishop is indeed in residence, but His Excellency is at his oblations. You will repair to the kitchens. You will take a meal and wait for a reply. If the Bishop needs time to compose his thoughts, you will take a bed in the servants' quarters."

Mercy, a real bed: That would be a first.

The kitchen proved a well-scrubbed inferno of roasting meats. The property's extensive staff seemed accustomed to visitors, and no one stared at Dirk or talked to him. A fleshy young damsel with hot pink cheeks, her bare arms freckled with orange, slapped before him a dish of veal stew with potato dumplings. He ate with gusto. A youth in a blooded apron bolted through from some stables with the news that the Baron's son and his university entourage had just arrived unannounced and would be sat at table that evening. Eight more heads. "Ach," said the head cook, "I am to prepare vegetables and potatoes with what, my toes, while my hands are finishing the strudel?"

"I can peel potatoes," said Dirk. He took out his gnome-hasped knife and pushed aside his bowl for later.

Because the Bishop sent word that there'd be no immediate reply to Pfarrer Johannes Albrecht's request for compensation for damages, Dirk Drosselmeier might have left the schloss von Koenig that evening. But the idea of the young kitchen maid—wringing bread flour out of towels in the doorway—gave Dirk pause. As he delayed, he was put to work again, and so without a formal arrangement he became a member of the summer staff.

Dirk fell in love, first, with the notion of his own bed, which stood in a row of five in one of the men's dormitories above the kitchens. It came with its own pillow and its own hay mattress under striped ticking. After a while Dirk became enamored, second, with the notion of sharing this bed with someone. The pink-vermilion kitchen assistant, Hannelore, so often stood in his path, scowling and smelling delectably of onions and rampion, that he wondered if she ought to be his first. He was uncertain how to begin.

19.

Upon a knoll overlooking the lake, quite apart from the schloss, a Catholic chapel minded its own business under shaggy hemlocks. The von Koenig dynasty once must have adhered to Rome, though to judge by the look of decay no one was currently devout. Or not in the summertime.

Dirk had no language for architecture. The building was small. Its bell tower was capped with a wooden dome in the shape of a turnip, through neglect listing as a real turnip will. Narrow colored-glass windows lanceted the stone walls, but from the outside they looked mostly umber. As the doors to the place remained locked, he could neither confirm nor ruin his uncertain faith by seeing for the first time sunlit stained-glass windows from the inside.

One afternoon toward the height of summer, when the dogs lay about drooling into their shadows, Dirk took his leave of the pantries. He was keeping an eye out for Hannelore, who sometimes strolled down to the boathouse with an expression that suggested a winsome sort of boredom. Dirk was passing the vine-gripped chapel when he drew up short. The door stood open, and a single voice issued from the shadows. The noise was plangent, persuasive, but of what? Unforgettable—indeed, he never did forget it, his whole life long. Told sharply never to approach or address the von Koenig family or their guests, Dirk nonetheless was drawn in. He stood and stared with his eye, but his ears were staring harder.

A figure with rolling locks was hunched over a stringed instrument of unusual size. Of music, Dirk had known only the reedy wheeze of Pfarrer Johannes's harmonium, with its tendency to bust a valve and leave the parish chromatically impoverished as it brayed through the militance of foursquare anthems.

This sound rolled forth. The strung melody seemed just the length of a line as sung by a human, breaking where a human voice would break for breath. As his eye adjusted to the shadows, Dirk saw the musician—a young man in a high-collared white shirt and billowy sleeves rolled to his elbows—who was caressing the exposed sternum of the instrument with a bow. He might have been bestowing loving attentions to a kneeling figure. Dust in the nearly empty room swirled around him; colored light from an Annunciation window made him crimson; from a Transfiguration, verdigris.

He finished at last, that crimson and copper-green one, and turned to Dirk.

"I don't mean to interrupt," said Dirk.

"I didn't stop till I was through," replied the man. The voice was refined, the glance bold. "You look as if you've seen a doppelgänger."

"I should go."

"I'll play another in a moment. I'm resting the pads of my fingers. Out of practice."

"What is it?"

"Bach."

"No, I mean—?"

"A violoncello. You've never seen a 'cello?" Dirk shook his head. "Come, have a look."

"How does it do that? How do you do it?"

"Bach is the genius; the 'cello is his voice. I'm only the keyhole through which it pours. Mostly I try to keep out of the way and let the message work through me."

This was beyond Dirk. "But it sounds—" He couldn't find the way to say it. Some memory of—something—speaking beneath or without words. "Bach is a Christian musician," he tried, flailing.

"Yes, Bach is Christian, but the 'cello suites are more like Euclidean arguments."

"I don't know what you mean. What do the suites argue?"

"I don't know, but they do it so convincingly! Don't you agree?"

The statement seemed nonsense—how could you be convinced by something wordless? Yet Dirk paused, and then nodded.

The man began to tighten the pegs on the head of the 'cello, coaxing the instrument into tune. "I'm Felix," he said, between repeated iterations of nearly the same note. "At Wittenberg with the Baron's son. Guest of the household."

"I'm nobody," said Dirk.

"A music lover, anyway. Want to hear another? The E-flat major." Without waiting for an answer, he lifted his chin and raised his bow, and he brought forth the haunted disquisition. Dirk settled on a bench at the side and closed his eye. Luminous colored patterns played upon his more capable eyelid as, outside, clouds shuttered and unshuttered the light through some Revelation or other.

20.

Upon leaving the church, Felix said, "I come here often to practice because the sound against the stone is profound."

"Oh," said Dirk.

"I'm told to put the key here," said Felix, showing Dirk where it was hidden. "Come see me again. I shall play more for you."

"I don't know if I can tolerate more," said Dirk. But perhaps that sounded rude.

"You can tolerate more," said Felix. "I'll prove it to you."

That evening the Bishop departed for Meersburg, and thence, it was said, across the great lake to Constance. The subject of a reply to Pfarrer Johannes hadn't been broached again. This left Dirk as an independent lad upon his own road, as Pfarrer Johannes wasn't going to come after him any more than the old man and old woman in the forest had done.

Dirk wandered by the lake edge, hoping Hannelore might happen along. Sharpening the horizon to knife-edge, a moon was rising in a sky tinted Siberian iris, making of the water of Obersee a black restlessness.

The world was a set of alternations, resistance and persistence, writ up in lake and the distant Alpine peaks of eastern Switzerland. In fact, the world was no easier to understand than Bach.

It seemed that the world was no more wonderful than Bach.

It was no less wonderful, either.

Magnificent imperturbability, exactly sized, one to the other.

What did that mean about Bach, about the world?

21.

He lay down with music in his mind, but not many thoughts about it. If there were words with which to consider music, he didn't know them. He thought of Felix bending over the 'cello and coaxing from it such testimonies of longing. Or perhaps there was no such thing as meaning to be found in those lines—not aspiration, not any human feeling. Perhaps the suites were just congeries of certain notes shaped by different keys and modalities. Nothing more than that.

But how could *nothing* masquerade as *longing*?

Dirk knew a little about longing. The man four beds down from him was a lesson in carnal appetite, and the woman who came to his bed with him answered it, like another instrument. She was a seamstress from Meersburg, and she showed up every fourth or fifth night. Despite all the other men in the room, who like Dirk turned their backs to the couple in the farthest bed, the junior plowman and the seamstress conducted their exertions with no sentimental comment but a lot of commitment to the cause. She fled before dawn. No one ever mentioned her existence to the field hand, but when he left to see her to the back gate of the estate, the others in the dormitory graded the performance and made snickery character assault.

By this Dirk knew that, should Hannelore ever indicate interest, he couldn't bring her to his own bed.

This week Dirk had been set to fastening loose roof tiles on the barns before the winds of winter could fling them away. There were only so many tiles that needed tending. When he'd completed his task, he avoided the overseer's office, to which he usually reported, and went skulking about the kitchen yard. He hoped to find Hannelore at a task, and there she was, shelling beans.

"The idiot from upslope," she commented. "What do you want?"

He wanted her to lower her dress off her shoulders and lift it above her knees so it was only a bolster of fabric around her middle; he wanted to look at her front and back and all around, and to stroke her up and down. "Nothing," he said.

"Good, because nothing is what you are going to get." She kept to her work, though Dirk noticed that she slowed down a little. "Where are you going when this is over?"

"When what is over?"

"The family doesn't live here in Überlingen the year round. The winds off the lake are too cold. They do have chambers in Meersburg, but primarily they root themselves in Munich. Will they take you with them?"

"I haven't thought to ask."

"Well, don't. Why are you looking at me like that, squinty?"

"You are a pleasure to look at."

She scowled more fiercely than ever. "I've both my eyes on the miller's son. Don't get notions. I find you scrappy and impertinent."

"Will you come walking with me?"

"And leave the beans to shell themselves?"

"If I help you it will go faster, and then we can walk."

"I don't want a stroll, but I'm tired of doing these beans. And this is my last chore before a break." She shifted on the bench, which Dirk took as an invitation to join her. He learned quickly. They worked in tandem like a four-armed automaton. She smelled of sweat and late strawberries, sweet to the point of stinging.

Returning from the kitchen where she'd delivered the shelled beans and discarded her apron, she shrugged at him and scratched her hip and pointed a thumb out the kitchen-yard gate. They left and walked together in the dozy mid-afternoon heat. All the guests and the family were napping or otherwise being quiet. A few children ran about on the lawns with a puppy, but they paid no mind to the servants, and Dirk and Hannelore returned the favor.

Dirk tried to put his hand in Hannelore's, but she would have none of it. "So public here on the road, anyone could see, and tell the miller's son." She snorted.

So at the abandoned chapel Dirk said, "Wait," and he got the key from its hiding place and opened up the door. He closed it behind him but didn't lock it, for he didn't want her to feel she was being imprisoned against her will. "This is private enough," he said.

"No one comes here." She sniffed at the wood rot and the mold and perhaps the ornamentation. "Who would?"

He put his hands on her shoulders. "My name is Dirk."

"Of course I know that, I asked. Dirk Dummkopf, I know all about it."

"I'm not slow."

"Well, you're not hasty," she replied, and took one of his hands off her shoulder and put it against her bosom. He marveled at the size of her breast, at the feeling of mobility of cloth riding over the skin riding over firm yet tender mass. Then she sighed and undid the top two ties of her shift. "Your hand belongs inside the clothing. I see you've had no experience."

"I've watched you for a month now."

"And you haven't noticed I have another one of those on the other side? Pity about the gruesome eye. This is like teaching children how to roll on their stockings." She guided his other hand. He wasn't sure if he should be tender or testing, but he so loved his hand upon the curves—they were exactly the right size for a man's hands. She put her own hands on her hips and whistled while he closed his eye and let his palms float like swan's down upon the waters. The sides of his thumbs brushed against her nipples, which went hard. He wasn't sure this was welcoming to her and he withdrew his hands.

"Are you worried about consequences? I've been down to the dock before, you know; I'm readied." Her voice was still hard but her words seemed chosen by kindness. He thought he knew what she meant. "Are you going to kiss me?"

He kissed below her ear, on the edge of her chin; he kissed her nose, the knuckles on her clenched hands, which now were nearly tucked inside of her elbows. She seemed open and closed at the same time. He was confused, but he expected this is what was meant to happen.

"You fool, kiss my mouth," she said. He didn't want to approach that bitter mouth. He dove toward her neck and put his arms around her waist, but that seemed to lead nowhere particularly.

"You're abashed by the open space in front of the old altar," she said at last. "I suppose I can understand. Come, we'll climb to where the choristers used to sing. We can disrobe there and lie down."

She found the door to the choir loft and led him by the hand. His heart was racing. The stair-hall was dark, the steps dotted with mouse turds. The thick dust made him sneeze.

In the loft she spread out some moth-eaten vestments on a pew and sat down. She lowered her blouse just as he had hoped she would. She took off her wooden shoes; her bare, callused feet looked like swedes. Hannelore's face seemed bright and sad in the gloom. "Well, come on, I have just so long," she said, and lay back upon the pew with an arm over her eyes.

Dirk had never had the coarseness—or courage—to peer at lovemaking in the men's dormitory: how a man might lie with a woman. For a country boy, he was rather vague on the mechanics of sex. The old woman and the old man had kept a single pig and a cow and some chickens, and despite all his years in the pulpit, Pfarrer Johannes Albrecht had never lectured on methods of human intercourse. Dirk knew he was to lie with Hannelore, though there was hardly room on the pew. If he lay right upon her he might squash those lovely breasts, which now were rolling to each side as if they'd prefer to be set on the floor with the shoes and wait till this business was concluded.

"Come on, then; have I to teach you what your candle is for?" asked the girl.

Gingerly, trying not to settle his full weight upon her, he suspended himself like a plank above her. He used his hands to take some of the weight off her torso, but she arched her hips and battered his midriff with hers as if to get his attention. "Are you entirely made?" she asked, beginning to work at his buttons.

"Oh, my," he said. He hadn't fully considered his own nakedness; he'd thought it was just hers that mattered. She managed to push his shirt back off his shoulders and mostly expose his chest, which to him looked silly and unadorned, dull above her more baroque design. She ran one hand through his hair, which made his scalp tingle. She lightly danced her touch up his sleeves to his biceps, and where her fingers came near to his underarms he got ticklish and began to laugh and he collapsed upon her.

"You *are* a novice," she said, with some disappointment, he thought. He wondered what he could do to pretend otherwise when the door below them flung open. Light off the grass swam into the chapel. Scraping noises, a dragged chair, some thumps, a few expressive sighs.

Then Dirk heard the first declaration, and realized that Felix had escaped his other diversions and come to rehearse the Bach 'cello pieces again.

"Shit," whispered Hannelore, though her expression was mean and gleeful.

Dirk had drawn back, though Felix wasn't positioned far enough forward in the aisle to be able to see them even if he should glance up.

Dirk pulled his shirt more or less back to rights and sat up very softly.

"Coward." Hannelore didn't speak out loud, but he could see the word her mouth was making. She sat up softly, too. As the 'cello piece grew louder, she stood and beckoned to Dirk to follow her. Leaving her blouse and shoes where they were, she tiptoed back to the staircase. He hadn't noticed that the stairs continued beyond the loft. Up they went, out of the gloom and into the stone bell tower that was open to the winds on four sides.

"Someone will notice us!" he protested.

"No one is around at this time of the day, and who would think to look up and see if someone had crept into the tower of this abandoned outbuilding?" She dropped her skirt and stepped forward over pigeon droppings and rotting coils of rope. She was entirely naked but for the mask of ferocity and charity upon her face. He froze as she removed his shirt and then dropped his leggings. "Do you want to do this or not?" she said. "I'm not persuaded. You have to persuade me."

"Yes," he said. "I don't know how."

"Is that so? I'd never have guessed; I thought you were Casanova's cousin."

The wind sweeping up the lake played a tenderness upon the skin of his torso, his buttocks, his legs and forearms, it was a different attention than that which Hannelore was showing him. The effects were at odds; she was rough with him and the wind gentle, coercing; he couldn't seem to decipher the moods of which, the needs and suggestions of either. The music, though distant, mounted to an urgent encouragement.

"Is it that we are in an old church? Is that it?" said Hannelore in a dusky voice. She was handling him as if he were ingredients for an impromptu supper, hurriedly. "Are you afraid of some ancient threat of blasphemy? Copulation in the holy sanctuary?"

He had no words anymore. A ratcheting itchiness inside nearly hurt, and he didn't know how to relieve it. She was being kind and troublesome. Below Felix was making love to the 'cello with the assurance of a maestro. Dirk hated himself and wished he were anywhere else.

"Don't you believe in Christ?" she said, and rising on her toes, began to settle herself upon his prick. She was soft and annihilating, a damp wondrousness affording a new aspect of mystery. The surprise he felt was both elation and terror. That the world could turn itself inside out, pull itself through itself like a thread through a needle.

He never answered her question, and she drew away from him, or he from her; he couldn't tell even which muscles belonged to whom. "I can't be bothered," she said at last. "The miller's son won't strike me if he finds out, for your appetite and your fork are not at the same table."

She left him there, but not without kissing him first. She taught him how to kiss on the mouth. Perhaps if she had started there, things would have been different. He waited, naked, in the stone tower, slowly growing chilly, his penis clocking downward. He watched her hurry across the grass. Her blouse and her skirt were proper enough. She carried her shoes in her hand. She didn't look back to see if he was watching her. She never spoke to him again.

That night he wondered if he had some sort of obligation to find the miller's son and kill him. Was that how it was done? But honor was a hard sum to do in one's head when one has had no lessons in it, and he wasn't sure whose honor had been besmirched. Perhaps it was his own.

22.

The summer had begun with a bear vandalizing a chapel associated with an obscure Protestant confession. It reached its apotheosis in a thunderstorm that rattled the windows in their casements and raged over the roof-beams of the schloss.

The lightning was so insistent that Dirk in his cot thought to raise himself on one elbow and look across the taut forms of three restless laborers. In the final bed, high-lit with electrostatic flares as from giant lucifer matches, the farmhand and the seamstress were at it, roused to greater lust by the drama in the atmosphere.

Oh, is *that* what is meant by making love, thought Dirk, and probably blushed.

The lightning became more frequent. The thunder seemed
to stop directly above the house. No stranger to summer
storms, Dirk found this one too close, nearly taunting. Despite
the activities across the room, he finally sat up in bed, found his
clothes, adjusted his eye-patch, and left.

He went down one staircase and felt safer. He went down the
next and arrived in the kitchens. A light was on. He entered anyway.

The 'cello player was foraging for bread and mustard and a bit
of sausage. Dirk had never seen a member of the family or their
guests in the kitchen, but Felix in his nightshirt and bare calves
seemed unperturbed by the situation. "Are you underfed or over-
excited?" he asked, holding up bread in one hand and some wurst
in the other.

Dirk shrugged. He accepted a hunk of bread and a heel of the
sausage. They sat down together at a table.

"These last days of summer, they always supply their strongest
storms at night," said Felix.

Thinking of the aggressive coupling under the eaves, Dirk
nodded.

"Are you returning to Munich with the family? If so, perhaps I
shall see you when next I come down from Wittenberg with Kurt.
We leave tomorrow, you know."

"Kurt?"

"The Baron in line—the Baron's son. Surely you know Kurt?"

"I don't know the family," mumbled Dirk. "I am a jack-of-all-
trades, privy to no one's attention but the overseer. I don't know if
I'll be brought to Meersburg, or to Munich. Or perhaps I'll be sent
back to the village from which I came in the early summer."

"See if you can get a job being manservant to Kurt," said Felix. "You would like Wittenberg."

"Why would I do that?"

"It's full of music. You like music."

"I'm not sure that I do. I'm not sure that I have any feeling for music at all. I'm just interested in what it . . . what it . . ." He paused.

"What it means?"

"What it—suggests."

Felix grinned and leaned a little closer. "And what does it suggest? Are you suggestible?"

"I don't know. It seems to indicate . . ." He waved his hand in the air, spilling a blob of mustard on Felix's knee. "Otherness. I don't know how to say it. An otherness, an apartness—like what we know, but transformed somehow."

Felix leaned back in his chair, as if they were old companions. "Well, take it from me. You would enjoy Wittenberg. I could meet up with you there, too. You and I, I am guessing we are *simpatico*."

"I don't know what that means, either."

Felix just smiled at his bread. Then he said, "The world is breaking free of smoky Roman superstition and glassy Lutheran rectitude. The heyday of the French rationalists, that, too, is gone, gone as Napoleon. A new attention is being paid to how things seem and how they feel. Have you read Goethe? *The Sorrows of Young Werther*? It's been taken up by university scholars of my generation, it proposes passion in life, not hesitation. It proposes engagement, not detachment. We must live life, not merely regard it. A happy satisfaction at being alive. Unless you kill yourself, of course, the way Werther does. But please don't. We must be brave and try to find our way. It may not be the way proposed to us in the past. Don't you think?"

That was what Dirk had been attempting in the belfry of the abandoned Catholic chapel. His efforts hadn't brokered a happy satisfaction at being alive.

Felix grabbed Dirk's hand and clasped it in both of his. Dirk stiffened. "*Simpatico*, it's Italian for 'sympathetic.' Hearts beating to the same pulse. That's what music does for one, you know—I mean, for two. For more. It trains hearts to lean in the same direction. Sympathetically."

Dirk pulled away. The lightning made a black-and-white image of Felix's open face, his bed-tousled hair, the Adam's apple bobbing as he swallowed the crust of bread. His skin from neck to the second button, for the first was open, was papery and slightly damp from the humidity in the summer kitchen.

"Well, look me up if you come to Wittenberg, or I'll see you in the Munich house, I expect, or the Meersburg salons. I'm a long-time hanger-on to this family. They're good to guests," said Felix, relenting. "There's some ale in the cold cupboard, I believe. Pull two glasses for us."

Dirk pulled two steins of ale and set them both before Felix and turned away to climb the stairs in the darkness. The midnight lightning was over, the thunder receding. He could hear his heart. Whether it was sympathetic or not, he had no idea.

23.

He never did speak to Hannelore again, true, but that didn't mean she had no effect on his life. Toward the latter part of the summer, in Meersburg, it became whispered loudly that the unmarried kitchen maid might be with child. Too early to show, but she was telling. The miller's son, it seemed, had become a romantic casualty of the season and therefore he would accept no credit of paternity. Hannelore was keeping silent as to the identity of the father. When Baron von Koenig pressed the point, the over-seer conducted interviews of the staff.

It became apparent that someone had seen Hannelore leaving the defunct chapel by the lake, carrying her shoes, looking disheveled.

Additionally, it was the opinion of many in the kitchens and stables that young Dirk Drosselmeier had been observed mooning about the girl from time to time.

But further questioning revealed that Felix, the bosom chum of Kurt von Koenig, family scion, had been rehearsing with his instrument in the chapel all summer.

A family retainer hastened to Wittenberg to resolve the matter. The advocate returned some days later with a statement. Felix had admitted the child to be his own, after all, and he supplied a settle-ment to be paid upon the unwed mother. Such things were done in that set, apparently.

Dirk pondered this as he collected his items—three shirts now, and a buttonhook, and a junky old knife that needed sharpening. He remembered the walking stick that had belonged to the old man in the forest, the woodcutter. It was more useful now that Dirk was no longer the slender slip of a kid, but a young man, and ready for a young man's life. At least he hoped so.

For the first and only time, Dirk was called for an interview with the Baron. "Your last chance," said Baron von Koenig, "to own up to your responsibility and to claim this child as your own."

"I was given to understand that your houseguest Felix has al-ready confessed to that?"

"Stahlbaum is a quixotic character. His motivations and his behavior are untrustworthy. Perhaps he was giving cover to you, as he could see for himself you are in no situation to take on a family. I understand from the maiden that he was friendly enough with you."

"Hannelore hasn't named me as the father," replied Dirk. He'd learned a little about dignity. "I'm not a father. Neither of her child nor of any other."

"Keep it like that, you'll be a lot better off," growled the Baron, who probably wasn't such a bad sort, thought Dirk, but seemed to be tired of dealing with the progression of pregnancies that summertime at the lake perhaps provided all too regularly.

"Am I to proceed with the household to the autumn address?"

"I'd been inclined to bring you, but not now. Deserved or not, a shadow falls upon your reputation. We strive to be a strict Catholic household, at least in town. You wouldn't think to return to your parsonage in Bavaria?"

"If a scandal attaches to me? It would dishonor Pfarrer Johannes. And I've been given no useful message to deliver to him. So, no, I don't think I ought to return."

"I supposed as much. Well, as it happens I was visiting a paper merchant in Meersburg to arrange for a volume of the scientific findings among some friends of mine. Adventures in atmospherics. The merchant mentioned he is in need of an assistant. I shall send you there with a letter of controlled enthusiasm. Maybe he'll find you suitable. If not, God be with you upon your own road, if He can find you there."

The Padlocked Garden

24.

Dirk was surprised to find how deeply he resented being let go from the retinue that served the von Koenigs. With only a letter of introduction in hand and some back pay in his pocket, he was turned out upon the dusty road in the direction of Meersburg. It wasn't to be a long journey, but he found it grating to watch the family entourage wheel past him without acknowledging him. Salt and brine them all.

An older farmer, carrying thumps of rain-dampened hay in a wagon, picked up Dirk eventually. "Going near enough Meersburg to make it worth your while, and the company is welcome, if you're going to talk," said the fellow. It seemed, though, that he didn't really care if Dirk talked. It was more that he wanted an audience for his soliloquy. So Dirk fed him the occasional interrogative syllable, tinder in an oven to keep it going, and more or less failed to listen to what the farmer said.

However, when they passed a substantial church building positioned over the lake, a great basilica structure painted a pale strawberry, the farmer commented, "You want religious paintings and such, there's the place. The whole congress of heaven is painted floating on clouds right above you. The ceiling of the nave.

You'd think the wind up there would have disturbed at least someone's flowing robes so you could get a good look at the particulars
of angels, but God's uncanny breeze keeps everyone modest."

"You can let me off here, I would like to make a visit," said Dirk.

"Not to bother with all that. Pilgrims stopped coming a few
years back when the Cistercians were chased out. The place is
boarded up. The canopy of heaven will still be aloft, but you can't
get in the door to see it."

The things that could be seen versus the ones that could only
be imagined. Dirk still felt he didn't have a grasp on what divided
the two armies. Was it a function of God's revelation, or of personal talent at seeing? Things invisible to see, they were still there,
weren't they? Birds maybe could see them. Gnarly schwarzkopfs
hiding maliciously in the underbrush could spy on cold transparent truths. Old farm-dames with second sight, maybe. But Dirk
couldn't see the invisible, not yet. He couldn't even see plain old
what-not.

"And so, here we part. I'm headed out the road toward Daisen-
dorf, and must be there before dusk turns to night. Meersburg
starts up beyond those fields. Can you make that out?"

"That much, yes."

The farmer bit his moustache. "I am obliged for the company,
young man."

"It was no bother to me."

Dirk dismounted. He heard the farmer chuckle and mutter to
himself something like, "No bother to you! Well, that puts my
mind at rest."

The vineyards gave way to a medieval gate. Meersburg mounted
from the lakeshore in switchback lanes and stepped alleys. Over-
hanging half-timbered buildings loomed in a rangy, busybody
manner—or that is how it seemed to Dirk. (He was beginning to

pay attention to how things seemed.) Citizens were disinclined to give directions, but eventually Dirk found his way to an alley off a cul-de-sac road above the lake, on the far end of town. It was almost too late to knock, but he had no other ideas for lodging, so knock he did.

The burgher answered his own door. He took the proffered note and read it in the falling light. "I'm not the governor of the poorhouse nor do I host a reformatory for lounge-abouts, but come in," he grumped. He was untucked in his dress—he'd gotten up from table. A nearly visible fug of sauerbraten and wet dog hung agreeably in the passage. The home beyond its severe façade seemed comfortable enough. Mitteleuropean *bourgeoiserie.* Dirk was brought round through some pantries to a kitchen, empty but for a few prowling cats. A desiccated fowl from an earlier meal sat in a covered pot. "I'm at table with the little lords," said Herr Pfeiffer. "The Frau is indisposed and seconded to her chamber. Help yourself to some supper and find a blanket in the chest. The morning will be time enough to sort out your particulars."

Dirk ate and then he stretched out among shadows and the drying pots some kitchen maid had already seen to. How many times in a life, he thought, will I lie down in a darkness whose character I cannot imagine, to see what daybreak reveals of my new circumstances? Or is that every day of my life?

He itemized what he could tell of this establishment by stretching out on a stone floor. A smell of char and of some oily polish, perhaps for leather or laundry. The distant sound of young boys laughing and thumping up a staircase. A sense of guardedness here, bolts thrown at the kitchen door as well as the street door. But the upper part of the window remained unshuttered, so the moon traced three angled crosses upon the slate floor.

In the morning his life might change again. There was something new to learn as long as he felt recurringly off the mark, belated, distracted. Walking with an invisible stone in his shoe, or speaking with a stone in his mouth and mistaking it for his tongue.

25.

He met the boys in the morning. They proved to be little garlic scapes. That Franz, that Moritz. Overly beloved, poorly handled, noisy as Romany brats, catapulting shots of black cherry conserve at the cats. Dirk feared he had been let into the house in order to become their tutor. A grave mistake if so, as he had nothing to teach them.

"What's this?" said Moritz the Visigoth, rampaging through Dirk's small satchel and discovering Dirk's knife.

"Give it me," said Franz, the Mongol Horde. He was eight years old, the big brother. His columnar head sported a froth of perfect curls that grew straight up but didn't spread. He looked like the top inches of a stein of foamy beer. He snatched at Moritz.

"Mine," said Dirk, lunging. "Leave my things be."

"It has a face, a nasty imp head. What's it got between its knees, eh?" asked Franz, peering.

"More than you have between yours," said Moritz, who was only five.

"He'll slice you of his own accord if you test him," said Dirk. "Hand it here." He folded the leather wrap around it again.

"Are you Papi's new run-around?" asked Franz. "You'll have thighs like Eastertide hams, going up and down these streets. No one lasts more than a few months. We can show you where Papi hides the key to the wine cellar."

"This is my room now," said Dirk. "It's been given me while I'm here, and you aren't allowed. Stay out."

"It's our house, we can go anywhere." Moritz climbed up on the windowsill and Dirk pulled him off lest he fall three flights.

Franz said, "We can come with you to pick up the bleaching compound today if you want company. I can show you how to find your way. Moritz can show you how to get lost." Moritz was poking the rest of Dirk's deflated satchel with his foot.

"We make the best paper outside of Munich, and also including Munich, too," said Moritz.

"If you're not fired by then, you can come to Oktoberfest with us, and get bread dumplings," said Franz. "Our mother won't go; she thinks it's a festival for peasants. So Papi won't go either, he can't. He says Mutter comes first and the world follows if it dares, that is what he says."

"When she's not listening he says that. When she is, he says, Darling Mutti!"

"He loves her, you clod, what's wrong with a husband loving his wife?" The older brother whistled derisively. "Come, why don't we let the rabbits out of the hutches and see if any peregrines notice." They tore away. Dirk tidied up and went for his assignment. Herr Pfeiffer was waiting for him in a small office off the stairs.

26.

You come with a lukewarm recommendation from the Baron, but beggars can't be choosers, and we've exhausted the stock of available help nearby," said Gerwig Pfeiffer. The man was a cheery enough sort, if beleaguered. Perhaps his establishment had more work than it could handle. He rubbed his scalp until his hair was flyaway thistle, and mopped his sweating temples with a cloth he kept in a saucer of water. "Everyone wants to read these days, Dirk, can't keep up," he explained. "Gluts of broadsheets. For us merchants of paper, it keeps idle hands busy and it renders holidays scarce."

"How do you know the von Koenig family?"

"You mean how does the merchant hobnob with the nobleman? I sell paper to the Baron for the printing of transcripts of his scientific companions. The wealthy have peculiar hobbies. Commerce is commerce." Pfeiffer began to lay out for Dirk a few metes and bounds of the trade. Dirk prepared to earn his keep through the gathering, soaking, sieving, pressing, and bleaching of rags into paper. And the sizing, trimming, bundling, carting, and delivery of it. At least until something better might offer itself.

Pfeiffer broached the topic of general finance. What constituted a profit; why profits ought to be reinvested into the business. Who kept the books (Pfeiffer himself) and the keys to the warehouse (Pfeiffer again). Who brought the takings to the countinghouse (guess who).

As Pfeiffer was about to go into a disquisition about the autumn schedule, the door behind Dirk opened. Swiveling on his stool, Dirk prepared to stand up in case it was the mistress of the household. A swish of skirting brushed against the doorsill. She may have been startled to find a visitor, as she didn't come in. The door closed softly.

"Ah. So now you've witnessed my wife," said Pfeifer. "The lovely Frau Pfeiffer. She enjoys being shy. What are your experiences with bookkeeping?"

"I'm not good with children."

"That's not what I asked you."

"I can try to learn about bookkeeping, I guess."

"Numbers obey. At least *something* adds up around here."

27.

Shy meant more than shy; it meant clandestine. Dirk was lodged in the Pfeiffer establishment for almost a week before he caught a real glimpse of Frau Pfeiffer. Well, he had the place itself to learn as well as its *ménage*.

The boys dragged Dirk throughout the house, upstairs and down. A cook lumbered in and baked and roasted things and left them out on the table at noontime. A girl drifted by at dusk to wash down the boys and wash up the dishes and store anything uneaten. Though Dirk sometimes heard steps upstairs, or in the hall behind closed doors, Frau Pfeiffer failed to emerge.

He didn't know if the establishment was characteristic of the area—he'd so little experience with houses. (The von Koenig schloss outside Überlingen had seemed like a palace-in-training, while the Pfarrer's cramped suite of rooms had been too spare of comfort.)

The property, though shabby, was generous enough to have not one but two wide buildings squeezed upon it. One behind the other, with a space between them. The tall, timbered house and offices fronted the road with a formal walled garden conferring a sense of status—slightly shabby status, because the garden was overgrown and the gate to the road was in need of painting. In the shallow courtyard behind the house, though, scrappy chickens pecked and herbs were hung to dry and broken equipment fell into further disrepair.

Beyond this cloistered utility yard loomed the twin structure, of similar dimensions to the house. It was fronted with open porches looking down at rusting harrows, a butter churn, and stacks of firewood. For another family it had been a genuine barn; Pfeiffer apparently used some of the upper rooms for the storage of supplies. As Dirk wasn't sent out there, he didn't know for sure.

Most of the houses in Meersburg proper had swollen to the margins of their properties, it seemed. This short way out from the center of town, the walled garden with a street gate was an anomaly: neither rural orchard nor coachyard. The boys told Dirk that their mother often spent whole days in the garden. No windows from the house looked out on it, and the walls were high enough to promise privacy all around—excepting the gate, of course.

On the sixth day, a Monday, a girl arrived to do the washing. She was a pasty thing with hair tucked so tightly under her cap Dirk couldn't guess at its color. She hollered at Dirk to clear the boys away, they were splashing in the water, which was a labor to draw and to heat, or didn't he know that?

He took them out. They walked the streets of the upper town and then wandered down to the water. The great steamboat that had brought Dirk here at the start of the summer was nearing the jetty, making a silhouette in front of the ice-grey Swiss Alps in the distance. Dirk and the boys climbed on the rocks, enjoying the spray and the noon light. After that, they made a circuit of the town by the lanes that had grown up outside the medieval walls. By the time he had exhausted the boys and returned them to the household, the laundry maid was done with the washing and had already hung it to dry on ropes slung between house and barn. She sat down with Dirk, the boys, and their father, and they all made a late lunch out of headcheese, mustard, and brown bread.

"Take them up to the nursery and read to them or something," said Pfeiffer when the meal was through. "I have to go see someone about an unpaid bill of lading."

"I don't think I am a governess," said Dirk.

"I don't think so either, but try," replied his boss.

The nursery, which doubled as a haphazard schoolroom, faced the courtyard between house and barn. Settling the boys with graphite and paper—there was always a lot of paper in this house—he turned when flashes of light began to arc across the walls. In the summer heat that lingered into early autumn, the glaring white sheets had already dried, it seemed. With large motions, the laundress was harvesting the dried sheets and table runners.

"Tillie," called Moritz, "let me see if I can hit you through the sheet with this ball!"

"If you muck up this laundry," began the girl, Tilda, but left the threat unstated.

"Sit down and draw," said Dirk, "or I'll teach you something about hitting."

He stood at the windowsill and watched. The sheets were like pieces of cloth paper, in a way. Shining panels. He noticed four hands above the lines, untying knots, folding the bedding away. Frau Pfeiffer was helping.

He might catch a glimpse of her if the laundry came down in the right sequence. He watched as, behind the remaining panels, the two women worked together, folding great cloths in a kind of shadow-puppetry dance sequence.

Now this one must be the last. He would see what she looked like. Perhaps she was monstrous, and kept to herself out of courtesy for others.

Not yet—what revealed itself wasn't Frau Pfeiffer but yet another panel more like a banner than bedding. That is to say, it was a sheet upon which something had been painted. Dirk made a *tchhh* sound, and the boys looked up.

"Good work, Mutti!" cried one of them.

"Whatever is that?" asked Dirk.

Tapered hands, more refined than a washerwoman's, loosened the pennant from its ropes. The sheet swooped around in a zephyr caused by quick movement, and Frau Pfeiffer disappeared through a door into the barn before Dirk could learn anything of her but that she could move swiftly.

"It is Mutter's drawing, and here's mine," said Franz, so Moritz pushed in front of his big brother to show his own work.

"But what was it a painting of?" asked Dirk. "I couldn't see."

"Oh, something," replied Franz, "or something else."

28.

Several mornings after this, Dirk approached the small salon where Herr Pfeiffer oversaw the affairs of his household and his trade. The door was halfway open. Dirk paused, not to eavesdrop but to wait for an acceptable moment to enter.

"But you've taken in another hobbled goose, I hear." A woman's tones, arresting to Dirk because they didn't sound like anything he'd ever heard before. It reminded him of his first exposure to the voice of the 'cello. Hers was a pearly instrument that made of workaday German something more velveteen, throaty. What she said, the way she put things. Emphases, sudden diminuendos. "I've seen him, you know. He wears a mark of the woods."

"He'll do just fine here. Trust me on this. He's not a local boy."

"I can tell that. Is he altogether put together?"

"He's a good lad, and no known family. Don't fuss about it."

"Well." There was a silence and the sound of fingers drumming on a tabletop. "I am trying to ask you your business with this boy."

"Ah, Nastaran. He is taking over the duties of the lad who had to leave to tend to his grandfather in the Thurgau."

"But sleeping here in our own home? Is that proper? Are our affairs to be public property?"

"The past assistants were all local, as you know very well. They all had plenty of scope for backstairs chatter if they'd been inclined. But they weren't, and this one isn't either, I can tell. Now, were you here to ask for more supplies?" The husband's voice tired and consoling. "I will get you what you need."

"You can't give me what I need." Oh, the 'cello in that sentence. "But you can get me a pot of blue the next time you are in Munich. I'd welcome that."

"What shade?"

The silence went on for so long that Dirk began to inch backward. Then she said, "I want the sky, Gerwig. Either you know the color of the sky or you don't."

"You should rely on it that I don't, my love. Give me a sample of cloth or paper and I'll see if I can match it. I'll undoubtedly get it wrong, but perhaps not so wrong as to cause offense."

She was up and through the door so quickly that she'd have bumped into Dirk had he not retreated. All he saw was an ebbing of dress material on the bottom step before his eye could really focus. She rose out of sight as if in an updraft. He waited a moment and then approached the chamber, rapping lightly.

"Oh, you just missed the Frau. She is longing to meet you," said Pfeiffer, peaceably enough.

"I'm surprised not to have had the pleasure yet."

"Oh, well, pleasure." The husband was ruminative, riffling some papers. "She is a retiring type, the Frau Pfeiffer. I can tell she will come forward soon. She isn't used to having someone else live in the house. Our previous help has always come from nearby, and left in the evenings."

"I don't enter the barn. But in the house you haven't told me what rooms to avoid, if she doesn't care for company."

"She'll do the avoiding, never fear." But he relented. "She's from a different tradition. She will have nothing against you, but your lack of connection with anyone we know personally will take some time for her to overcome. In her society, she wouldn't have generally met someone like you." He sighed, and added almost under his breath, "Or me."

"I am uncertain . . ."

"She keeps to the garden and her own chamber, across the hall from mine." He looked up under his bushy brows. "You'll have deduced that we accommodate Frau Pfeiffer. I'm sure at your age you know what relations between a man and a woman are."

"Oh, I'm not questioning—and, no, I'm hardly in the situation—"

He laughed. "Well, if you don't, you will soon enough. It helps keep the peace that the Frau and I should retire to separate sleeping chambers. But don't worry about affection. I'm devoted to her, and always will be."

"It's hardly my place—"

Gerwig Pfeiffer stopped humming. "You're quite right. Let's to this day's lesson in availabilities of glue, shall we? There are three sorts we use, depending both on the wetness of the atmosphere and the quality of the rag content we've boiled up. See here." They bent over their work. Upstairs, a door slammed, once, then twice more, as if practicing outrage.

29.

The next morning Herr Pfeiffer had to be out to meet a steam-ship arriving with a shipment of rags. It was a drizzly day, and the boys were cross to be kept inside. Dirk hunted about the nursery for something to entertain them. He discovered a stack of woodcut prints. They'd been discarded from some printing job, probably for misalignment, as they all tilted at the same angle. The boys had used charcoal crayon on some of them. Dirk selected an image of a man beating a donkey. He cut the page up into fourteen or fifteen segments and shuffled them. "Now you are to put it back into the right form," he told them.

"I wonder if the donkey will have run away," said Moritz.

"How could he do that?" asked Franz.

"Dirk's scissors have cut through the harness."

The boys weren't much amused by the puzzle, but they dallied and fought over it. The pieces of paper got gummy and stuck to their fingertips. It was a bit of a disaster.

Then a voice from across the utility courtyard: Frau Pfeiffer calling for assistance. Her tone was even. Moritz rose to go, but Franz was bigger and spilled him on the floor to get by. The older brother ran upstairs at once—a covered bridge-way spanned the courtyard on the third level, so those on high floors in either build-ing wouldn't need to go down and up so many stairs.

Moritz was sulking when Franz returned, carrying a small clay flask with a wide neck. "Mutter would like you to open this, if you can."

He took it. Something heavy and liquid inside. The mouth of the jug had been covered with a square of cheesecloth. Wax had been melted across the top to keep the vessel secured and, perhaps, the liquid from spilling over or drying out or spoiling. "What is it, do you know?"

"Paint, I think. But I don't know the color."

Dirk tried to wrestle the wax off, but it had hardened to stone. He pulled the leatherfold out of his pocket and unwrapped his gnome-head knife, and he set to work carving chunks of wax off the edge.

"Let me," said Moritz. "Franz got to bring the paint. It's my turn."

"I'm bigger," said Franz. "You'd only stab yourself."

Dirk wouldn't hear of it. "It's not a very sharp knife, but it's sharp enough. It could slip. What does your mother use the paint for?"

"To paint with," said Franz."

"Well, think of that. I really meant: What does she paint?" His hand slipped and a short line of crimson showed up along the edge of his thumb.

"It's red paint, then," said Franz, not understanding.

"It's the red paint we all have inside us." Dirk went to the window, to rinse his hand in the rainwater that still splashed down.

"Stop," cried Franz.

"It's only blood," said Dirk, but pivoted as a chair overturned.

Moritz had grabbed the blackened knife and was hounding his brother with it. "You never let me do anything you rotten stinking shitty!"

"Gott in Himmel, give me that!" roared Dirk, and joined the chase. The boys were too quick, and tumbled out of the room and halfway up the stairs hollering.

With Dirk only steps behind, the brothers raced across the rain-spattered span. They careered onto the porch of the barn's third level, where they were stopped by the emergence of Frau Pfeiffer. Dirk recaptured the knife by encircling it with one hand. With his other hand he froze Moritz's fist to prevent an accident.

But then it seemed everything had frozen for an instant, a tableau made more theatrical by the sound of rain.

Perhaps it was merely her garb, which wasn't the closely fitted and over-stitched apparel of her fellow goodwives in Meersburg, but a weird and billowy shift and a pair of loose pantaloons below. Maybe a man's shirt of a sort Dirk had never seen before. Upon her scalp her dark hair was roped, only loosely and off-center, exposing a neck of bleached oak.

"What are you doing to me?" she asked her sons, in a voice and tone that Dirk couldn't characterize. A kind of ribboned smoki-ness. He wasn't musical enough to think beyond that.

The boys hung their heads and hung back till Franz said, "He was trying to kill me."

"I wasn't, only hurt him," insisted Moritz. "Anyway, it was the knife, not me."

"Did you open the jar?"

"Dirk is working on it."

"Bring it to me when it's open. And please don't shriek. Any-thing but shrieking. If you must kill one another, do it silently. It's much more effective that way."

The scarf-like clothes rippled as she disappeared. The door closed without the sound of a latch dropping. She had neither spoken to Dirk nor looked at him.

30.

And then, as if enough had decided to be enough, the next morning Frau Pfeiffer knocked on the door of the office and entered before her husband had a chance to raise his eyes from the page.

She stood with her eyes down and hands folded, one upon the other like a pair of nestling doves. "Forgive me for my intrusion," she said to the floor. Dirk heard in her words what he'd missed earlier. It was accented German. She was from elsewhere.

By now Dirk had come across polychrome carvings of the Virgin and Child in the Catholic churches. One splendid, fourteen-inch example had sat in a nook in the chapel at the schloss von Koenig. Wood could see what stone could not. Marble eyes were blind, but wooden eyes were only cloaked. Frau Pfeiffer had eyes of polished chestnut that retained a deep gleam of greenwood. Pliability.

"Never an intrusion," said her husband, evenly.

She was done up like a grandee in a roving theatrical troupe. At once a maharani and a hausfrau, a peddler and a djinee. Dirk had never seen the like. Musulman, Ottoman, *opera buffa* wife? Queen of the harem and Friday night barkeep?

She wore a proper, kitten-grey Brunswick gown, its waistcoat of contemporary style—just flanking the hips—but beneath its split sleeves spilled a voluminous silk blouse in a pattern of unkempt garden—roses, coiled brambles, irises, narcissi. Several bangles of brass or silver or white gold sloped toward her elbow. A scarf was loosely fastened around her mouth as if to keep her words and expression curtained.

Her bonnet was simple, even homely, but at her neck was gathered a scarf the colors of water reed and apricot.

"I feel I should now be introduced," she said.

"Oh? Why now?" asked her husband, a wry twist of his lips on the side of his mouth used to accommodating a pipe.

"He has helped me with my color."

Herr Pfeiffer turned to Dirk, who felt himself going pink. "Franz brought me a jug of paint to open."

"Well, then, it's cozy enough already. My dear wife, behold Dirk Drosselmeier. Dirk, Frau Pfeiffer. As you live and breathe."

"I am in your debt," she said to Dirk. "It is not easy to open color." She rolled her gaze over him at last. In the serene light dropping from the clear high windows of the office at break of business day, he felt almost noticed.

31.

Gerwig Pfeiffer often sent Dirk on errands. The young man began to map out Meersburg in his mind as he crossed from Unterstadt to Oberstadt, along the Steigstraße or down the sets of stone steps. Always around a corner or outside a window, the teal or oily-grey waters of the rippling Bodensee—Lake Constance— lurked with a hint of menace. Dirk realized that Meersburg did business across and upon the broad lake as if it were a commercial square. He didn't like the lake much, though.

Sometimes Dirk took the boys with him. They held his hands. He wasn't interested in children, though he did notice them. Despite being younger, Moritz was the keener, the broody anarchist. Franz was paler, more stolid, perhaps more cowed by life. He chuckled, when he chuckled, with closed lips.

As they hopped and skipped beside him, the boys recited verses from *Des Knaben Wunderhorn*. With joy I walked in a green wood. *Ich ging mit Lust durch einen grünen Wald.* They didn't know the whole thing. Above and beyond Meersburg, the vineyards and orchards seemed a distant set of flanking angel wings, antithesis to the annihilating lake, which wouldn't hold color for long, constantly slipping into new disguise as if to hide its elemental nature.

Glancing above the rooflines, Dirk wished he could spy the

steeper hills of Bavaria his homeland. But what was home to him? The only Alps were those of western Switzerland across the lake to the left, looming, when mists didn't obscure them, like a thundering army in glacial advance. Or a battlement prohibiting passage, padlocking the lake-dwellers into place.

32.

He didn't eat with the family. He didn't eat with the help. Somehow he didn't fit in with either. This seemed the usual way in his life, and he didn't mind.

The Pfeiffer family lived close to the bone. Their home was large, handed down to them from some forebear, but it was in need of attention. Walls that hadn't been whitewashed since the turn of the century were mottled with a green rash. Windows with cracked panes were fitted with cedar shakes. Dirk suspected subsidence in one corner of the house, as all the balls and tops that the boys dropped tended to roll toward that quarter.

In the first month alone, two separate chairs lost their footing and deposited colleagues or family upon the floor.

Despite the pleasant commotion and daily decay, Herr Pfeiffer managed to run a business. He worked from home many days, dispatching Dirk to deliver a bill or to collect a shipment of supplies. Sometimes the paterfamilias oversaw processes at the rag baths, which were housed in an old fishing shed near the jetty. On these days, Frau Pfeiffer kept to upstairs chambers. She read light fictions and sometimes could be heard weeping over them. The housemaid rolled her eyes and the boys ignored her, and pestered Dirk instead.

"Are they going off to kindergarten soon?" Dirk asked Herr

Pfeiffer one day when a nasty autumn storm looked to be blowing in across the lake—some Alpine drama heading north. The threat was keeping everyone housebound.

"Oh, no. Mutter wouldn't have *that*," he said.

"Never?"

"Never so far. Moritz, he isn't suitable."

"Then they will want a tutor?" Dirk was risking his own employment, as he knew himself to be unequal to the task.

The Frau chose this moment to appear upon the stairs. She paused, struck by some private consternation. A non sequitur would result, Dirk predicted, and it did. "The moon bowled down the length of the Thurgau slopes last night."

"Did it now," said her husband. "You were up late, to notice that."

"Is he questioning the boys' training?"

"I mean no harm," said Dirk, addressing her for the first time.

She continued looking at Pfeiffer. "You've only to move an inch one way, and all the world shifts an inch in the other direction."

"I'm afraid it's coming to that time of the year," he said, shuffling some papers. "You'll be all right for a week. Dirk will be here."

"Dirk," she said. Now she turned to look at him, and proceeded to the bottom step. "Is he diligent, Gerwig? Dirk, are you diligent?"

"I am attentive," said Dirk, hoping that was the right answer.

"He'll do just fine." Pfeiffer sighed. "It's only a week, Nastaran."

She moved on in a soft whuffing of scarves, and went out into the walled garden. She was framed by the open door. A needling rain was beginning to fall, and winds stirred the leaves of the Russian olive tree, which made behind her a pattern of irregular chevrons, silvery and silky. She opened up her hands as if to collect pearls liquefying from the sky.

"I never came across the name Nastaran before," he said.

"Persian," replied Herr Pfeiffer. "I am told that, in the tongue of her homeland, it means 'wild rose.'"

"Wild," said Dirk.

"Rose," insisted her husband, and then told Dirk the real reason he had been hired.

33.

She couldn't be left alone overnight, that was the thing. She was a somnambulist. Dirk didn't know what that meant.

"She walks in her sleep."

"Surely that's not possible."

"It is a rare condition, but a genuine one. She finds herself in a dream, you see, and in a dream she rises and moves. We must always keep the windows locked on the upstairs floors, and we bar the door to the crosswalk to the barn, lest she take it into her vacant mind to sit upon a sill or rail and try to step upon a breeze."

Dirk said, "Are her eyes open?"

"They are open but unseeing."

"I don't know what that means."

"It means," said the paper merchant, "while I am away, some-one must stay near her, to guide her homeward if she goes out of doors."

"In the middle of the night?"

"It has happened, so."

"But surely to keep attentive is the job of—a husband—or a governess—or a lady's companion of some type—"

"She won't tolerate a governess of any sort," said Pfeiffer, sadly. "She is afraid of losing me to some more capable woman. I know what you're thinking: Why not some ancient biddy, some cross-eyed housewife needing a personal income? But my wife won't have it. She admits a sense of her own—particularity. Besides, a certain amount of physical strength could be needed in a crisis."

"Is this situation regular?"

"Annual. It gets worse at this time of year, but in the deep winter her body seems to notice the cold even if her mind doesn't, and there is little chance she would go barefoot into the snow. So it's in the autumn that I need help. Her remark about the moon suggests she notices the season is changed. This is also the time I go to the university at Heidelberg and to Munich to collect my orders for the spring, which work keeps me busy all winter. If you become a true apprentice, you can take over that job of travel for me someday. For now, I need you to stay here and keep—what was your word?—attentive."

"Where is she going when she is walking in her sleep?"

"She cannot accept that question." Pfeiffer sighed. "She only partly believes me when I tell her she has been sleepwalking. She can't remember her dreams, you see, so if it is something she is dreaming, she can't learn what it is. We must keep her out of danger." He leaned forward. "You do not know Nastaran yet, truly, but you must love her enough to keep her out of danger."

"I will."

34.

Herr Pfeiffer had taken leave of his wife privately upstairs, it seemed, for when the boys gathered at his hips for final embraces, and Dirk hung back trying to appear responsible, Frau Pfeiffer didn't emerge.

"You have your instructions," said Herr Pfeiffer. "You won't have any problems."

"But if there is a problem?" asked Dirk.

"Just treat the boys as you were treated yourself, growing up." At Dirk's blank look, the man continued. "You're a good boy, so your parents must have done their job right."

I'm not good, I'm just quiet, thought Dirk, but didn't believe it was sensible to say that aloud. "But what about Frau Pfeiffer? What if she becomes—indisposed? Or needs something I can't help with? Has she a friend I can call upon?"

"She has no friends," said her husband, heaving his leather carryall upon the carriage bench. "The Meersburg merchants and their wives aren't as open to the stranger among us as I had hoped. But she is used to all that."

"A minister she might trust?"

"She is unprofessed. The cook will be able to advise if it should come to certain womanly matters. But don't worry. I go away every fall. All part of the pattern. See to the boys, and attend to the Frau as I have instructed you, and I shall be back before you notice I'm gone." He headed off with a heave-ho, whistling.

The boys didn't run off to school. Their mother wouldn't have it. She thought Moritz too intense, and Franz was needed at home to keep him engaged.

So the boys plunged about the house and gardens. During the day Dirk kept an eye on them. Neither a hard job nor interesting to him.

During the nighttime, as agreed, Dirk assembled a pallet for himself in the corridor outside Nastaran's bedchamber.

On the third night of Herr Pfeiffer's absence, Dirk woke to the sound of a piece of furniture being shuffled across the floor. He knew that Herr Pfeiffer had nailed his wife's windows shut, but for a small inset of glass. Hinged on one side, it could be opened for air. Hardly large enough for a human hand to reach through.

So the only way Nastaran Pfeiffer could leave the room was to step over Dirk.

He lay so still in the dark he might have been trying to hear the fall of a shadow. The more he held his breath, however, the more the pounding of his own blood rose in his ears like a sequence of breaking waves. Once he thought he heard the noise of beaten air, as when a bird launches herself in a small wind whipped up by her own startled, urgent wings.

He might have heard another sound—a chair pulled here or there, and then bed curtains or blankets rustling.

It's she who has taken a lover, he thought; and somehow he has managed to come in through the window.

Herr Pfeiffer would want to know. Or he wouldn't really want to know. Dirk couldn't decide.

He was sure, waking again later in the night, that her door had never opened. She couldn't have stepped over him in her sleep without his knowing. She'd have bumped into him.

In the morning she came downstairs more composed than he had seen her so far. She didn't wear a bonnet today. Upon her brow, like a diadem, rested a stiffened, coiled gold braid. From this soft clamp fell a cloth of pale saffron with Oriental pattern. Her mouth and cheeks and chin were unveiled. As she walked, the head scarf fluttered loosely behind her shoulders. A look of billowing wings. A hawk settling.

The boys flung themselves at her and she petted them and sat while they ate their bread soaked in warm milk.

"I trust you slept well," said Dirk, politely, seeing to the boys' spills and crumbs.

"However could I know?" she replied. It was the most direct

thing she had ever said to him. "Only a spouse can report on whether one has slept well."

He had no answer to that. She pressed her point by saying, "Did *you* sleep well?"

Sure enough, he found he couldn't quite answer with confidence. He lied, perhaps for the first time. "I think so. I may have had a dream—"

"A dream is only a fancy. But lucky you, to fancify. If it is suitable to share with my family, tell us what your dream was about."

"I dreamed I heard furniture walking about in your room, and that you had turned into a bird, and left your room in the middle of the night, returning only as the sun was beginning to rise."

"*Did* you really dream that?" She turned to him with the scrutiny of a physician. Her look was neither alarmed nor suspicious. Her expression seemed to center itself in whorls, as peering down the cup of a peony or a rose toward the golden stamen seems to stabilize the gaze and intensify the act of seeing. Her next sentence was spoken with controlled force. "Do you know where I might have been going?"

"I don't," he said, and then, daringly, "perhaps you do."

At this she rose from the table and floated away. As she lifted her hems to clear the step to the passageway, he saw she was not wearing customary leather shoes, but dancing slippers in muskmelon silk.

35.

Having received no instruction in the particulars of the necessary entertainments, Dirk was aware he was failing the boys a little. They were becoming more rambunctious. Pottery shattered; language coarsened. It was a relief to hear from the laundry assistant that the harvest festival was about to begin. Dirk wondered about taking Franz and Moritz.

Franz said loftily, "Papi tells us that our festival is nothing as royal as the celebrations held in Munich for the marriage of Crown Prince Ludwig to Therese of Saxe-Hildburghausen. That was the first Oktoberfest. Papi went and got drunk for only the second time in his life."

"When was the first time?"

"He won't say."

Moritz mumbled, "The day he met Mutti."

Franz sat up like a trained poodle. "Can we go to the fair?"

"Let me ask."

Nastaran was in the kitchen. She was arguing with the cook. She wanted, it seemed, a pomegranate, or a few of them. "The harvest market isn't till tomorrow, and in any case pomegranates aren't native to *our* land," said the cook angrily. It sounded as if this was a conversation they'd had many times before.

"Pomegranates," insisted Nastaran, "and walnuts. I have a holy hunger. I need them."

"What you need," muttered the cook under her breath, "is something I can't easily supply. Oh, the mercy of good fortune, look who's here," she said to Dirk. "Lend me those lads as a hedge against unreason from Good Dame Precious Particular here. Boys, I shall set you to carving potatoes, how is that?" Distracted for a moment, the boys fell to, and Dirk turned for a few private moments with their mother, but she had already slipped away, bangles clinking and scarves rustling in the windless volume of the staircase.

"I want to talk to you about Oktoberfest," he called. Upstairs, a door closed.

"Dirk! I need your knife with the creepy dwarf so I can carve a monster out of a potato," cried Moritz.

"This potato has more eyes than Dirk does," muttered Franz.

36.

She was always disappearing. That was her charm and her allure, and it maddened him. Through the hasped gate into the dried and brittle garden; through the low door to the stone yard where the horses would be watered, had there been horses; behind films of cloth. He didn't think she was being intentionally seductive. Then, he didn't know much about intention. Or seduction.

37.

That night as he was settling his body down upon the pallet, he thought he heard the sounds for which the boys had waited all day. Heavy wheels over cobbles, curses and snatches of song and high laughter.

Dirk lay back upon the coat he'd folded up as a pillow. With his eye closed, he followed a parade pictured in his mind. A lady in green, not so much saintly as serious, attended by a swarm of birds burnished with torchlight. A congregation of pastors in formation, apparently right at home among this midnight revelry. A goat-legged impresario of sorts. A truculent bear on a chain, sometimes on four paws, sometimes upright. Prisoners in chains, singing. What a motley population the world could pretend to tolerate.

He was looking for Nastaran, for she must be there; she would be coming along any moment.

He was shaken from his vigil. He thought she had come to him at midnight, at last. But it was Franz.

"Moritz," he said. Franz was keeping his voice low so as not to affright his mother. He was crying. "Moritz has heard the caravan in the streets, and I think he has left to run after it, to watch."

Dirk was up at once. Taking the older brother by the hand, he slipped out the back door of the house. He left the door on the latch so they could return without waking Nastaran.

"Why didn't you come to me sooner?" he snapped at the boy.

"I thought I was dreaming," sobbed Franz. Dirk could hardly fault him for that.

Fortunately the progress of the caravan was easy to follow. The noise hadn't abated. Indeed, Dirk and Franz weren't the only midnight pedestrians. More than one curious citizen of Meersburg had come to darkened windows in nightshirt and cap, or donned a greatcoat and shambled out to watch the procession.

Dirk didn't know why anyone but a child would get up in the middle of the night and tiptoe along the cobbles in the moonlight.

We sleep with exhaustion, thought Dirk. We do this every night, don't we. And we wake with *such* exhaustion.

In guttering torchlight among the beery farmers who were beginning to angle their wagons in favored positions around the platz, Dirk caught sight of Moritz. He looked abandoned and cold. Franz reached him first, and it seemed to Dirk that initially Moritz hardly recognized his brother. But the moment passed, and Moritz became alert, and seemed only a little cross to be found. "Ach, I'm in for a thrashing," he said, slipping his hand into Dirk's. "I'm sorry."

"Why did you come outside?" asked Dirk, equably.

The boy shrugged. "We waited till evening. I couldn't wait till morning, too."

What doesn't arrive by day has to arrive by night, if it is to arrive at all, thought Dirk. "There's not much to see." Already the singers had quieted, the rumble of carts was done, and the whole party was laying out bedrolls under their wagons. Otherness subsided. Dirk felt as if the company dragon must have been led to the church graveyard, and the angels ascended to roost invisibly on the leads of the vestry. Ghosts in their disguise of moonlight, basilisks in the blue stone shadows.

They crossed the emptied streets. The town was now quiet, nearly serene. An owl, a breeze, a scatter of dried leaves across a lane, a barking cur. Then, Nastaran. By the fountain. She was trailing her fingers along the lip of the well. The crouching stone bear that emblemized Meersburg was holding the carven arms of the municipality and staring blankly beyond Nastaran. She was barefoot, dressed in gauzes, and her womanly form showed in the moonlight through the garments. Her brow was covered with a mantle that gave her the look of a biblical heroine. Her eyes were open but her gaze was not upon the well, not upon her boys, nor upon Dirk as he approached her slowly, as one might approach a skittish foal. A new patterning of cloud had come in; the sky seemed to be paved of softly luminous blue brick.

"Nastaran," he said with great tenderness, and reached out his hand. She might alight there in the cup of his palm, he felt.

She walked right by him. She could sidestep the winch and the housing of the pump, but she couldn't see him. Her shoulder and her right arm pressed into him, her unclasped breast rolled against his forearm. And then she recoiled, the back of her hand to her mouth in fright, her eyes twitching to locate herself in foreign particulars.

"Mutti!" cried Franz, and ran forward. She suffered herself to be greeted but she didn't clasp him. "Where were you going? Were you looking for us?"

"No," she answered, when she could speak. "I wasn't looking for you."

"Then where were you going?"

"You are still there," she said. "Already."

"I don't understand."

Hearing his mother's vatic remarks, Moritz looked up with a dark brow and spilled a remarkably foul and adult comment almost under his breath.

She gripped Dirk's arm and allowed herself to be walked toward home. Halfway there, she stopped and fastened a silken cincture to keep the panels of her blouse closed. Farther along, she dropped his arm and stepped a foot away from him, but kept pace. When they'd reached the house and secured the door, and the boys had been put to bed, Dirk poured her a little Kirschwasser. She drank a sip, and then stood to return to her room without further comment. Following, Dirk was too tired to be mindful of his manners. "But where were you going?" he asked her as she was turning to shut her door. He put his foot in the breach to keep the door open. "Nastaran," he said, with longing. "What are you looking for?"

With a few inches of space between their faces, she raised her dark eyes to him and regarded him keenly and openly. Her eyes were too damp, her face looked disarranged. She told him, "I don't know. If I could only find out—"

38.

Nastaran took to her room and wouldn't come to the door when Dirk knocked. The boys awoke at last, cross and dull-eyed, but wolfed their breakfasts and dressed to be brought out to the opening of the fair.

Perhaps the entire town had been awakened by the midnight commotion of arriving merchants and revelers. In the morning when Dirk went to the well, Meersburg seemed more than usually shuttered against him, the streets empty. What is a town but an assemblage of locked and secret chambers, he thought. The forest opens its arms more gladly.

In the scientific light of day, the midnight sense of mysterious presences had evaporated. Most stalls were heaped with ordinary harvest.

However, a few booths featured carved figurines, puppets and the like. Garishly painted. A population of mute and obvious toys. Mere figments of the exotic bestiary that had seemed to sweep into town by moonlight. Insults to them, actually.

Dirk watched how the Pfeiffer brothers paused over the toys. The old man in the forest—surely he used to carve figures? Not like these, though. Stout oaken gentlemen with mugs of beer, one in each hand. A wooden horse, two apes on its back. A doll that stood by itself, staring catatonically out of a porcelain head as perfectly ovoid as a grape. Her real cloth skirt featured real wrinkles. A few rod marionettes in the shape of officers with crested helmets. The boys were gentle, even reverential with the military figures. But Dirk had no coin with which to buy presents, so vendors shooed all three of them on.

Vexed at Dirk for apparent minginess, the boys ran off. He let them run. No harm could come to them now. However busy the residents of Meersburg, they wouldn't let danger come near a child, not even one with a foreign look in the eye, an olive cast to the skin.

Dirk was still musing on Nastaran and her concerns when he felt a tap on his shoulder. At first he couldn't even find the name on his lips. "Felix," supplied the young 'cellist. "Felix Stahlbaum."

The story of Hannelore and her pregnancy struck at Dirk, but lightly. He cared nothing for her. Or for Felix. Dirk did not hold out a hand or utter a greeting.

"I'm here for the festival," said Felix. "We've come from the university. Baron von Koenig is presiding over some municipal ceremony, and either receiving an honor or bestowing one, I forget which. He's also assembling a gaggle of his associates who dabble ineptly in atmospheric experiments. He sent for Kurt, and I accompanied him. I thought I might see you, if you were still in town." He looked with happy scrutiny, as if Dirk were a specimen of exotic snail or an oddly designed fern. "I'll stand you an ale. Look, that tavern has some benches set out. The light is nice. Come with me."

"I'm looking for some boys—"

"I thought you might be. Stop a while; whoever you want will pass by in time."

Felix meant something other than Dirk did, but it was true, Franz and Moritz wouldn't be far. Dirk could keep an eye on the proceedings from a bench. Warily he settled in the lackluster sunlight. Soon enough he spied Franz, watching some young louts of the town play skittles; Moritz hunched on the sidelines, too. Felix Stahlbaum looked to see what had caught Dirk's eye. "Who will be the winner?" he asked, amusing himself.

Dirk couldn't follow. He said, "Someone suggested to the Baron that I was—was with Hannelore."

Felix shrugged, toasted Dirk. "*Vive la différence.* You *were* involved with her. Weren't you?"

"But you admitted it was you all along."

"Who knows why we say and do what we say and do? I thought better of ruining anyone's life," said Felix after a silence.

"Because of that rumor, I lost my chance to stay on with the von Koenig household," replied Dirk. But then, he might not have been sent to the papermaker, and might never have met Frau Nastaran Pfeiffer. "No matter. What's done is done. I didn't know you realized I was in the chapel that day. That's all."

"The door was open. Who else knew where the key was hidden? Anyway, I tried to play up a storm for you, as I recall," said Felix. He yawned. "Sorry—a late night."

"For everyone," agreed Dirk. "You are still playing?"

"My Lehrmeister has me working over several string trios of van Beethoven. And I've just got my hands on a ravishing piece by de Saint-Colombe. Practice does get in the way of my theology studies, I am afraid."

"You will be a pastor? After you've fathered an illegitimate child?"

Felix laughed. "I intend to learn only enough theology to know how to sin more effectively, thus to become more deeply penitential. The darker the sin, the richer the value of spiritual recovery." He was speaking in a level of nuance beyond Dirk's apprehension: droll, insincere, affectionate. "No, I hope to become a better performer, to be worthy of the music I am learning. If knowing music can bring me relief, can—move me across the border—how to say this—can release me, perhaps, to write my own, so others may be moved as I have been—is there any other ambition? Theology and art aim in the same direction."

Dirk had nothing to say on the matter, so he slurped at the ale. Felix said, "What are *your* aims, young man?"

"I have no talents," said Dirk. "I only watch and listen."

"You have a talent of charm, I see you do."

"I cannot see—what did you say about it—across borders. I have never been able to see that. But I know someone who can, I think, but is stuck—cannot take the step."

"Music usually helps," said Felix. But he seemed to realize that remark was glib, and he relented. "Tell me what you mean."

Without naming Nastaran, Dirk told Felix about a woman from somewhere in the Near East, a woman possessed of a dybbuk of sorts, pestered by an incubus, that caused her to walk at night in her sleep. She couldn't name the destination, so she was haunted and trapped in this syndrome. If she could be released, Dirk said, who knows where she might go?

"Perhaps into a church tower with you?" asked Felix, knocking Dirk's calf with the toe of his boot.

"Franz! Moritz?" called Dirk, standing up.

"Wait," said Felix. "I have an idea. I heard of someone who might help. I don't know the man, and he has become elderly, but I'm told he lives right here in Meersburg. Would you like me to see if I can get an appointment for your mysterious somnambulist?"

"What must I pay you for your help?" asked Dirk.

"I'll think of something." He downed the last of his ale and tossed a few pfennigs upon the boards. "Though the von Koenig family is here only occasionally, the Baron knows everyone in Meersburg. Baron von Koenig will open any doors for me that I ask. I'm sure the door to Herr Mesmer's apartments are no exception."

Felix took down the address of the Pfeiffer household and left brusquely, without a good-bye. The cinnamon reek of rot that accompanies harvest was beginning to rise as the morning sun strengthened.

39.

The physician had a suite of rooms above the Heilig-Geist Spital in Vorburggaße. Dirk and Felix found the man settled in a wooden armchair upon a heap of faded cushions. He was in his seventies, perhaps late seventies. He said, "I am Doktor Mesmer. I am told"—glancing again at the letter of introduction unfolded in his lap—"that I am to be at your service, young Stahlbaum." He winced even to raise his right hand to grab Felix's.

"This is a preliminary visit." Felix glanced back at Dirk, who was standing behind him in the shadows. "I'd like you to explain to my friend what you might do to help the mistress of his employer's house. She suffers an odd ailment."

"I might do nothing to help her. Is that explanation enough?"

"He doesn't understand your theory and practice, and I'm not competent to clarify."

"I don't entirely understand it myself," said the old man. "Is that perhaps a flagon of schnapps you have brought as a present? A good deal of therapy starts and ends with a bolt of schnapps, I find. My nephew, who runs this hotel for the elderly, arranged my rooms right above the winepress, the rental cost of which helps support his whole operation. But little wine is pressed in my direction. It's a sore trial to me, the proximity of possibility. Very Tantalus, very Aesop."

Felix uncorked the flask and poured a portion in a gummy glass with a chipped gold rim. There was only one glass. Doktor Mesmer fortified himself. "I have been discredited in Vienna and I have been discredited in Paris," he declared. "Lavoisier was cutting, the bastard, but at least that visiting gasbag, Herr Benjamin Franklin, managed to be witty in his dismissal of my claims. I am parading my high-fledged associations for your admiration, in case you haven't noticed. How tawdry of me. Am I obliged to humiliate myself further at this stage in my life?"

"We won't keep you long. But you might help. I should be *so* grateful." Felix said that last in a way that suggested the mildest sort of menace, a pressure brought to bear upon a man who couldn't stand up from a chair without the help of a cane. Felix went on. "Where shall I start? Your work concerns a theory of affinity between animals as they meet and correspond with one another, is that aptly put? A sympathetic hydraulics of vapors and fluids, a depression of phlegms? A rising of invisible energies? I practiced these definitions last night to get them right."

"I see you like that part. The young always like that part," said Doktor Mesmer. "Sometimes my theory is known as animal magnetism. Have you a canary, perhaps, with a chronic malaise? Won't sing? Much can be achieved by understanding the psyche of the canary. Listen to your canary. Did you know *psyche* is the ancient Greek word for *soul*? Of course you did." He was mocking them, mocking himself.

"Tell us about the part that's come to be known as Mesmerism," prompted Felix.

"Ailments." The Doktor appeared to be addressing the schnapps. "Physical abnormalities. What are they? A blocking in the circulation of vital liquors? Perhaps. If so, an induced *crise*—a trance state—can sometimes be helpful at restoring vigor. This aids in recuperation and for a while it also allowed me to keep up with my debts. But, Herr Stahlbaum, I'm not about to treat your young friend." He glared over Felix's shoulder at Dirk. "I can see from here that he is beyond help. Those born dull remain dull. I shall not be sued for incompetence. I won't open myself to that indignity."

"I told you, it isn't him," said Felix. "And if we don't pay you for your services, we can hardly sue you if you fail to satisfy. Isn't that true?"

The elderly gentleman—charlatan or seer, Dirk had no way of knowing—sighed. His hands trembled, one on the stem of the glass, one on the letter in his lap. He said, as much to himself as to the young men in the room, "When Herr Benjamin Franklin came in, and I saw his prodigious intelligence and his beaver-skin cap, I wondered if I was having an elective affinity with genius or with a dead beaver. Can you trust anything that I would say?"

"You're lying about that little vignette." Felix settled his own felt cap upon his head. "I have affinities of my own. Might you see the person in question tomorrow morning at this hour? A respectable hausfrau?"

"I suppose unless I gouge my own eyes out with a cooking implement, I shall have no choice," said Doktor Mesmer. "I shall study up my old methods. You're leaving the flask as tribute, I suppose." He poured himself a second portion.

Dirk hurtled down the stairs, eager to get away. Outside the front door, Felix bounded after him, chortling. Felix pressed his palms upon Dirk's shoulders and launched himself in the air, like a boy leaping over a stile, and hooted. "So I have powers of persuasion of my own," he crowed. "Now you do your job, and persuade your Frau Pfeiffer to meet us here tomorrow."

40.

As it happened, while Dirk was out with Felix that morning, a letter had arrived from Herr Pfeiffer. He'd taken ill with a bowel complaint and was laid up, unable to begin the arduous return carriage journey until his vitals settled themselves. Nastaran was to forgive him and Dirk Drosselmeier was to continue to maintain the household as directed.

Frau Pfeiffer was convinced that her husband, finding his wife unmoored and deficient, had fallen in bed with an ostler's daughter or a courtly dame. Under the circumstances, Nastaran lost her usual resolve and reticence and she succumbed to Dirk's pleading. She presented herself at the appointed hour dressed like a proper wife, her wild hair swept upon her head and hidden under a tedious and sturdy bonnet. No circlet of brass, no veil of painted silk. The shoes were brown leather, stout as varnished aubergines. Her mouth and chin were bravely unveiled in the local manner.

"We want to come, too," said Moritz. Franz hung back in the passage to the kitchen, eyeing the gingerbread that the cook was rolling out.

"Stay here. Make me a gingerbread figure," said Nastaran.

"A man or a lady?" asked Moritz.

"You choose."

"I shall make a gingerbread nutcracker," said Moritz.

"Some gingerbread walnuts and pomegranates, too," said Nastaran. She wouldn't take Dirk's hand to manage the stairs or to climb into the carriage, and she told him to ride up top with the coachman.

"It isn't far, we could easily walk," said Dirk, a little hurt.

"I don't walk in Meersburg," she replied, as if she believed the walled city to be swarming with wild cats and wolves.

Somewhat to Dirk's surprise, when they arrived at the apartments of Doktor Mesmer, Nastaran refused to see the scholar without Dirk as a chaperone. "My husband wouldn't hear of it," she told Mesmer, though he looked too old to threaten a strudel. Felix, arriving late, was heard bashing about in the antechamber as Mesmer settled Frau Pfeiffer upon a leather-covered settee. Dirk took a wooden stool in a corner.

The woman told the Doktor scarcely more about her life than she'd ever revealed to Dirk. The old man seemed untroubled by her reticence. "If what we are seeking is to open the blocked channels," he said, "perhaps one of the channels that is blocked is memory. Now here is what I want you to do."

He wanted her to keep to a seated position, not a supine one, as she would not be sleeping, and certainly not dreaming. He said he would put her into a trance.

"It is not a condition I understand," she replied.

"Many say it is not a condition *I* understand," he answered, working up an expression of protruded eyes and withdrawn lower lip—for comic effect. Nastaran didn't react. His face relaxed. "Without delving into the science of it, for the science is obscure and has been both challenged and faulted, may I liken it to something else? A trance, in earlier days, might have been called an enchantment—a reverie—falling under a spell. Asclepius, the classical Greek healer, received wounded souls at his clinic at Epidaurus and wooed them into a healing calm. It is said that the visions of John, sometimes called the Apocalypse, were received in a trance state."

"I am not gifted with visions," said the woman. "I suffer the absence of them."

"Perhaps the absence of visions is also a gift. I do not know. But you fall asleep at night without dreaming, and you walk about without remembering. You put yourself at harm and you frighten your family, and when you wake you have no memory of the excursion and no sense of what you are seeking. How can it hurt to try to find out? And how much might it benefit you if you do learn what it is you're seeking?"

She was silent for quite a while, and then said merely, "I am ready, because I do not like to live in a state of panic and nameless longing."

At that moment Dirk could hardly keep himself from rushing to her and burying himself in her bosom. Enough that she seemed a Persian goddess disguised as a commercial traveler's wife, wrapped round with the severities of Baden rectitude. But her confessing to nameless longing—all the disassociated comments she'd made, the mysterious glances and close-harbored opinions—the contrast of effects bewildered him. He could only keep staring at her as Herr Doktor took a restorative swig of something smoky and aromatic.

The old man lowered the drape off its hook so the room settled into a watery, dusty gloom. The distant thrub of beer kegs rolled on cobbles, the complaints of fishwives—sounds of the scrag-ends of festival in the Schlossplatz—began to be muffled. A small, gold-ribbed Meissen plate with several plums of dark Copenhagen blue swam into view upon a table. Light chooses for itself what to promote.

Mesmer toddled across the room and opened the glassed door of a large standing clock. The hands had been removed from the clock face, but Mesmer tugged on the carved weights anyway. Their chains ratcheted up along cogs and dials. He nudged a pendulum, and as it began to tick timelessly, Mesmer inserted several tiles of pale wood. The effect was to augment the sound of the tock. Not unlike, thought Dirk, how the carved panels of a 'cello amplify the music of vibrating strings.

Mesmer must be striking some high glass cylinder with a mallet—Dirk couldn't see this happening, but he began to hear a repetitive note as of a glass bell. A candle guttered somewhere. An aroma of lavender and of torn leaves of geranium, that earthy, affronted smell. A flutter near the flaking rosettes of the plaster ceiling, as if a small bird had gotten into the room. Then the sense—barely an aroma, some other apprehension, maybe a certain pressure—of a thrust of native roses observed in a wildwood bower, and the soundless drop of a petal upon the forest floor, and another. Falling upon the browned needles and acorny mast of a woodland slope. Silting up against the carved haunches and screwed-up expression of a hunched figure, provenance unknown.

41.

He could hardly swim forward deftly enough to take in the words being spoken to the shadowy woman.

"Now, Frau Pfeiffer, I intend to say back to you what you told me, so would you like your chaperone to withdraw?" asked the old Doktor, stopping the pendulum with a crooked finger. He twitched the drape open only an inch, as if by slow degrees to reunite Nastaran with current time. The blue plums retired from their prominence, yielding to a general air of powdery shabbiness, as if the room— walls, carpeting, furniture, and occupants—were all woven in deteriorating brocade. A sliver of the pink façade of the Neues schloss showed itself along the left edge of the windowpane.

Nastaran waved a hand dismissing the notion; Dirk should stay.

The Doktor spoke slowly. He seemed now to realize that German wasn't Frau Pfeiffer's native tongue. He said, "Only you can know if I have helped relieve some internal constriction so that your fluids—your humours, if you prefer—might better align themselves."

"What did you discover?" Cold as stream ice, analytical as a magnifier lens.

"If I understand you correctly, you told me that when you walk forward in your sleep, you are trying to walk backward."

"I don't comprehend you," said Frau Pfeiffer, humbly, even pitiably.

"Backward to some time in the past, some place. Some garden. Some walled garden in a place called, I think, something like Bandar."

"Bandar-e Bushehr," she whispered. She held the pads of eight fingers and the nails of her thumbs at her lips, as if to guard any other word from escaping.

"You left a child there, among the roses and the fountains, among shrieking peacocks and other luminous birds. You walk at night to try to return to collect the child. To rescue her. You did not mean to leave her behind when you left with—was it I think— merchants from the Low Countries, from Holland? Amsterdam? Because of a family matter? . . . and there you met your current husband."

His voice was neutral, without scorn or blame.

"You could see the Persian Gulf, you could smell salt in the air. There was a tiled dome on some ecclesiastical building, a mosque or a shrine, that rose to the east, like the blue-veined breast of a sleeping mother. You could see it above the top of the stone wall. There was a pomegranate tree, there was a walnut tree. Someone used to tell you that the key to your life would be found in a wal-nut. You would collect the walnuts as they fell, but you hadn't the strength to open them by hand, and there was no brick or mallet or stone with which to strike them. I don't know who used to tell you that. I don't know much more, nor if I have said this very accurately at all. I am somewhat out of practice."

Nastaran was weeping, and her forehead nearly touched her skirted knees. Perhaps as much to afford her some privacy as any-thing else, Doktor Mesmer turned to Dirk and said to him, "Please take her home when she is ready. Then come back to me at once. I have something to tell you, and another thing to ask you."

42.

She wouldn't let Dirk go back to Herr Doktor, not right away. She spent the day in a parlor whose circlets of crown glass in leaded frames looked out at the mountains of eastern Switzerland across the lake. At evening she called Dirk to the open doorway but held him there, not speaking further.

"What is it I can do for you?" he finally asked, willing to hear any answer, any one, if it would stir her out of her spell.

"What is the key of which the Doktor spoke?" she finally replied. "The key in the walnut shell?"

"It is your key." He spoke with deliberate imprecision. Cautiously. He had no idea what he meant, except that if the idea of a key had come from her, the secret of the key must be hers, too. Hidden in her memory; in her heart.

"Someone must find it for me. I cannot find it for myself."

Someone? *Someone?* Why not *Dirk, you must find it for me?* He suffered a flash of irritation. He crossed the threshold of the parlor and walked to the straight-backed chair against the wall, where she sat enthroned, her hands wreathed in the lattice of its arms. She looked up at him and bit her lower lip. He knelt like a Siegfried or a Roland and bowed his head. Her feet were bare. He lifted one foot to his lips.

He left her in silence, in the near dark. She seemed not to notice.

He lay down outside her door once more, but if he slept, it was only behind his eye-patch.

43.

He hadn't realized it was laundry day until the girl accosted him in the stairwell.

"She's not coming to help me hang the bedding?" she asked, raising an eyebrow to the closed door of Frau Pfeiffer. "I can't manage on my own, and the cook is in a snit over a maggoty cut of beef."

"It's started to rain," he said. "How can you hang sheets to dry in the rain?"

"You come upstairs and help, and I'll show you."

The boys, who had been playing in the garden until the downpour, came thundering inside. They joined Dirk and the girl in traipsing to the very top of the barn.

The young laundress swung open high wooden doors in the back wall. The view looked over the alley and roofs, north toward Munich out there somewhere. A protruding beam and a pulley for hoisting bales proved the point: This had been a hayloft once. Despite the rain, a strong breeze pulled through on a flood of grainy-green light.

The tent-like space under sloping eaves was strung with cords for dripping clothes and sheeting during days like this, and probably in the winter, too.

The clotheslines on the side nearer the open doors displayed billowing, painted sheets. As Dirk helped the girl square off and drape the dripping laundry over the ropes, his eye sought out the work of Nastaran Pfeiffer.

The sheets were painted in two styles, quite unalike.

Some were done in black line, in the style of woodcuts by late medieval cartographers or court geographers. Nastaran must have had models to work from. Several, maybe all of them, were of Meersburg as viewed from the water, the way Dirk had first seen it approaching on the steamer. The lower town; the great broad flats of cliff-edge administrative buildings. The archaic angles of the tower of the old castle. The filled-in scallops of roofline, the hills beyond. Sculpted meadows and vineyards. Tight parallel lines to indicate shadow, dimension, progression toward a dim horizon. As an engraver on steel might do.

They might have been copied from a voyager's collection: "Towns of the Bodensee." They had a clinical exactitude.

The other paintings featured vague and flaming colors. As Dirk stared, the shapes organized themselves into coherence. Sequences of disorienting landscape. Flowering trees and sculpted hills progressed in a flat, unnatural evenness from the bottom hem to the top. No sky showed, no horizon, and each sequence of trees apparently ranging behind the foremost was articulated with the same degree of precision. Nothing became dim or smoky by distance.

The boys raced among them until the laundress spoke sharply to them. "It'll be on my slate if these scribbles and daubs fall and dirty," she said pointedly, though it was clear she thought it was Dirk's job to mollify the children. "Go on, help me with this last load and then get those heathens out of here. Why should housework always feel like a military campaign, I wonder?"

She may have expected Dirk to answer, but he didn't. After they'd straightened the final of the sheets—she could manage the clothing on her own, and if it was female apparel he had no business handling it—he grabbed the boys and said, "Let's do something messy—let's go for a walk in the rain."

"Will we splash in puddles?" asked Franz.

"The biggest ones we can find."

"The *biggest* one is the lake," cried Moritz, delightedly.

Off they went, sliding along the sloping streets and forgoing the long steps, heading for the Seepromenade edging the choppy lake.

The boys ran ahead, holding hands. Dirk slumped his shoulders. He was clear now of the mustiness of Doktor Mesmer's rooms, the sloppy drip of laundry in an attic, but not yet clear of the softness of Nastaran's sole remembered upon his fingertips. What could have drawn him to touch her, and what invisibility did he suffer that she made no response? He'd been intolerably forward, even immoral, but who cared—it hadn't been noticed.

At the end of the Seepromenade extended the jetty. The boys wanted to scamper out by themselves along the rocks and stand at the very end, but the lake water was deep there. They might slip on slick rocks, tumble, and drown. Then, he told them, he would have to fish out their corpses and go hang them up to dry in the attic with the other laundry. They howled with glee at the thought, as if he was the most droll person in the land.

He had rarely made anyone laugh. The sensation felt false.

They held hands and continued nearly to the end. No steamer in view today, no sailing or fishing vessels. Though it was still raining, the clouds were very high. Dirk looked across the agitated lake to the southeast, to the highest mountains he'd ever seen. The Swiss Alps. They raised their knobby shoulders, a wall between Meersburg and some garden in far-off Persia.

44.

Doktor Mesmer looked up as Dirk was announced. The old man had abandoned his breakfast and was fussing in an inglenook over a weird musical instrument of some sort, fitted with a lateral spindle. "My glass armonica," he said as he hobbled away. Tones of a mechanical shrillness faded.

"You asked me to come back," said Dirk.

"I didn't *ask*," said the Doktor. "Though, frankly, I didn't think you'd come on your own. I thought you'd have to be collared by your good friend and dragged here."

"Is there something more of what Nastaran said that you couldn't bring yourself to share with her? I would like to know, even though I am not her 'good friend.' I'm not her husband, only her servant."

The Doktor rearranged some limp cushions that appeared to have given up any ambition of providing comfort. He sat upon them. He crooked a finger to Dirk to draw a stool close. He wanted that his voice should not carry. Dirk obliged.

"The autumn and the winter are dark seasons for her," said the Doktor. "Perhaps she finds it is painful when her husband has to leave. I think this ravaging of her spirit is not occasional but is systemic—chronic, as the Greeks would call it. Chronic. Having to do with time."

"My mistress is in great distress. She talks of a key; is it a key to the garden you described? She asks me to find it for her."

"Perhaps. But I fear you will not do so. It is a key to a garden that no longer exists. It is the garden of her childhood. And no one can return to that garden."

"Your work—your therapy, if you will—does that not loosen the lock?"

"All I can do is lay out the map for her as best I can. She must identify the garden; she must find the key; she must turn it herself. Or she must accustom herself to living without."

Dirk struggled to put his own words in order before speaking them. "I learned a great deal by listening to you yesterday morning.

I think the reason that Nastaran is a poor mother to her sons is that she left her daughter behind when she sailed from Persia. She is distracted with grief. Surely something can be done about that."

"The child is dead."

"How do you know that?"

The Doktor sighed and patted his heart as if cucumbers had featured in the breakfast menu. "Don't you see? The child in the garden is Nastaran herself. Is Frau Pfeiffer as a girl. Who ever can give an adult a key to that lost garden? The child in that garden is gone. She cannot be rescued; she cannot be found."

Dirk slumped on his stool. "So there is no hope for Frau Pfeiffer?"

"I didn't say that. I don't know. I merely hope to massage the channels of memory and longing. Once reawakened, perhaps they can renew health of their own accord. We possess our own land-scapes, after all. Marking them out, I have come to believe, is a physic of the mind. Or of the psyche, in the Greek sense of soul."

"I am not a university fellow. I don't understand."

"Let me emblemize what I mean by turning to a separate system of metaphors. What, I ask you, does *music* do but bring us out of ourselves into a wordless, unauthorized zone, a country of un-marked borders? Have I mentioned I was quite social with the Mozart family of great renown? Young Wolfgang directed his *Bastien und Bastienne* in my very own garden. Music interprets mystery, my friend." As the Doktor spoke, it seemed to Dirk that the echo of the glass armonica returned, faintly. Perhaps it was only the memory of the echo—and perhaps that is what Mesmer was trying to propose could be useful: the memory of an echo. Better than nothing. Better than the memory of nothing.

Dirk swallowed. "She asked me to find the key."

"We all have our secret alphabets. Private codes of gesture and symbol. Perhaps there was an actual walnut tree in the garden of her youth. Who knows. All children want to know the hidden meaning of the world, until they grow up and resign themselves to it being unknowable. Every closed walnut that fell at her feet in that cherished past held, perhaps, more possibility than anything that has happened since. I can't say. In any case, I prefer now to talk to you about your own vision."

Dirk snorted. "My vision? As in a rosy past like Nastaran's? I have no *vision*. I hardly have a past."

"I want to ask you something personal. I'm curious. I've heard of situations like yours many times, but I've never met anyone before who has"—he seemed to struggle for the right words—"who has died, and then come back to life."

"I fear you are addled this morning, Herr Doktor."

"Sit back down. I am not done. Don't be angry. You spoke, too, yesterday morning. You do not remember? I'm not surprised. I want to ask you now about the knife, and the bird, and the lost forest. About how you died, and what you saw, and how you came back to life. Here, I thought you might need this. The French call it *eau-de-vie*. I had it smuggled in. I'm partial to it of a morning, but in this case I offer it to you medicinally. Do you need to lie down? Take your time. I can wait."

And then: "Now, tell me what you have remembered. Tell me everything."

45.

Once, Dirk heard himself say, once there was a boy who lived in a small cabin in the deep woods with no one for company but an old woman and an old man.

He was a foundling, a child of unknown provenance, and the old woman and old man cared for the boy kindly until the day they decided to kill him. At the old woman's command, the old man turned his woodcutter's axe upon the boy.

"And then?" asked Mesmer.

"It's a story, and that's all I know," said Dirk, in a foul dark tone.

"But the old man lived."

"I suppose."

"And you lived, too."

"Oh, *me*?" Dirk surprised himself with his own mocking tone. "I was merely telling you a story. Me, I'm from someplace else."

"Where?"

"It doesn't matter. Anyway I'm not the type to husband my memories. Are you thinking I am wounded as Nastaran, with her ferocious past of locked walnuts? I'm more like a spider—or a burdock—I cling with strings and hooks only to every passing day. I haul little or nothing along with me."

The old doctor said, "The Latin word for luggage is *impedimenta*. But we all carry things, whether we know it or not. I think you carry your own death, uncompleted. Or revoked temporarily. I think—please don't flinch like that, it makes me feel I haven't adequately tended to my morning ablutions—I think you're one of those very few people who have ever died and come back to life."

"I see the *eau-de-vie* has much to recommend it."

"You cut. You wound. Sarcasm is to be expected in the young and stupid. Patience, please. And listen to me. Human literature has always spoken of certain—passages. Transitions. Transports. Homer tells of Odysseus going into Hades to interview Achilles; and without intention to blaspheme, may I remind you that the Christ descended into Hell? Dante saw the fiery pit in his great poem. But those are legends and lore; they are faith and fictions. Not everyone is a character in a story, Herr—what did you say your last name was?"

"Drosselmeier."

"I have a wide circle of medical associates. True, some no longer answer my petitions for a loan . . . that's a different matter. In the interest of truth we must be willing to be called a Dr. Slop, a charlatan, a 'verray parfit praktisour,' as Chaucer has styled the Physic in his tales. I don't care what they say of me. Mozart was beastly. What was I talking about?"

Dirk suspected the Doktor cared deeply about what was said about him. The old man regained his thought and rushed on. "What is missing from the imaginative histories of the ancients, and likewise from the venerable faiths? Tell me."

"I don't know. Perhaps: reason?"

"Wrong. What's missing from the literature of our species are the stories of the peasants. The filthy illiterate. Those with no firm address, no surname. No one to impress, nothing to lose. But the poor tell stories, too. Ordinarily, only women wise with herbs, or father confessors, or we doctors—only we ever hear those stories. And what we hear! There is such a thing, it seems, as dying and visiting the other land, and coming back to life.

"When I helped Nastaran to liberate the seized channels of memory, you were here, too. When she fell silent, you spoke. You told me that you had been murdered, and you went to another place, and something happened there. And then you came back. But you were not the same."

"Did I also tell you where I hid that crock of golden shit I meant to go back and reclaim? Please remind me."

"You are trying to shame me. I'm too brazen to be shamed, and I'm too old to bother with you if you won't cooperate. There was a tree you cut down, you killed. It was a sacred tree in a severed forest, and in dying, you yourself went to the lost forest."

"I don't understand your words. A severed forest?"

The old man put his fingertips together like the ribs of a fish, and tapped his thumbs five times. "In dying, you lost something, I think, and you also gained something. You possess something I don't have. I have curiosity. But you have knowledge."

"I have a headache."

"*Must* you be stubborn? Of course you must: It is your youth. Most of the people who have experiences like the kind you've had are much older, some of them at the end of a long life. When they come back—oh, through a tunnel, they sometimes say, or down from a great height where they were floating above their bodies, or out of a blinding white light at once peaceful and abnegating— they are often furious at being revived. And they can be terrifically different people than they were before. But I never heard of it happening to a child."

"What causes this—this detachment—to happen?" asked Dirk. Unconvinced, he was looking for a way to undercut the mad Doktor's assertions.

"I once knew a man who was struck by lightning. Those who ran to him said his heart had failed. It was stopped for ten minutes as they carried his body through the barley. At the edge of the meadow, startled by a wild boar bolting from a ravine, they dropped the poor corpse, and the heart in the corpse began to pound again. The man recovered, and raved about his journey into the other ness. But I saw that he was never the same. He would not look at or address his wife, and the comforts of the pulpit and the pew were as burning coals on his ears and heart. He sat in a doorway like someone twice his age, unable to work the fields anymore, and he died again several years later. His hand tangled in his beard, as his face remained unshaven from the day of lightning unto the night of the actual grave."

"I suppose I shall have to remember to shave, no matter what comes." But Dirk's voice was less strident now.

"Shall I tell you another case? This one is hearsay, but from a reliable observer. A man of probity."

The boy didn't nod, neither did he shake his head to forbid it.

"The woman was not gifted in noetics." At Dirk's shrug, Doktor Mesmer said, "Noetics. Having to do with knowledge and canniness. I am trying to say that she had all the perspicacity of . . . of a shrub. A bucket. A slab of mutton. I'm told her speech was slow, and her sentences rarely reached a verb. She was good for nothing but carrying rags for the rag man. An itinerant without a real home."

"The poorhouse ought have taken her in."

"Now, this middle-aged woman had a dreadful swelling in the forehead like a bald peach pit. People avoided her. They said the contusion was the stump of a devil's horn, and though she'd been able to break off the prong, the root remained, poisoning her. My colleague, a fellow in Vienna, offered to try to cut it out for her. He promised her enough liquor to make her pass out, which appealed to her. Perhaps she hoped she would die under his knife, and dying dead drunk would be better than life. Or perhaps she was too dull to disagree with his proposals. At any rate, the operation went ahead, for her benefit and for his medical curiosity."

"Did she awaken as a knife plunged into her skin?"

And here Dirk remembered the axe in the old man's leg, and his awful screams.

"I will admit my colleague drew a veil over those unseemly details. I think ropes may have been involved. But the important part is that the dreadful devil's root was indeed removable, and the head bandaged, and the woman seemed to leave this valley of sorrow and lie stony and limp upon the board. She was cold as a riverbed in March. Then, I'm told, after an hour or so of death, quite suddenly, she revived. She survived a prodigious loss of blood, she slept for seven days, and when she woke up . . ."

"Waking up, that's good . . ."

"She spoke in a language never heard on earth. No one else could understand her for the rest of her life. But she spoke— voluminously. Like a cataract, night and day, even in her sleep. It made her distressing to be with, as she stared at those around her with maddened eyes, entirely unable to share whatever it is she had seen while she was dead."

"What happened to her?"

"In the end they had to lock her in a tower room. I believe she slipped and fell from a high window."

"I still don't know what this has to do with me."

The old man mopped his brow with a stained cloth. "You said things while—oh, why should I be falsely modest—while Mesmerized. As some folks call it, admiringly or not. You said things that led me to think you have had a similar experience. But you were young. You were a child. You went someplace and came back. Would it bother you if I asked some questions?"

"I oughtn't stay too much longer."

"You can come back another time. I made notes. I can wait."

"Do it quickly. My life has many turns. Perhaps on the way home I will be struck by a woman throwing herself out of a high tower, and I won't see you again."

"You killed a tree; and then the tree killed you."

Dirk waited. Motes of dust revolved in the lamplight. The drawn curtains gapped at the top, revealing a dart of dulled sky. He said at last, "That isn't a question."

"You went to a forest. It was not a forest of the mortal world."

"Dreams are not of the mortal world, Herr Doktor."

"If it was not a dream, where did you go?"

"If I have no answer, it must have been a dream."

"You spoke to someone? A spirit of some sort, maybe a spirit of the forest? What the Greeks called a dryad? Or was she called Pythia?"

"These are questions?"

"Did you speak to a wood-nymph?" Then: "If you don't want to say, tell me this: Did you talk to someone else?"

"You're making fun of me. You're horrendous."

"Young man. I know what it means to be ridiculed. I wouldn't turn against someone the same weapons that have been raised against me."

But Dirk couldn't quite believe him, believe any of this. He got up and left the room without replying, or even nodding farewell. Tore down the stairwell of the seedy Heilig-Geist Spital, past the suffering old souls with their whimpering or catatonia, and threw open the door into the safer, untheoretical world.

46.

The closed drapes of Herr Doktor's chambers had hidden from Dirk a change in the weather. He found himself slipping on a doorsill and sliding several steps into a street gone ghostly with snow.

At this time of the year! It must have raged in across the lake. A few dark ravens swooped at the height of attic windows from one end of the lane to the other, like spies on a mission. Otherwise the neighborhood was deserted.

He stumbled any which way, circling through the Schlossplatz and under the archways into the Marktplatz. For a moment the sun was a white thumbprint upon a blue-white pane of ice. Then, skirls of snow rose and fell again, until the curbs, the hitching posts, even the timbered window lintels and iron lamp-posts disappeared in annihilating impasto.

He sensed the opening up of the square, somehow, perhaps by a characteristic of echo if nothing else. Though how to move across it diagonally to find the right lane that would lead back to Nastaran and her sons—that was impossible and would remain so until the squall moved on. He ought just stop and stand, or lean against a building. A surprised blue sky would blink overhead momentarily and citizens would start to come out and laugh at the assault.

He moved sideways with his left arm out, to find the nearest wall and then trace it to a doorway or portico where he could huddle a moment, but no wall rose quickly to steady him. He tried to remember if a set of steps led out of the square. The old town had its drops and climbs. He didn't want to lose his footing. He couldn't remember. This wasn't his town. He would never know it intimately enough to be safe here.

It seemed for an instant that the sun had swollen and come nearer, trying to find him through the storm. A disc of white gold bumbled above him, hovering and uncertain. A touch of pale apricot, a circlet of dissolved flame—it was hard to draw into focus. He couldn't determine what it was as it plunged, nearly overhead, with a noise separate from that of the wind.

Then he was knocked sideways off his feet by a carriage of some sort, a sledge without horses or the like. Propelled by some arcane and invisible hand, it bumped and scraped and even bounced along the snow-gritted cobbles at a velocity unusual in a town square. Dirk fell heavily against a doorway—and caught the whiff of balsam and of some strange incense, a charcoal opiate. He felt himself lift, then drift, as if he were an integument of the wind. Absorbed into the separate whiteness of unconsciousness.

47.

The snow parted, retreating and lifting like ranks of theatre curtains. It didn't stop falling, but it became less swirling and blinding. The forest emerged, crept forward. In a clearing a few inches above the white ground hovered a basket of woven wicker and bramble, large enough for Nastaran and her husband and her sons, though not perhaps for Dirk.

He approached the carriage. No wings, no stilts or feet, no cord or pulleys—just a rustic box in the air, a tray with high sides, hovering and slipping sideways.

Either his eye became accustomed to the light or the figures just appeared, colored shadows printed upon the obscure landscape. Within the vehicle: a woman with fierce coppery hair, her pale hands upon the balustrade of the basket. Next to her, crouched upon the rail, a hunched wizened figure, scowling. The woman wore green, the brave irresponsible color of new ferns. The other creature looked blackened as if by smoke.

Dirk stood, he didn't approach them, but the basket drifted nearer.

"How long will you take?" she said to him.

"To do what? To die?" he asked.

"To live, to give us life." She was cross and fiery.

"He's the wrong one, he hasn't got what it takes either to live or to die," muttered the squatting creature.

"You have a spark inside you," she said to Dirk. "Let it go out or let it loose, one or the other. What is your life for? You chose to live, you *chose* this world! What *is* this half-living? Even a mouse has more intention."

The sour companion interrupted. "Mercy on the human. He didn't ask for us or our demands. Leave him be, leave him alone. We're fucked."

"I don't know what you are asking of me. I don't know who you are," Dirk replied.

"You have the means to find out." She folded her arms. "You don't try."

"Open your heart, open your mind. Open your mouth," said the gnome-thing. "Open your trousers. Open your ears. Open your eye."

"You took the knife," said the one perhaps called Pythia. "You took it from us. What is a knife for but opening?"

"A knife can be used for killing, for severing," said the hench-man. He began to stand up. "Or for cracking open the nut-case and finding the kernel. Someone has to do it." At full height, standing on the rail, he was only a little taller than the dryad or goddess. He lifted his head from where it crunched into his neck. His flanks were ragged fur, and from his matted hair could be noted two curv-ing horns. "Aren't you ashamed to be so lost? We have our own sorry excuse, but you?"

"I died a long time ago," said Dirk. "The old man tried to kill me, but I died before he could manage it."

"Listen to me." The woman spoke in a cold voice. "We're all severed—we are, the forest is, you are—it's the nature of the world. Some agents can recover. For themselves, for us, for others. What are you waiting for?"

"Lost is not an address, it's not a permission to fail, it's not an excuse." With shocking vigor, like that of a young warrior, the creature hopped upon the ground and approached on cloven hoof. "It's a reason to read the world." His breath was meaty, his animal nakedness unnegotiated. "Panic," he said, either a prediction or a directive. "Panic." Leaning backward so the goat-man wouldn't be able to press his hands upon his lapel, Dirk stumbled. "Open panic, open the past, open *something*," snarled the creature.

48.

Dirk started, jolted by the hand on his lapel. The forest was gone. Its intensity, its panorama turned inside out—a landscape of hills and wildness brushed up close, as close as clothes—it was all gone.

He felt raw and empty—not as if he had voided himself, but been extruded from—from something. From the forest. From life. An all-too-familiar malady.

A hand on his lapel, gripping, shaking it, another touching his face.

"A happenstance such as would delight von Kleist, or that American, Washington Irving. Those who object to the coincidences that drive a romantic novel should think again!" said Stahlbaum.

He was on his hands and knees in the snow, roughing blood back into Dirk's cheeks. Laughing. Now talking not to Dirk but over his shoulder to someone else, calling something. Now turning back.

"Are you alive?" said Stahlbaum. Stahlbaum—oh, Felix. Yes. Felix.

"What is happening?" muttered Dirk.

"The collapse of Icarus, brought down not by sun but wind

and snow. It's a mercy we weren't killed. You, too, as we all but ran roughshod over you. Think of the odds!" Felix waved one hand behind him. Now the snow was thinning. The squalling clouds hastened eastward. A wasted light returned through paler, higher clouds. Off to one side of the square lay the remains of a large wickerwork gondola and what looked like gently burning sails subsiding into the snowy gutters.

"We were air-ballooning, Kurt and I. We launched from the von Koenig place outside Überlingen in hopes of crossing to Switzerland, but scarcely had we risen above the roof-beams of the estate barns when a brutal storm rushed in from the Untersee. It pummeled down the valley and caught us sideways, sweeping us into Meersburg—exactly where we didn't want to go. Then, I don't know, perhaps we got punctured on a steeple. We could see nothing!—we were twirled about like mad Viennese waltzers!— and we buffeted against cornices and slid down the roofs, ending quite by accident in the square. Catching you on the side of our downed runaway chariot in the bargain. You! It might have been anyone in town, it might have been no one. For all I know you provided a brake in our velocity, though you took quite the thumping for your kindness. Now what do you make of that? Destiny or accident?"

Dirk was sitting up and rubbing his eyes. Irregular rips in the cloth of cloud showed ribbons of mocking blue. He could see the younger von Koenig, that university friend, dashing his boots against the cobbles and tearing at his hair. People were emerging from doorways, laughing and pointing. A white collie raced up to the impromptu bonfire, wagging its tail in delight and leaping like a witch at Walpurgisnacht.

"I thought . . ." said Dirk, and stopped.

"What did you think?" Felix looked at Dirk with the same sort of expression that the dog was giving to the conflagration; there was appeal and puppyishness.

"I thought you were in the basket."

"But I was. Until it tumbled me out on my hinterbacken. Look, are you really all right? I'm afraid we smacked into you pretty hard. You went over like a tree felled for a ship's mast. You look in shock."

Dirk shook his head.

"And I was going to try to run into you—! Though not today. I got a note from the Doktor who said he was looking to talk to you. I was going to alert you."

"I've already been to see him—he was saying things—"

"Oh? You surprise me. He alluded to a surprise or two, and wanted you to come back, but he didn't know where you lived. He didn't think you'd come back on your own, as you left so suddenly with Nastaran."

"I wanted you to pull me up. To take me with you."

"Too late for that. I'm not going anywhere now. The heated gas has all escaped. Look, Kurt is having a fit. I should help him."

"Did you ever hear of someone—called—the Pythia?"

"You look as if you've seen a ghost."

"Where is the forest?"

Felix rocked back on his heels, pursed his lips. "Maybe you should see a physician? Or down a stiff cognac?"

"Maybe I should return to Mesmer." Dirk began to cry. "I left in disarray."

"It's being startled, it's nothing, there now, straighten up, man."

Dirk stood on weak knees; Felix leapt to support him. "I'll take you back. Least I can do after smacking into you. Anyway, I'm curious; Mesmer may be Herr Doktor Quack, but he always turns over a bright thought or two despite himself. Wait here, hold on to the wall while I go tell Kurt what I'm doing. He can manage on his own. He'll hire someone to clear away the mess. What that boy won't do for a lark! The Baron will beat him silly with a cane. His father meant that hot-air assemblage for a gathering of scientific enthusiasts this weekend, I think. And it was hard to acquire, and dear. It came from Paris. We were taking it on a trial run. Without permission."

Dirk watched Felix walk away. The young 'cellist was hobbling a little, too; he was hiding his own bruises in the interest of taking care of Dirk. The tears began to seep again; Dirk hid them in his collars two or three at a time, and had dry cheeks by the time Felix returned, offering an arm.

49.

Are you willing to try again?" asked Mesmer. "If you can attain the proper calm and detachment after your hard knock in the street, I shall interview you."

"I'd like to stay," said Felix.

Dirk shook his head. "But don't go far. Come back in when I say."

Felix left the room and the Heilig-Geist Spital, looking for a coffeehouse and a broadsheet, and promised to return in an hour. Mesmer again lowered the drapes, and did something with glass balls that made a shimmering sound, like rounded prisms if there were such a thing, and in terrific curiosity and fear Dirk closed his eye.

When he opened it, Felix had returned, and the Doktor was drawing back the drapes with a palsied hand. "Do you want to say what you saw?"

Dirk shook his head. "I have no words for it."

"You had many words for it half an hour ago, but I don't know what they mean. I believe you mentioned the Pythia."

"I don't know who that is."

Mesmer glanced at Felix, who obliged. "The Oracle of Delphi," said Felix. "The famed seer of ancient Greece—"

"I never heard of such a creature—"

Felix rushed on. "She foretold the fates of kings and men, and spoke in riddles or spoke in plain tongue, as her visions allowed. Why did she speak to *you*? Frankly, I'm cut to the quick."

"Stop, young man," said Mesmer. "We must proceed with diligence. Reticence. Which means let *him* tell *us*."

Dirk grimaced. "I'm not sure what an oracle is."

"Or Pan?" asked Mesmer.

"Pan?"

"A sort of satyr, as you described him, half goat, half youth?"

"He was no youth! Old as a dwarf in the Black Forest." These words spilled from Dirk's mouth. They were almost the most definite thing he had ever said aloud. His eye widened at the sound of them.

"You have seen them before," said Mesmer. "When you died as a child."

"That's balderdash."

"You took something from the Pan. You took his knife."

"I . . . thought he *was* the knife?"

"We often mistake the object for its essence. Philosophy will clear that muddle up in time. Do you know why they come to you?"

Felix couldn't help blurting out, "He's possessed! Dirk hears voices . . ."

"Shut up," said Mesmer. "He sees visions. It's not the same thing. Nor is it the same thing as memory, I think. Not like

Nastaran's vision of her childhood garden. Maybe this begins in memory, but a different sort of transaction is occurring. Do you know why these two come to you in their forest?"

"Their forest," said Dirk. "Why is it . . . the way it is?"

"Do you want me to tell you what I think you said to me when you were—otherwise? Well, mesmerized?"

Dirk looked at Felix, whose face was beaming—jealousy, pride, curiosity. Dirk shrugged his shoulders, and sighed, and nodded.

So Mesmer told them both.

"The Pythia—the Oracle at Delphi—lived in as quiet a way as she could manage, given she was the most famous woman in the ancient world. To see her, crews rowed the triremes of kings up the strait of Corinth and anchored at Delphi. Slaves hauled tribute uphill to the temples of Apollo and Poseidon, among others. The visiting kings fasted. They cleansed. They paid out alms. They sometimes forgave debts. Quite a few of them found prostitutes lower down the hill but more of them did not even go looking. Then, usually heavyhearted from a question about some political or military mission, some concern of a royal house, like lines of succession or a proposed military allegiance, the great man of state would go alone into the temple of the Pythia.

"Having spent the previous night in a sacred grove, the priestess would also approach the house of prophecy and settle herself there. A vent of holy smoke roiled from a fissure in the earth below. She would fall into a trance. She would speak as the gods directed her to speak. Often when she awoke she couldn't recall what prophecy she had made, and when it was told back to her she rarely took pains to decipher it."

"I said all this to you?" asked Dirk.

"No," said Mesmer. "This much is known by scholars of the

ancient world. I am sketching it out for you to suggest the significance of your experience."

"Shhh," said Felix to Dirk, "let him go on."

Mesmer: "One day, back in those times of Attic glory, I don't
know how long ago, the ludic demi-urge Pan traveled from Arcadia,
which is to the south of Delphi, and requested something of the
Pythia. I'm not sure what, but does it matter? Who knows what
we really ask of one another? Pan may have been in search of
sexual favors, perhaps, or word of the prospects of some cunning
king or lithe maiden in which Pan had an interest, unseemly
or otherwise. Pan is the god of rural heights, with tenderness
toward shepherds and their sheep, but his eye strays to mortal
maids and the naiads and dryads, too. With his goatish under-
carriage he seldom enjoys romantic success—not even with the
sheep. Who are not as stupid as they look. I hope not to offend.
I shall continue.

"The Pythia refused Pan his suit for reasons of her own. Perhaps
he'd propositioned *her*. I couldn't make that bit out. But Pan
stamped his hoof in anger and started a panic. *Panikos*, you know:
the mischief of Pan. That tremor that causes sheep in a meadow to
scatter, that causes human hearts to tremble, and fingers to drop
goblets to the floor, that causes Gaia's seizures. Gaia, the great
earth herself, in all her moods and mysteries. Today's scholars think
the Oracle at Delphi was a handmaiden of the ancient goddess
Gaia, whom Zeus and his broody, inbred, self-involved cohorts
ignored. Gaia, perhaps, took umbrage at the insult to her priestess,
the Pythia. Panic: the sense of being in the grip of—something
terrific—sometimes terrible, sometimes overwhelmingly sweet
and capsizing."

"I know of panic," Dirk averred in the quietest voice.

"So what I am telling you is that this has become your story, this is what you have said to me. Are you listening? The Pythia picked up Pan and threw him down with such force he was embedded in the ground. Like a knife. When Pan struck the earth, Gaia shifted and groaned in her hips and breasts, causing an earthquake as dreadful as that of Lisbon sixty, seventy years ago. That bad. The very paling of the hillside at Delphi split. The ground up high separated from its moorings. An entire hill-face of forest slid as one section of soil, one portfolio of many kinds of trees. Severed from the ridge-top, it dashed itself down upon the temple housing the Pythia. The Greeks have always known the trees are full of spirit—the dryads—but when this slice of forest rolled over the great vapors that Gaia sends up to inspire the Pythia, to tell the future and to warn blind humans about their blind behaviors, the severed forest was liberated from its common imprisonment, chained by roots and memories. Though enobled, it was also made migratory by the gusty inspiration of Gaia. It was free, but it was exiled. It couldn't reclaim its homeland—"

"None of us can get back to childhood," murmured Felix, "not Nastaran, not you, not I—"

"Hush, you. Or I'll strike you! I'm trying to say this to young Drosselmeier while it is clear. The forest was liberated, but it was homeless. It was—it is—free, and forlorn. A sacred grove, peculiarly lacking in fundament. Searching for—I don't know. A place to be established."

"The Little Lost Forest," said Felix. "It sounds like one of those household tales published by those lexicographer brothers. One of the märchen, a folk belief, a fairy story."

"How could I have said anything like this?" asked Dirk. "You're mad."

"You told me all this," said Mesmer. "For when you died, that day in the forest when you were a small boy, you went to the sacred grove. The Little Lost Forest, as your friend has it. You took some-thing from that unreachable land. I believe you may have it still."

Dirk said, "I believe you have been hitting the schnapps for reasons beyond the medicinal. You're making a joke of me. Come, Felix. I can't be party to this nonsense."

"'What fools these mortals be,'" said Mesmer, a bit sadly.

"But wait." Felix grabbed his cape and held Dirk by the wrist to keep him from bolting. He pivoted Dirk back to Mesmer. "Was there a motive in their releasing Dirk from death? Was there a gift they gave him, a challenge they set him upon?"

"Life is challenge enough," snapped Dirk, "come—"

"You're right to ask," said Mesmer. "If you never see me again, young man, listen to this anyway. Some good may come of it. Or not. They want a home. This magic woods—the unrepentant Pan, the unforgiving immortalized Pythia. If that's who they are. The male and the female demi-urges. The progenitors. Pale Eve and swarthy Adam, if you prefer. They cannot go back. None can go back—neither the figures nor the trees of the sacred forest. That congress of inspirited trees! Migrating now for several thousand years, stumping with the speed of glaciers up the hard-scrabble Balkans, wading through the Carpathians, forging the streams and storming the valleys a foot or two every decade these hundreds of years—they have now reached a time and a world unknown ever before, an edge of mills and factories. The lip of industry. Europe has become too populated for them. The living timber that wanders . . . it wants you to colonize a place for it. However secular it becomes, the world still needs a sacred grove. You were there. You saw it. They have given you your life in ex-change for your mission."

Dirk slammed the door as he left. Felix was laughing on the stairs behind him. "If this doesn't call for a mid-morning brandy—a ballooning catastrophe and a Greek tragedy, all before luncheon! At this rate, a trip to the beer halls and a raunchy evening of music and frolic and—wait, where are you going? Wait for me, Dirk!"

50.

Felix caught up with Dirk; Dirk shook him off, saying, "You've set me to be a laughingstock. You . . . you privileged fellow . . . you will cavort and chortle with your university scholars over my ignorance and simple nature. Gullible, that's the word. I won't be your toy."

"I don't want you for my toy," said Felix. "Come, this is no ruse. I only tried to get you help for your Persian hausfrau. How could I know the discredited old coot would uncork a vintage experience of yours? What, do you not believe these things that Mesmer has said? 'There are more things in heaven and earth, Horatio . . .' I think you must believe, on some level, or you wouldn't be so angry."

"Leave me be."

Felix put a hand on Dirk's shoulder so forcefully that Dirk had to stop and wheel about and face the young man. Felix: "If you say there was *nothing* in what Mesmer told us both, I'll drop the matter and never mention it again. All I ask is that you tell me the truth."

Dirk didn't answer for a while. The early snow was already melt-ing into wetness. It made the world, white and airy when coated by snow-storm, into a warren of dark varnished streets, an ogre-size kuriositätenkabinett built of stone and stucco. In which Dirk was a scurrying mouse, no more.

"Well?" asked Felix.

"He told back to me something about a dream I must have had, long ago," said Dirk. "I would rather leave it there. I haven't thought of it in a decade, or more."

"What will you do next?"

"What is it to you? Hadn't you better go find the friend you abandoned? Von Koenig?"

"I'm going to go find my 'cello, and play up a storm." Felix regarded Dirk with sudden coolness, as if he were a specimen of another order of being. "I should be grateful for a vision. I have to try to make my own with my music. I knew I liked you for some reason. You have something I lack."

"Go to your 'cello, then," said Dirk, and spun away. Though there was little he would have liked more than to lie on the floor beneath the belly of the 'cello, eyes closed, and let music wash over him, purge him, coat him.

51.

As Dirk kicked along the lanes, he watched the snow-melt coursing in the sunken gutters. In Meersburg, a dropped piece of paper was an insult to the neighbors. An unpolished boot-scraper upon a doorsill, reason to call the sheriff. A shoddy paint job on the street door was unpatriotic if not treasonous.

Dirk knew all this, and lived within the registers, though it wasn't how the forest lived, not at all.

He was surprised therefore, turning into the lane that led to the Pfeiffer establishment, to see that the trees rising above the cloister garden wall had gone bare all at once. Underfoot, as untidy as a forest floor, lay yellowed, slick leaves; he kicked through them. It made him sick to see the instantaneity of death.

He was suddenly alarmed, and ran the rest of the way down the lane, along the garden wall.

The boys were swinging on the gate.

Dirk: "Is everything all right?"

"Of course," said Moritz. "Mama is in the garden sewing the leaves back on the trees. We are going to have sauerbraten tonight; can't you smell it?"

Dirk pushed through. Nastaran stood on a chair she had dragged into the garden. Her lifted arms made a perfect expressive O.

"The boys say you are re-leafing the trees."

She allowed herself to take his hand and climb down. "The brutality of this German world. A wind decides the season is over, all in one morning, and annexes my garden without permission. I am not going to let it happen." She had string wrapped around one wrist, he now saw, and on the ground sat a basket of gilded fruits, were they? She saw him looking. "Last year Herr Pfeiffer saw some Lauscha baubles in a market in Munich. He brought them for me to hang on a fir tree at the Nativity. But those are frail; they break when a wind blows upon them. I prefer to make my own." She reached down and lifted one for him to examine. It was a hard walnut painted over with gold.

"You scared the boys. They thought you were hanging the leaves back on the tree."

"I've tried that. They don't stay." Nastaran was laughing at him, maybe. An openhearted smile, at last. Everyone has one to give the world, at least once; this he believed.

"When did you make these?"

"When I can't come outside during the day."

"Why can't you come outside?" Bold of him to ask.

She took a while before replying. "Too little here of what I might want to come outside for. But this helps, doesn't it? Look, the wind turns them, the sun dances. It is a magic garden."

And now he saw it. The well-clipped trees were all dressed in invisible silks suggested by the formality of lines of string and by the golden walnuts hung at various heights. Who dares to try and best Dame Nature at her beauties, he wondered? Only someone who is ill.

"That Herr Doktor," said Dirk. "He said the key to your unhappiness was held within the walnut." But Dirk was wrong to have mentioned unhappiness in this rare moment. Her face took on a pensive look.

"That is a Doktor's way of speaking," she replied. "He means something other than what he says. Why should there be a key in a walnut? And anyway, how would I get it out? To smash a walnut with a hammer is to crush what is inside."

"What is inside the walnut shell?" He wanted to know, but he wasn't sure that was the question.

"The walnut? When mixed with pomegranate, is the sweet grainy sauce of a *fesenjan*, a stew in which spring chicken is served. With pistachios and honey the walnut is baked in pastries fit to offer a Shah, or Mullah Nasruddin himself. It is put out in small bowls on the carpet at the end of the meal. It is sweetened and fermented with hazelnuts, and my father serves it to his brothers as my mother clears away the meal." She made an effort to control the shaking in her voice. "Your friend, Herr Doktor, he has loosened much in me. The past is a temptation." He could see her trying to become everyday. "The past is too much to bear. Surely you have such a walnut in your own life, something that holds the key to all your past ease and safety."

"I have had little ease and safety in my life."

"Doesn't even the comfort of well-known foods evoke your

treasured innocence? What your mother cooked for you? For my boys it will be gingery sauerbraten. For me it is *fesenjan* and *baklava*. What is it for you, then?"

The wrong question for him. "There wasn't enough to eat. There is nothing to call me back there. It wasn't a garden. It was a dark, fierce woods, dangerous, and I died there."

Then she sat on the chair she had hauled from the house. She gestured to her handiwork. "This is crude and shallow, but it's all I know how to do. It brings nothing back to me. It mocks me and proves futility."

In a small voice, Dirk replied: "I have said the wrong thing. Forgive me."

"There is no right thing to say."

She tried to control her anger. "My father was a merchant in the Persian port city of Bandar-e Bushehr. In a last attempt to improve his finances, he traveled to Europe. He told me he hoped to find other trading merchants, ones who might offer more favorable terms. Now I believe he took me abroad so I wouldn't live to see him impoverished, perhaps murdered for failure to pay his debts. Herr Pfeiffer and I met in Amsterdam, in as accidental a way as you and I have met. For a month his attentions distracted me from nostalgia, and by the time I woke up, we were married. All I have from home besides a trunk of clothes is a *dotar* made of walnut wood, which I have no talent to play."

"Did Herr Preiffer hope you would learn to play a—a *dotar*?"

"This is all distraction. I shall tear it down." Her arm shot out like a scimitar and caught the nearest walnut and wrenched it, and smashed it upon the gravel walk. Being a walnut, it did not break, but lay there like a gold button off an ogre's waistcoat.

"Stop," said Dirk. "It may mean less to you than you want. But it means something to them." For out of the corner of his eye he saw Franz and Moritz; they'd finished swinging and come back in the garden, and were running around the perimeter, leaping among the golden walnuts like a pair of ignorant spring lambs who cannot yet control their limbs.

52.

Dirk had never heard such a parcel of rubbish in his life as that romantic fiction perpetrated by Doktor Mesmer. But how curious. While Mesmer may have actually garnered some thoughts from Dirk—however disassociated from reality they were, goat-satyrs and oracles and meandering sacred groves!— the old charlatan must have taken an image or two and used them to plant this spurious *capriccio* into Dirk's untutored mind. And now—now there was some truth to it, even if it was only the truth of a story that, once heard, becomes history. You might forget a story, but you can never unhear a story.

By that token, you might forget an event, but you can never go back to living as you did before its hidden influence was applied upon you.

Pan and the Pythia. The lost forest. What a saddlebag of crap!

Still, when Nastaran began to run a fever a few days later and took to her room, admitting only the cook with goblets of steamed lemon water and honey, Dirk distracted the fretful boys with a story.

"Tell us again about the Little Lost Forest," they said. Dirk realized they were talking as if it were a living character in a story-book. As if it had agency, desire. "Tell us where it is now." Dirk, with his limited sense of European geography, talked the forest up the slopes of Mount Olympus and down the other side. He made it a silent partner in some Balkan war between the Tribes of Good and Evil. The next night Dirk proposed that the homeless woods had witnessed the crowning of Charlemagne and saved the day because when the Emperor thought he was dreaming in a forest grove at midnight, it was really the Little Lost Forest hiding him from his enemies, those wicked (wicked what? Sicilians? Lombards? Saracens? Oh, the English, the wicked English!) . . . those wicked English enemies, who wanted to find him and cut off his head and steal his crown.

All the while Dirk hoped his voice was carrying, and that Nastaran would hear what a jolly helpmeet he was being, and take some sort of comfort. It seemed the only kind of comfort he could offer her, and from such a hurting distance.

He unwrapped the old knife from its leather wallet. Where had the funny thing come from, really? He had grabbed it from the hut in the forest where he had spent some early days, once upon a time, with an old man and an old woman. The old man had been a woodcutter, and this knife had been his knife, and Dirk had stolen it and bravely run away. He couldn't remember why.

It made a nice story, or the beginning of a story. Dirk didn't know how it went on, though, so he didn't bother to tell that one to the boys. He used the knife to carve them a few rough figures of soldiers. It seemed the blade wasn't dulling with time, but growing keener. A trick of its metallic makeup.

53.

Another letter from Pfeiffer. He was delayed still. His ailment had grown into a pulmonary spasm. He could not sit up without a punishing cough. He couldn't yet leave his bed.

Nastaran folded the letter into her lap. They were sitting in the orchard garden. "Who else, I wonder, cannot manage to leave his bed," she murmured in a costive voice. It was the bitterest and also the healthiest Dirk had ever heard her. He set the boys to playing with the few little wooden soldiers coming home from the Napoleonic wars. Dirk had carved them poorly; they were little more than pegs with identifying noses. Still, the boys personalized them with crude and consistent behaviors, different for each. Dirk made up a story about a river they must forge here, see, on this broken branch, across this scarf that will be a stream, all right?—no one must fall in or the others will have to save him! Then Dirk retired to a bench in the frosty sunlight.

"All this is making a menace for you, but it needn't be," said Dirk. "Nastaran"—he had not before dared to use her name without an honorific—"no one adores a wife more than Herr Pfeiffer does you. Otherwise he wouldn't have taken such pains to bring me into your household, so I might be an assist to you."

"I am a sore trial to him, with my airs and vapors and, and, the offenses I take. I would leave me were I him. I would leave *myself* if I could."

"Did your experience with the Herr Doktor afford you any relief?"

She grunted. "We are all migrants. We are exiled from the place where meaning *meant* something."

He waited, picking at calluses near his fingernails.

"Look." By way of explanation, she rotated a hand at her boys. Across the garden they were squatting beside the plugs of wood, moving them this way and then, while conducting muttered negotiations of the utmost seriousness. "Do you realize that they live someplace that we don't?"

He felt he almost apprehended what she meant . . .

"Those boys and us—we only seem to be sharing a life here. The young are entirely separate. They are someplace else right now. They won't join us in our lives, really, until they are grown. And by then, who will they become? People I don't know. And I may not even be here when they get here."

"Where will you be?"

She didn't answer, but it was a normal silence this time, not a troubled one. Perhaps Herr Doktor Mesmer's peculiar methods *had* massaged some paralyzed process within her back into operation. Dirk reached out and covered the hand in her lap with his. She didn't twitch, neither did she add her other hand to clasp his.

"Those who sit in the house of grief will someday sit in the garden," she said.

"This garden?"

"I was reciting a ghazal from the *Divan* of Hafez. 'The bruised soul will find honey.'" Then she added a few more lines in Persian.

"We have that much in common, you know," he said. "We're both exiled from something long ago."

"Maybe you did die once," she said. "When it is my turn, I will not come back the way you did."

The boys shrieked. A soldier had fallen into the raging torrent, and one by one the others jumped in, too. Whether to rescue their drowning colleague or to relish the solidarity of a community suicide, Dirk couldn't tell.

He couldn't carve a magic key into Nastaran's secret garden. He couldn't open any golden walnut that might harbor such a key. But perhaps Dirk could make a figure that could open some ordinary walnut. It was the possibility of hope that mattered, he knew.

He took his hand from her lap and put it in his pocket. He felt the knife with the carved figure squatting on the blunt knoll of its handle. He imagined that it could speak, but the language it talked in—some obscure tongue, a *lingua hellenica*, or maybe a *lingua magicis*—how could he know that argot?

54.

Then Nastaran took him to the small office with the dusty drapes and Pfeiffer's bookkeeping ledgers. She opened a locked drawer and withdrew from a sack of pounded grey leather a healthy fistful of coins. She sorted out a few gulden and a scraping of florins. She wrapped them in a cloth and handed the parcel to Dirk. He wondered if he was being asked to find other employment.

"You need to take the boys to visit their uncle in Oberteuringen," she told him.

"I haven't heard about that from Herr Pfeiffer," he replied.

"At this time of year, their father usually does it, but"—she looked about with a studied theatricality he hadn't seen before in her, as if to suggest she was just noticing—"he isn't here." She shrugged. "If we wait till he bothers to recover and then to return, the snow may come and the chance disappear. Their uncle is expecting his nephews, and I have written to say you will arrive with them within the week."

Dirk hadn't been made head of household in absentia. He had no authority to protest. Nonetheless, he raised what few objections he could come up with.

"Herr Pfeiffer wanted me to stay and keep watch on—" But he wasn't sure how to finish the sentence respectfully.

"On the household," she answered for him. "But with the boys out of the house, no harm can come to them."

"You pace in your sleep," he said forthrightly. "*You* could come to harm."

"Their father can make the trip there and back in one day if he starts early. It isn't far. Though usually he spends the night with his brother. In any case, I shall ask the laundry maid to stay the night here."

"But—" He was sputtery. "I was told you never wanted another female overnight in the house—"

"Not while Gerwig is home, of course not. Unseemly. But if the house is empty of men, that caution is lifted. You weren't hired to defy me, Dirk."

One more try. "I couldn't find that place on my own. You forget I'm not from around here."

She stood and closed the drawer with her hip. It was a violent gesture. "I already asked your friend, that fellow who took us to see the dream doctor, if he had time to accompany you. It seems he is taking a term off from his studies. He has told me he is more than willing to make the trip with you."

"When did you see *him*?" Dirk found himself feeling outraged.

"I sent a note to that Doktor, who must have sent it on to the Gasthof zum Bären, where the young scholar is staying. Right in the Marktplatz. He came to visit me at my request yesterday when you were out with the boys."

Dirk could hardly think of what to say. She hadn't spoken to Dirk for the first ten days of his residency in her home, and now she was inviting Felix Stahlbaum to call on her when her husband was away and her family otherwise engaged? This was novelty indeed, this was alarming.

"We met in the garden," she said, as if she were reading his thoughts. "For only a few moments. He was not hard persuaded. Between the two of you, there must be enough language to ask for directions. It isn't very far."

Dirk didn't know how to think about that. "I have never had children of my own. You'd entrust *me* with them?"

"Has my husband been wrong to entrust them with you so far?"

"Well—luck has been in attendance."

"They adore you," she said. "Haven't you noticed?"

"I amuse them," he said.

"When they are playing their games, as in the garden the other day—I would want to be there with them. Back in childhood, or so the doctor says. But even if I could get there, somehow, could I shrink in age and stature, I still wouldn't find them *in* their childhoods. For when they play, they aren't even in their own childhoods—they are some other where. Someplace else. In the game you set for them to play. The bridge, the stream, the other place you invented for them. If I wanted to join them, I'd have to go to the size of a mouse, and become one of their toys—for they live at the scale of their toys. They are twice removed from us, you see. Contact is impossible. But you have their confidence."

One last try. "I really don't think that Felix would take time away from his studies to accompany me on a trip like this. We hardly know each other, and he is committed to learning . . ."

"You'd be surprised, Herr Drosselmeier." Her use of his surname was an assault. "Your university friend is compliant and generous. And up for adventure. He said for you to call for him at the Gasthof zum Bären. He'll be expecting you."

He was angry, shut out. She turned away from him. What could he add about dislocation—he'd never belonged in the first place, really. He knew that.

55.

T he chatelaine of the gasthof directed Dirk to a coffeehouse in a nearby lane. Felix looked up from the table in the corner as Dirk entered. He had commandeered the one spot in the room that daylight could reach at this hour; he sat in a scatter of dust-motes. A much-read journal was folded under his elbow. It was as if he had been expecting Dirk that very moment. A Viennese-style pastry lay half-uneaten on a plate. Felix pushed a fork toward Dirk as he claimed the chair opposite.

"We're to have a lark, I understand," said Felix.

"Your studies will suffer."

"I had already written my professors and advocates not to expect me back for the rest of the term. Family matters, I told them."

"But is your family in need of your attentions?"

"I'd have no earthly idea. Generally, we aren't in communication." He waved an attendant for another coffee. "The truth is, I've become uncertain about the direction of my vitalities. Music and scholarship are rewarding but somehow, I fear, unsatisfactory. I'd rather discover what hasn't yet been charted on the ruled lines of music manuscript pages or in the venerable bleatings of sages. Something of my own."

"And you intend to learn something original by chaperoning two young boys to visit their uncle in the mountains?"

"It's over the next mountain, isn't it, where adventure always seems to begin? It's always off a little way. Rather than, say, starting with two fellows sitting in a coffeehouse waiting for the pretty maiden to arrive—ah, there you are, Fräulein. What's your name, then, when you're off duty."

"My name is spoken for," she replied pertly enough.

"Well, Miss Spokenfor, may I call you Engelbertine, which is a name nearly as pretty as you, you bright angel?"

"Would there be anything else I might supply." She put her hands on her apron, flat against the curve of her belly. It was a protective stance of decorum that had the effect, unintended or perhaps not, of straining the fabric of the upper apron against her bosom.

"Dirk?" Felix waved a spoon in a nonchalant circle in the air. "Name your request."

Nearly anything could raise a blush in Dirk. "This coffee will suffice, Fräulein," muttered Dirk into its steam. The young miss hurried off to see to a noisy crowd of burghers who stood stomping at the door, chafing their elbows for warmth.

Dirk said, "How did Nastaran engage you in such folly? You've met her, what, twice? You owe her nothing. Besides, I'm a country cabbage compared to your high-flown friends like Kurt von Koenig and those other sharp fellows at university."

"I'm easily persuaded to be nice if I think I can get something in return. Like nearly everyone else in Europe."

"I have nothing for you."

"You don't see yourself, do you?" For once Felix's voice lost its playful affect. He leaned over the table and looked sturdily at Dirk. "You only seem to read in yourself what you have *not*. Didn't that exercise with Mesmer show you something that I saw right away, the first time my eyes fell upon you? What you *do* possess? In ample fashion?"

"Ignorance?"

"Capacity, maybe. I don't know what to call it. The Scots might say glamour."

"Glamour!" Dirk felt his blush return. Felix laughed.

"I didn't say beauty! Though some might. I meant glamour in

the sense of . . . enchantment. Otherness. Enticement. Maybe it's merely the eye-patch."

"Nothing more than naïveté. I'm a proper clean-souled Christian, touched by no folk hexes, no matter what else you've heard."

"Mesmer brought out into words something I had seen in you from the first. Some—attachment—some—sensibility. A genius of . . . of access, maybe? I haven't the words for it at all. I suppose that's what attracts me to you. Could I learn it from you, it would benefit my music and perhaps my mind as well."

"You're speaking some tongue I don't understand." But despite his intention to warn Felix off the trip, thus canceling it, Dirk grabbed the fork and picked at the pastry. He ate a sloping edge of it. Raspberry, sour cream, crusty torte pastry. The tart and the succulently sweet. By the time he'd marshaled his thoughts about Felix's plans and was ready to register an objection, Engelbertine or whoever she was returned without her apron. Abandoning the other table now the customers were all served, she sat down in a chair between them. Whether spoken for or not, the young woman seemed eager to address Felix. Dirk couldn't command his attention again. At length he stood up, and he left them nattering away. There seemed nothing for it but to make this foolish journey to Oberteuringen and be done with it. Get back to Nastaran as quickly as possible.

56.

The following morning, the cook having supplied him with a hefty luncheon wrapped in cheesecloth, Dirk commandeered Franz and Moritz in front of the Pfeiffer establishment. "Smarten up, soldiers," he told them. They threw their heads up and stamped their feet as they had observed soldiers doing.

Nastaran came out of the street door, an exercise Dirk had never seen happen in the Pfeiffer household; normally the family and servants used the garden entrance. The woman had thrown around herself a black shawl with a mortuary aspect. Below the shawl, Dirk glimpsed some loose and gauzy pantaloons. Her lower calves were bare and not at all pink, but sallow down to the ankles. Her feet, unshod, were stained with a pattern of curling leaves.

He wanted right then, before everyone, to kneel and to take her foot in his hand again and bring it to his lips. How like a spoon with a razor edge is human need.

Before he could speak, he heard the trap rattling along the street. Felix had arranged a carriage to take them the first leg of the journey. Out of the steeps of the city and into the more rolling upland meadows. There, it was hoped, the road would continue at a lesser grade of incline, making a trip on foot easier.

The boys shouted as Felix leapt out, showing off an outrageously cheerful and crimson cape. It whipped about his shoulders. "Brave travelers, prepare to advance to adventure!" he declaimed. "But take farewell of your mother first, don't be nasty little weevils, go on now."

They ran to Nastaran and lifted their cheeks for her kiss. She put one hand on Moritz's left shoulder and the other on Franz's right. Her hands were ornamented like her feet. She spoke in what Dirk supposed to be Persian. The boys nodded solemnly, trying to keep from craning to watch the pair of jittery horses, but their eagerness got the better of them and she let them both go.

"Madame, we shall guard them with our lives." Felix bowed with a flourish of his silly plumed hat. He was using the voice of pretend with her. She neither scowled at him nor broke the mood in any other way, but made a gentle obeisance in return, at a careful distance.

"You'll freeze your feet there, now, Mistress," said the laundry maid in a voice almost beneath hearing. She chafed her own elbows as she stood at the garden gate and watched the palaver. She had arrived to stay overnight and keep an eye on things just in case Dirk didn't return in time. But he was determined to be home by evening if he could. He didn't mention the need to beware of Nastaran's sleepwalking; it didn't seem his place to do so.

"You will take care of yourself," said Dirk to Nastaran, coming a little nearer, lowering his voice for privacy.

"That is what you must expect of me," she replied, turning her face upon him at last. What he'd come to recognize as kohl was smeared about her eyes, lids and lashes alike. The ornamentation made her eyes bigger but seemed much farther away. "You take care of *them*. That's all you can do."

It was a dismissal and a challenge at once. He lifted his hand to her as she hurriedly fastened the black shawl around hereslf more tightly.

He unfurled his hand and gave her what he had for her. It wasn't much.

"It won't have a golden key in it," he said, "but when you open it, it will smell like Persia."

She rolled the common walnut in her hand. "I have no way to open the past," she said.

"The smell will bring you back," he told her. "I will open it for you when I come back. I promise. Keep it safe till I return."

The horses nickered and paced, Felix made a trumpet voluntary with his lips meant to sound like melodic farting. The boys screamed with joy. The last warm breeze Dirk would feel in some time coiled in from the lane, smelling of baking bread and simmer-

ing pork and apples. Nastaran dropped the walnut in the neck of
her blouse, between her breasts, it seemed. Dirk could barely get to
the carriage on his swoony legs—he had to lean on that old staff
he was still hauling about. He had thought it might come in handy
while hiking along a high road; here it was being useful already.

Felix hollered an instruction. Smitten by his antics, the boys
didn't turn to wave good-bye to their mother.

57.

But at the edge of Meersburg, when the landscape began to
open out into stubbled fields of hops and pastures for oxen,
Felix rolled his hand in the air, bidding the driver to continue. Dirk
said, "Between us we don't have coin enough to hire a trap all the
way to Oberteuringen."

"I received my seasonal allowance. Settle down your nerves,"
replied Felix, patting Dirk on the knee and pulling the blanket up
around their waists. "I know you by now, Dirk. You won't want
to spend a night on the road worrying about her well-being while
you're gone. We'll make of this trip as quick an operation as we
can. Perhaps even get there and back in one day if we're lucky."

The boys had tired of kneeling up and looking through the
muscovite window at the road reversing itself behind them, or
leaning out to spit at sentinel dogs. "Tell us more about the Little
Lost Forest, Dirk," said Franz. Moritz put his thumb in his mouth
and nodded.

Easier to do that than talk to Felix, who always seemed to Dirk
to contain several identities simultaneously, to go by the evidence
of the contradictory emotions displayed by his smile, his eyes, his
hands. Felix's intelligence was one thing, his rapscallion nature

another, and his unsolicited affection a third. Too much for Dirk. He leaned forward to clasp both boys' hands as they slumped in the seat opposite. Felix relaxed with one arm behind his head to pillow it. A smile cousin to a smirk played along his upper lip.

"I forget what I said before," said Dirk, looking for a prompt. What sat with them, what made a difference? He himself had never been a child, he now realized; what did he know about what children wanted to hear?

"The Little Lost Forest was lost," said Franz.

"In the forest," said Moritz.

"Walking from someplace, Rome or Greece, I forget, one of those places . . ."

". . . ultramontane?" supplied Felix.

"Shhh," said Dirk, delivering a backhanded slap on Felix's upraised knee without turning around. "The forest was—it was severed, it was orphaned. It was a place without a home. Does that make sense?"

Moritz shook his head. Franz nodded. Felix lit a pipe, pretentiously.

"It was . . . migrating. It was wandering slowly north through Europe. And in the forest were two spirits, who came from ancient times and who were carried away—"

"Like us," said Moritz, indicating the carriage.

"Except they weren't youngsters. And they weren't happy."

"We're not happy," said Franz cheerily enough. "Something has to happen now in the story. It's stuck."

"I forget who the spirits were," said Moritz.

"Me, too," said Felix, elbowing Dirk in the ribs.

"We have to have names for them," said Dirk, buying himself a little time. "One is a kind of satyr of sorts—"

"—I'll just bet he was," muttered Felix.

"Will you let me be? He is an old acquaintance of highland shepherds. He likes to run along meadows and scare the goats into a rush. Like an invisible wolf on the margins. But he's not intent on hunting them, just having fun. His name is Pan."

"Are the goats lost, too?" asked Moritz.

"No, they're still keeping the grass shorn around the ancient temples. They're well behaved now that Pan has stopped panicking them."

"No fun for the goats," said Moritz.

"He likes to make trouble, that's true," said Dirk.

"Who's the other one?" asked Franz. "Is it a boy?"

"No. She's a beautiful young woman, maybe the ghost of a tree that someone cut down."

"A dryad," supplied Felix.

"Her name is Dogface," suggested Moritz.

"No, it is Pythia," said Felix. At Dirk's scowl he put up his palms. "Sorry. Your tale. I'll be quiet."

"Pan and Pythia," said Franz. "Pythia and Pan. Are they married?"

"No, they hate each other too much. But they are isolated together in the Little Lost Forest as it slowly sweeps its way north. It was in Bavaria not long ago, I think, and maybe it is in Baden now."

"Can we see Pythia?" asked Moritz. "Will she scare us?"

"She's beautiful beyond compare," said Dirk. "She's like your mother."

"Oh, her. Well, what about Pan? Can we see him?"

"He's tricksy. Here, look, he's a little like this." Dirk fiddled in his coat pocket and withdrew the old knife with the carved figure crouching atop it. What a big head, and bulbous eyes, almost leering.

"Why does he look like that?"

"He's—he's—" Dirk was stumped. "He's ancient but he's not old. He wants to stir up mischief."

"He's not the only one," interjected Felix. Dirk shot him a look. Felix continued, "I mean, isn't Pan the mascot of every university boy-scholar since the School of Socrates? Why do he and the Pythia not get along, do you think? Is it simply that she is sacred and he is profane? She is all arbory by the valley stream, and he is the wind in the uplands? They hail from different tribes, like the *Montaguesi* and the *Capuletti*?" At Dirk's bewildered look, Felix said, "Juliet and Romeo of Verona, from families with different interests and allegiances?"

"Pythia wants—evenness," said Dirk slowly.

"Civic order. Civilization," intoned Felix. "And Pan wants anarchy and riot."

"Who wins?" said one of the boys, and the other, "And how do they fight? Do they have swords and cannon?"

"They don't fight. They only have each other, whether they like it or not. And their shifting homeland."

"Oh no," said Moritz. "They don't fall in love, I hope."

"Yes!" said Felix, smacking his knee. "Pan uses his knife to open the Pythia's golden walnut, eh, Dirk?" He raised an eyebrow and licked his lips.

Dirk snapped, "Why is it always like that for you?"

"Because I'm young and I'm male and I'm alive. Obviously. Aren't you?"

Dirk couldn't really answer that. The little boys were relieved though that romance wasn't the *sine qua non* of the tale. "What they both want, despite themselves, is the same thing," said Dirk. "They want a place for the Little Lost Forest to grow large enough that they can both live there without being in constant argument. They want it to be a place all its own. Not lost anymore."

"The forest is scary though," said Moritz. "Wolves."

"Baby wolves are nice," said Felix.

"But their mothers," said Franz.

"Mothers can be very nice." Felix smirked. Franz and Moritz exchanged glances.

"I hope there isn't any wolf at all," said Moritz.

"There isn't," said Dirk, a little desperately. "There's only a mouse. But he's the king of the mice, did you know that?"

They began to look a little more interested despite themselves. A mouse was the right size. Felix closed his eyes and pretended a huge snore, and soon it was no longer pretense.

58.

After they'd eaten their lunch and stopped to pee by the side of the road—insisting Dirk get out with them and stand nearby in case of wolves—the boys gradually fell asleep in a heap. Felix finished the crust of one of their loaves and stretched out his legs to rest his calves on Dirk's lap. Dirk shucked them off.

"That's not much of a story," Felix said. "Is that all you learned about the Pythia from the strategies of the venerable Mesmer?"

"You used to be nice. Why are you so dismissive?"

"I want her to be wildly fecund. Louche, licentious, the female equivalent of Zeus, taking whomever she wants. Pan won't be enough for her, even if he is a satyr of sorts. She needs a god."

Dirk grunted. "Do they teach you pagan texts at university? Imagine superstitions having a place of honor there. Are your professors and ministers so flummoxed by Christian thought that they have to relish primitive lore from the childhood of the world?"

"The old-fashioned stories have always been with us, Dirkie. The cross was planted in the mouth of antiquity so modern faith could begin; but the old beliefs mumble from the ground. Those who halt their incessant prayers can hear the old stories telling themselves out loud. Indeed, I think that is what you do—that is your genius."

"Genius!" He felt a hotness rise from his collar. "All this is nonsense meant to amuse the boys. Or stultify them into sleep, as I've done."

"Don't feel too elevated, now," said Felix, kicking Dirk companionably. "These stories belong to Europe and to the world. Like Odysseus on his ten-year magical voyage, amid the likes of Cyclops and mermaids and Circe the witch—Odysseus coming back to Penelope the faithful wife. A world story. You know about all that?"

"I don't want you to tell me. I'm more curious about why you even care. Why do your masters at university care. Greece is a long way away and a long time ago."

"Ach, it's not just the German and Prussian states that pay attention! England suffers an advanced state of Hellenophilic tumescence, you understand. Concupiscence. I know, I've been there. My uncle took me to the home of a great architect in London who collects artifacts of the deep past—stunning marble torsos and intelligent faces, scallops from the rooflines of buildings, pillars and such. Bodies almost too beautiful to be human. *Ideas* of being human rather than portraits of individuals such as the Dutch and the Venetians give us. The whole building is a mausoleum of ancient faith—or maybe it isn't faith but *trust* in human capacity. I'm not sure."

"But how does a rage for the raw niceties of Greece infect modern Munich and Berlin?"

"And London, and Paris, and overseas, too, I'm told. It's a good question, Dirk. You might be university material after all. Maybe it goes back to the Lutheran rebellion against Rome."

"How could that possibly—"

"Once Gutenberg and his printing device were able to make the Gospels more widely available, not only to bishops and monks but also to the pious everyman sinner, the curious among *hoi polloi* wanted to know more. Mighty Luther himself worked on a translation of the Holy Book from Latin into German, did you know? So it's just sensible that the scripture-crazed devotees of the New Testament would need to go back to the original sources to ensure sound theology. And in the rush to learn Attic Greek, Germans discovered more than the foundations of the Christian faith. The Hellenic classics are stuffed with fundamental thought, oh, on government, and philosophy, and aesthetics, and architecture, and drama, too. As well as stories for children."

"Hmmm," said Dirk, but uneasily.

"You scoff, but really, *do* you know the *Odyssey?* Athena argues with the god Zeus for permission to intervene on behalf of Odysseus, as the great warrior struggles home from the Trojan wars. And when Zeus agrees, how does she manage her meddling?"

He expected Dirk to answer. Dirk shrugged.

"Athena disguises herself as an old woman. She helps him out with magical interventions. She then transforms him by giving him a disguise so complete that even his *son* and his *wife* can't recognize him. Only his dog. Who does this sound like to you, this Athena?" When Dirk didn't answer, Felix said, "Who do you think really *is* the fairy godmother in those tales by the Brothers Grimm, those household märchen that they published to such success, but Athena herself? You must know Aschenputtel, the cinder-girl in the hearth? There's a French version written up by

Perrault—Cinderella, no less—and in that one, the girl is elevated by divine manipulation, she is so glorified and disguised that her own family can't recognize her. Just like Odysseus, hidden in plain sight. The fairy godmother is Athena brought forward. Who else but Athena at the girl's side to help with a carriage magicked up from a garden gourd of some sort, with mice for horses, and a rat for a coachman."

Dirk rolled his eyes toward the coachman clicking the horses up front, but Felix chattered on. "The old gods steal secretly into our own times. Just as your Little Lost Forest is doing, with its Pythia and its Pan. What I'm interested in—do you want to know?"

"No, not really."

"What I'm interested in, Dirk—" He shifted his rump on the seat and looked at Dirk so intently that Dirk couldn't look away however much he wanted to. Felix pulled off his grey leather gloves and took Dirk's face in his hands and pulled him within a few inches of his own nose. "I want to know why the Pythia and the Pan would show themselves to you, who don't even know of their provenance, and who hardly care about it."

"I care," said Dirk. He could hardly breathe. "I care. I do care."

59.

The uncle was clearly a much-loved fellow. He hoisted the boys, one under each arm, as if they were squealing piglets, and romped around the barnyard with them. His wife, a stout friendly Frau with a cheery wall-eye, laughed at the reunion. Her fists clasped in a knot at her waist, and her bosom and belly shook as if well accustomed to the exercise.

"You'll stay the night?" Onkel Peer asked of Dirk and Felix.

"You ought to do; there's weather on the way," said Tantchen Isabelle. She glanced skyward, though it was impossible to guess from which direction she thought trouble might be approaching. She seemed to be surveying east and west, past and future, all at once. "I'll make up a mattress."

Felix insisted the coachman could see them back to Meersburg by nightfall. "I've an assignation arranged for this evening, mustn't miss it," he said. Oh, thought Dirk; and with whom? Old Mesmer, seeking out more secrets of other people's lives? As if he could read Dirk's mind, Felix said, "If I arrive on time, the von Koenig family expects me for dinner and a concert, Dirk. You could come, too."

"They won't welcome me, and I wouldn't accept if they did." But before they could argue the matter, the coachman declared he had no intention to push his horses through bad weather. Should the lads intend to return to Meersburg by nightfall, they could do it by foot if they started at once. They might be there by sunset if they didn't dawdle. The coachman would hunker down at Onkel Peer's stable and return to Meersburg in the morning.

As Dirk wasn't eager to leave Nastaran alone for a single evening if he could help it, he bade the young Pfeiffer boys a brisk good-bye. They were too busy romping about with their uncle to reply. Tantchen Isabelle refreshed the food parcel with slices of ham and a few apples and brown bread with seeds. Then Felix and Dirk set off on foot. The sound of the boys' laughter haunted the farmland behind them until the road turned at the heel of the hill.

They strode with vigor. After the first half hour had passed in companionable silence, their pace slackened. Dirk asked Felix more about his interest in music and how he had come to settle on the violoncello as an instrument. Felix liked to talk about himself, so Dirk heard more about the university student than he'd ever heard about anyone before. There was the uncle in London, and a surviving grandfather somewhere on the Hanseatic coast. Felix's parents lived alone in a village northwest of Munich. Their humble home looked out on the Dachauer Moos, a marshy sort of badlands that gave off a redolent stink. Felix abhorred it. Profoundly dispiriting. His parents had had no other children and seemed perpetually surprised to have given rise to Felix, as if they'd expected only to serve the Lord and not to serve supper. Vater Stahlbaum was a verger at the church of Saint Jakob in Dachau, which had a door handle shaped like a fish. He whipped young Felix once for liking the feeling of the fish in his clasped hand so much that he stood outside stroking it over and over instead of entering to receive the Sacrament. "So many ways to come to the holy truth," finished Felix. "Now, your turn."

Dirk thought, I must be capable of saying something; I must be capable of knowing something about the world now I've lived in it a bit longer. Surely friendship is built on the sharing of private histories. One has to start somewhere.

"I was born, I don't know where. Or of whom. I was a foundling in a basket, and raised in a forest by an old man and an old woman until, I forget why, I ran away."

"Were their names Pan and Pythia? They sound like the same pair of people. Old and cross and full of mystery."

"Isn't that anyone's parents?"

Felix snorted with surprise, as if Dirk had just given an amusing disquisition in classical Greek. It was only relief, Dirk guessed— relief that Dirk was capable of an actual opinion.

But pry and prod as Felix did, Dirk couldn't reveal much more about his origins. The old man and the old women were self-sufficient. Indeed they might have suffered some sort of fear of society, as they lived like hermits and never went to town together, and avoided all manner of travelers in the woods as best they could. "The only time I really remember someone at the waldhütte," admitted Dirk, "was the day before I left. A man was wandering along looking for someone to share the common stories of the district, and he found the old woman and listened carefully to stories she told. She was good at storytelling, I will grant her that much."

"Like those philologists, the brothers from Steinau, who produced the *Household Tales*. Die Gebrüder Grimm. I wonder if it was someone following in their footsteps. Or if it might have been one of the brothers himself? You should ask your Mutter."

"I don't know where the old people are. Or if they are alive, even. They were old when I was young."

"So were my parents, and they're still alive. Sort of. We should find your old folks. We could go on a hunt. Where do they live?"

"They are as lost as the Little Lost Forest," insisted Dirk, and would say no more about them. Luckily, Felix's crimson cape started to whip about his shoulders, flapping and snapping too noisily to talk above. The subject was abandoned as the travelers turned their faces into a strengthening and sharply chillier wind.

Within another half an hour they began to think perhaps Tantchen Isabelle had been right to suggest they postpone their departure for Meersburg. A rainy slick began to fall. "We'll not make Meersburg, and I'll miss my concert," said Felix. "At the rate this is falling, if it turns to snow before we regain the main road, we'll lose the track, too."

When that happened, they knocked on the door of a farmhouse in whose windows a few cozy lights shone. No one answered the knock, and Dirk wanted to turn away, but Felix said, "We'll perish in a snowy chasm, clutching each other for warmth until we die, and what good to Nastaran will you be then?" There was sense to his argument, but Dirk let Felix be the one to try the handle of the door, which opened to him easily enough.

"Hello; we are harmless strangers in this sudden storm," called Felix, for the house had the aroma of occupancy. Food in the kitchen before them, laid out and half-eaten; a fire in the kitchen stove, and an iron kettle of water on the boil. A cat playing with a half-dead mouse looked up at them with scorn, and the mouse escaped for a few more moments of life until the cat could return to its game. "Hail, are you at home?" called Felix again.

A step on the stairs, and a beefy farmer with bloodied hands stumbled into the room. "Has the midwife sent you two bekloppts in her place? Where is she?"

"I don't know, we're not her lads," said Felix. "If she is on the road, she's imperiled by this sudden snow squall. We've come to ask for your roof over our heads until morning."

"Do you know about midwifery?"

Felix shook his head in mock horror. Dirk said, "I saw a cat give birth to kittens once. That's all I know."

"You can't stay here, my wife is in knots and the house is too small—take the water up to the chamber and let her hold your hand if she will—"

"You have too much trouble already; we'll risk the storm," decided Felix, grabbing Dirk by the hand. But before they could back away, the door opened behind them and a bony-shanked woman came huffing in. Her skirts were tucked into her waistband, as if making allowance for having had to ride on some donkey or broomstick, whatever had come to hand. "Your Frau, she couldn't have kept her legs closed another twenty-four hours, either nine months ago or tonight? It figures. Country women have no sense of timing," she snapped. "What are you lads gaping at? Go tend to my mare before she breaks loose and bolts."

"The wife in a bad condition, and you're late yourself." The distressed husband held up his reddened hands. "I've been doing what I could."

"Haven't you done enough already? Give me a quarter hour to assess the situation and I'll holler down when I'm ready for the knife." She lumbered for the staircase. The man paled and collapsed into a chair, which collapsed onto the floor. Dirk and Felix helped him up and Felix lit his pipe for him and stuck it in his mouth.

"Go do as she says, and stable the mount," said the farmer. "Blankets in the loft. You can stay there. You won't want to be near this home. If you hear screaming, pay it no mind. I've sent the other children to their granny. Grab some food as you go, and don't come back until morning unless I summon you. The goodwife will sleep on the kitchen floor if there is sleeping in her immediate future. I doubt it."

The night seemed to have come in. A mangy horse with a disagreeable expression allowed them to lead it around the corner of the house, where a set of sheds and barns, already settled with a white pall, were dissolving into vortices of snow. Inside, several other animals, two cows and two horses and some sheep. As he'd learned to do last summer, Dirk milked one of the cows and then the second, so he and Felix had warm milk to share in the one tin cup. Then they shucked off their sodden freezing garments and hung them to dry on pegs along with the farm implements. They climbed a ladder to a loft where, in the hay, they found several blankets and even a couple of ratty sheets, which, once the mouse droppings were flapped away, were comfortable enough. Felix had stripped to the bone, but for modesty Dirk retained his shirt, which fell to his mid-thigh, and that was something at least.

60.

irk had brought to the loft with him what was left of the staff as well as the knife with the gnome-figure handle. The crutch was almost useless now, as the narrower, earth-ended point of it threatened to splinter. The thicker part, though, the bole that fit naturally under the arm, was still solid and good. So Dirk broke the staff across his bare knee. With the old fabled knife of his childhood, he set to scraping at the hardwood knob.

"What are you making?" asked Felix, wrapping himself in a brown blanket and lying on his side, his temple propped up by his curled fist. "Is this another of your secret talents?"

"Another?"

"I mean, besides talking to the spirits of the sacred grove?"

"You ridicule me, you toy with me," said Dirk in sudden heat. "For certain I'm a superstitious dummkopf, but why must you mock me?"

"You're anything but that. How many ways do I have to think of to say it? You're an oddity among young men, Dirkie. Your thoughts are already knitted into your skull, while other lads I know haven't yet learned that a passing observation is preamble to thought. I *admire* you. I'm lying here wishing I had a 'cello to play some composer's heart out, but I don't. Here you are on your own, and you? You set about to find a knife and a piece of wood and begin to make something out of nothing. If that isn't magic, I don't know what is. Don't you see I'm envious as hell? You destroy me."

Dirk kept to his task. The wood turned under his shivering hands. A shapeliness lived within, a secret he wanted to find.

Felix groaned and rolled over and threw his arm over his eyes.

The door to the barn opened and the farmer came in. "She sent me out here to build up the fire for you," he called up to them.

"Mostly she wants me out of the way for the next little bit. You didn't even find the stove? I keep it going in the worst of the winter for when the ice harvesters come by to work the lake."

Felix opened his eyes. His clothes were all down on hooks. He wasn't going to climb naked down the ladder to help. Dirk sighed and put aside the carving and the knife, and with his shirttails flapping, he descended to the ground level. "It's the normal stove operation; keep this grate open for air; feed the wood through here. The wind can find a thousand chinks in the roof. Believe me. The wife has sent me out here to think things over on more than one night, so I know what I'm grousing about. But with the stove going you'll do all right."

"How is she?"

"The midwife won't say a word until there is a good word to say. That's how they work. Bragging can taunt a hex to lurch into the fray and turn it all around. There we go. How is that?"

A small red blaze of heat threaded into the cold. It would be enough.

"If my cape is dry, bring it up to me, Dirk," called Felix.

"One the lord and one the lackey, it was ever thus," said the farmer as he opened the door into the wind. "Keep yourselves warm, fellows."

Dirk draped the cape over his arm, pinched an awl from a workbench, and climbed up to the loft again. He flung the cape at Felix's head in something like anger, though he didn't know why. "What *are* you making?" asked Felix, scrabbling out from behind the red cloth.

"A nutcracker."

"For me?"

"*You?* No. For Nastaran."

"Oh." Felix replaced the rough brown blanket with his red wool cape, which Dirk now saw had a silk lining. He had rich tastes for a boy with a minister for a father. Very nice against the skin, no doubt.

He returned his eyes to his task. The figure was roughly cylindrical. Dirk blocked out volutes that would indicate arms held in martial strictness at the figure's sides. The easiest sort of headpiece would be a Napoleonic conical piece, or a fez of some sort to indicate the mysterious East of Nastaran's longing. A lancer helmet of some sort. Identity wasn't important—indeed, Dirk wanted to avoid specificity. This could be the agent of a private brigade, coming to her rescue.

"Why a nutcracker, of all things?"

"To open the proverbial golden walnut, of course."

"Ach. Of course. Stupid of me. I see how the jaw will pivot open by lifting the coat-tail. Clever. But look, when it's in its resting position, the cavity where the jaw will descend is exposed. It's an open box. No heart. The heart has fled."

Dirk answered after a while in a lower voice. "Its heart is in its throat."

"We'll see about that."

Dirk fashioned the tunic to tighten at the waist. He scored a diagonal across the chest to indicate a bandolier of sorts, or a sash for the display of medals. What campaigns might an army of one attempt? The rescue of a sorrowful woman, nothing more vital than that. Quickly the booted feet found themselves grounded on a disk that would help the creature stand at attention, should Dirk do the job well enough. The knife whacked and flicked. Dirk brushed the cuttings off the blanket. The iron stove clicked as it warmed. He kicked the blanket down to his naked feet, sitting up at attention as Felix began slowly to drowse in the heat and in the luxury of his silky cocoon.

By the time Dirk turned his attention to the nutcracker's face, the wind had begun to howl about the barn as if in protest. Then it shrieked in a high-pitched note. Felix, who had rolled on his side to face away from Dirk, rolled back again. "That's her, you know."

"Her?" There was only one *her* in Dirk's mind. Then he realized Felix meant the farmwife in labor. "Jesus's mercy," he muttered, putting down his knife just for a moment and gripping Felix's hand. The oil lamp was guttering now. Dirk didn't want to risk ruining the nutcracker in shallow light, so he set aside the creature, which could already stand on its base, and stuck the knife into a crack in the floorboards, blade down. The gnarled ironstone creature that formed the grasp was angled as if watching the travelers balefully. Dirk took a resting position beside Felix. He lowered the lamp but didn't want to blow it out fully. Against the sound of screaming, which turned and returned in the wind, he felt defenseless and alone.

"It's become warm up here," murmured Felix. In response Dirk murmured a good night. He told his eye to close.

Some minutes later. "Are you quite cozy?" asked Felix in a low voice.

Dirk didn't answer but willed his breathing to come more slowly. If he pretended to be asleep he would eventually learn to be asleep. He had no more talking in him today. He concentrated on the nutcracker in his mind, what it might do for Nastaran. It would only be a sign of Dirk's adoration, of course, but she could keep it by her bed. If she worried about getting up and walking about in the night, looking for her childhood, the nutcracker would be there in Dirk's stead, to guard her and protect her from terrors and affrights.

Dirk could never enter in her cloistered room with her, so the nutcracker would be his emissary.

He would borrow the paints in Nastaran's attic studio and give his creature a bright red coat, and black boots, and a yellow brim to the military helmet, and perhaps epaulets if it wasn't too late to work them into the shoulders.

And perhaps a feather from a thrush. He must make a small hole in the front of the cap to take a plume.

"Come here, the red cape is large enough for two," whispered Felix.

Dirk had no way to consider what Felix was saying. For a moment he stopped breathing entirely. He'd have to answer Felix. And he couldn't answer Felix in any way at all.

He must feign a deep, deep sleep. He released a breath through his nostrils as slowly, naturally, as he could. His eye-patch was toward Felix, his good eye squeezed shut on the far side.

"You are dreaming of her, of course," whispered Felix. "I might have known."

So Dirk's carefully paced breathing compellingly implied sleep. Good. He trained his thoughts on the nutcracker. Perhaps it could have a sword.

"She is so beautiful, in her fluid pantaloons, her shawls."

Why was Felix talking about Nastaran in the middle of the night in the warmth of a barn loft in the teeth of an early snowstorm?

"Her eyes so warm . . ."

Yes, but . . .

". . . and her breasts, both of them so warm—so full."

To keep his breath even, Dirk had to harness every scrap of intention in his human form. It was too late to draw the blanket back up to his waist. His nightshirt clung to his thighs and, rucked beneath his bottom, was pulled tightly across his groin, which was responding to the whispery seduction.

"She must drop her shawl when the summer evenings are warm, and anoint herself with perfumed attar of roses here, and there, and there." Felix's voice was the haunt of a 'cello, and as his voice grew ever fainter, he leaned nearer and nearer to Dirk's ear. "It must be hard to resist her. You must be hardened to her—you are hardened." And so he was. If one could blush in the midnight, Dirk would be blushing. Though concealed, his cock was slantwise to the roof-beam, held and articulated by the fabric of his shirt tucked under his hip. Felix, to judge by the location of his hushed voice, must be on an elbow, looking down upon Dirk. It was unbearable. Felix meant to talk Dirk into somnolent ejaculation, and watch all the while. Whatever did they teach at university?

"If she were to bend down and kiss you—to take you into her Oriental mouth—"

Dirk rose one shoulder into the air in a pretense of nocturnal stretching, and rolled on his side, back to Felix. His shirt had slid up a little, exposing most of his rump, but at least his cock was now hidden from view. Aching like a pistol readied for the duel, he bore it with such dignity as he had reclaimed for himself. He was shivering not from cold but the shock of such impertinence. Felix flung the red silk cape over them both, and their legs touched once or twice, Felix's knee indenting into the back of Dirk's knee, trying to slip between his thighs, but Dirk twitched himself away with as much naturalness as he could. He endured the exhausting moments until Felix, finally, seemed to fall into a genuine sleep.

All the while the nutcracker and the knife of Pan stood watch over Dirk, the one a protector in roughed-out form, the other a leering lecher. The distant screams continued for a while, every now and then, until they stopped or Dirk fell asleep, or both.

6I.

𝔍n the morning the two young men dressed in haste without speaking to one another. The cows were desperate to be milked but this morning they seemed spooked by Dirk and wouldn't let him near. Felix grabbed Dirk's knife and sawed off a small tendril of wool from an inattentive ewe, and pocketed the scrap. "You'll see why," he said.

The farmer met them crossing the snowy yard to the house. He had a hank of bread smeared with butter for each of them.

Dirk didn't dare speak, but Felix mumbled through a mouthful of breakfast, "Did she make it?"

"She did," said the farmer. "Both of them, daughter and mother. A bit battered this morning, and sleeping the effort away."

"Can we see them?"

"Felix!" said Dirk.

"Room looks like a surgery on the verges of Waterloo, but sure, if you're quiet," replied the farmer. This wasn't his first child, Dirk remembered.

The midwife was folding blankets and beginning to rinse rags in water boiled over the hearth. "You'll not take those gentlemen up the stairs!"

"Your job was done last night, mine starts this morning," replied the farmer, and up the stairs they tramped, as quietly as possible.

The mother lay in damp sheets pulled up to her chin. Her hair was mostly pinned to her head and a night-cap with untied straps had come awry. Next to her on the bed in a wicker basket, swaddled in greyish toweling, a morsel of a face was puckering and squinching. It looked like a bloated, hairless mouse, a raw pink radish. "Isn't she lovely?" asked the farmer.

"Where did she *come* from?" asked Dirk. A question he had asked before in his life, he seemed to imagine.

"If you don't know that, your friend can instruct you on the way back to town," said the farmer, ushering them out. "The weather has broken and the snow was light, for all that wind; you'll have no trouble keeping to the path."

Dirk turned and looked once more before descending the stairs. The mother looked like an angel that had been shot out of the sky with an arrow. He could no longer see the baby over the sides of the basket, but he could feel its presence like a radiant chord, a sweetness of otherness.

62.

They stopped for a lunch at a tavern just above Meersburg, open to a view of the great lake, blue and brown and green with the mountain steeps reflected in it. They hadn't spoken too much on the trip. "Not a very restful night," Felix had groused as a kind of excuse for his silence. Dirk had not offered an opinion.

Yet at table on a sunny terrace—for the day was returning to one of those shocking seasonal warmths that the mountains can sometimes boast at autumn noontimes—they each downed a beer and finished a cheese and a half, and four sausages and a pickled onion between them. Felix called for a second tankard. Dirk settled for some sliced apples in honey. Then he picked up his carving and sat in the sun, struggling with the chin.

"You have a little skill at this," said Felix.

"The wood is working with me," said Dirk. "I think it *wants* to be a nutcracker."

"I know, wood confides in you. How will you stop the chin from dropping out?"

"Look, I'm trying to keep a pin of wood in each jaw. When someone works this handle, which looks like the back end of a bird, its tail-feathers, maybe, or the drape of an overlong coat, the chin will go up and down, pivoting on these pegs."

"Won't it break?"

"I'm using this awl I found in the barn last night to gouge out what I can, so the jaw and its handle are detached from the rest of the fellow. Two pieces of interlocking wood carved from the same block. It's a tricky business but the wood is strong, and the knife is talented."

"Your hands are not instruments?"

Dirk looked up. "Only midwives, I think." And he smiled. "If one of the pins snap, I could replace it with a nail and it would still move like a hinge. But the jaw will be stronger if I can keep the pieces separate and interlocking."

"Your lady love will adore it." Felix's voice was uncharacteristically small. "She will hold it in her lap." He put his finger in the pot of honey and smeared the lower lip of the carven figure. Then he pulled the twist of wool from his pocket and pressed it until it adhered. "There. The beard will hide the lack of a heart."

"Is it a flaw to be heartless?" asked Dirk, pointedly.

A small brown bird came down in the silence and stood on a gatepost at the edge of the terrace. "Hey, where are your mates?" asked Dirk of the bird. "Aren't you off to Africa or the Levant with them?"

"She'll never give you what you want, you know." Felix seemed in quiet, business-like despair. "Will it be enough, to have made her a present? Will that see you through?"

"See me through what, Felix? I've never been able to imagine three days ahead of myself my whole life. I don't know any more of life than that infant in the basket does. I'm just doing what I can from day to day. Handholds and landfalls and anything to grasp onto. Nothing gives much purchase, does it?"

Felix shrugged. His red cape seemed larger today, and he was lost a little inside it.

The thrush, if that is what she was, hopped from the post to the edge of the table, and brashly worked at devouring a scatter of crumbs. Her movements were a kind of dance, hop skip hop triple skip. She looked at Dirk, as if trying to see if he was a bread crumb, and then she departed in a flurry of wing-feathers. One fell behind on the stone terrace.

"Here," said Felix, picking it up. "Here is your plume for Herr Nutcracker."

Using the awl, Dirk routed a pinhole notch, and threaded the feather into it. Now the nutcracker belonged to them both, somehow. Dirk finished the corner of the jaw, and began working the tip of the knife into the back of the throat. "This is the last integument, and then the jaw will have life," he said. His palm was closed around the black-iron imp, but the knife-head seemed warm to his grasp. "In . . . just this . . . this final bit . . . and, is it presto?"

"Presto!" said Felix. He reached over and gripped the handle of the nutcracker and lifted it up, before Dirk, using the tip of the knife, could finish clearing out the last of the shavings from the nutcracker's throat. The mouth swung open on its solid jaw pins. "I sing of the Golden Walnut!" cried Felix in a pretense of triumph. Several other travelers on the terrace turned and looked. Then Felix slapped the handle back into place, and the bulbous lower lip of the wooden nutcracker smacked against his upper lip with a satisfied grin. "It works!" cried Felix as the blade of the knife fell out of the nutcracker's mouth, broken off of the cold lifeless dwarf-shaped handle that had held it for so long.

63.

They parted at Kirchstraße in the center of town. Felix would continue on to the gasthof and the von Koenigs, and make his apologies for having missed the concert last night. And then, he said, he would wander back to university, probably, and rejoin his fellow scholars.

"That's a big change from yesterday," said Dirk, trying to sound interested but eager to hurry home.

"As you said earlier, who knows what is to happen three days out?" said Felix. "Maybe I'll suddenly come upon enough of life to be able to play the 'cello with conviction."

"Conviction? Is that all it takes?"

"You mock me. You've learned to mock." A wry grin worked its way forward between Felix's clamped lips. "Hope for you yet, I suppose."

"You'll be playing for the crowned heads of Austria and France by the time you're twenty-five," said Dirk.

"I'll be married to Hannelore or Engelbertine or some such goddess," said Felix, sullenly, "and we'll have eight of those little pinched newborns like the one we saw this morning. And the screams to make them come out right! . . . Dirk, give me something to remember you by. Please."

Dirk had driven his hands into his pockets, feeling for something, so could not resist when Felix gripped him by the shoulders and kissed him so fast and hard his teeth rattled in their sockets. He pulled away. "Here," Dirk said, opening his hand. Felix caught it. The broken knife-handle, the dead carved little figure, staring up at nothing. "Take it, Pan, it is a thing of the past."

They parted, moved to opposite sides of the street without further comment, as the last of the melting snow ran cold and clear in the gutters, and a cart filled with squawking chickens in cages came up the street between them.

Dirk then turned toward home.

It was, as he probably ought to have guessed, too late, far too late. In the absence of family and a chaperone with any sort of authority, Nastaran had tried to release her childhood from herself through her own steps, taken in the middle of the night to the edge of the jetty that faced the barrier Alps. To the edge of the lake, and past the edge. Whether this was an accident during somnambulism or clear-eyed suicide, no one could ever say.

Part Two

Intermezzo

64.

He stayed in Meersburg another eight years, until the boys were more or less grown. Well, Franz, anyway. Perhaps Moritz would never emerge into anything like competence.

Gerwig Pfeiffer didn't join the others at the quay to see Dirk off. Whether this was because in his stolid silences Herr Pfeiffer still held Dirk accountable for Nastaran's death, Dirk didn't know. Or perhaps the old man just wasn't interested. The boys came down in the cart with Frau Pfeiffer the Next. She was a hearty proxy of a wife, not so much a pillar of the community as a footstool.

"Well, that's that, then," said the second Frau Pfeiffer. Her Christian name was Cordula. She handed Dirk's lunch to him, and then assumed her customary stance, her wrists wrapped around her forearms and her elbows angled away from her waist. This, Dirk always assumed, was to air the skin on her upper arms, which tended to a farmwife gloss in the summer. "We'll miss you, Herr Dirk. You shall always have a home with us."

She was everything Nastaran was not, and nothing like how Nastaran had been, except in one way: Cordula kept a lot inside. The slant gleam in her eye was a sign of intelligence and probity.

Franz was now through school. (The first thing the stepmother did was throw the boys into a rowdy schoolroom with an anarchic teacher who taught them Greek and archery and sums and Psalms. Franz had thrived, Moritz become shriveled.) The older boy was ready to apprentice with his father in the paper trade. Not knowing how to perform a gesture of authority, Franz clasped Dirk's forearms with both his hands, and then pushed a purse of cash upon him, all sudden, as a bully might land a thump. Dirk allowed only a grunt of thanks, so as not to further discomfit the boy in this shift of authority between them.

He turned to Moritz, who was kicking the rim of the cartwheel and looking down along the lake into hazy glare. The Persian force in the younger brother was emerging in his plum-like, deep-set eyes. "I don't know why you have to go now," said Moritz. His tone suggested a correlative assumption . . . *since you didn't have the nerve to leave eight years ago when you deserted your post and cost us our mother.*

"You're grown," said Dirk. "Or nearly. The paper trade is your family work, not mine."

"What is your new work to be, then?" They all watched the paddlewheel steamer approach with near noiseless plash from around the promontory, hugging the shore and heading for dock.

"I don't know." Dirk had resolved not to tell the boys or their father that he hoped to find his way to Persia. What he was looking for, he didn't know. A lost land. A home without the stink of familiarity. He realized this seemed a conundrum impossible to resolve. He might try, though. He, too, had grown up.

"I want you to have this," he said to Moritz. He had waited until the last minute to decide, and only now had the courage to reach in his satchel. Franz and his stepmother stood a step away; they understood this transaction was more important than sausage or guilders. Dirk took out the Nutcracker. Once Dirk had finished the figure with a gritted cloth and sand, he had used Nastaran's paints to color the piece into individuality. He replaced the thrush feather of the plume every year or so, and he had oiled the hinged jaw with linseed and lemon juice to keep it from splitting or drying out or chafing. It had gone from nutcracker to Nutcracker, and, in the stories Dirk used to tell when the boys were younger, to "The Nutcracker," or "Nutcracker, he . . ." The creature had evolved from *it* to *he*.

He had a touch of Pan about him still, did Nutcracker, but he wasn't Pan. Maybe he was the bastard son of Pan and Pythia. "Here. For you."

Moritz didn't look at Dirk or at the Nutcracker; he turned his chin and looked back over his shoulder, eager to be done with this. "No."

"I want you to have it. Really."

"You want a lot of things. Too bad."

Dirk was waved away by Franz and Frau Pfeiffer. Moritz hunched in the cart with his back to the lake, his face lifted to the sun, his eyes closed. Not *rigor mortis* but *rigor vitus*. Broken as his mother had been broken, and for something like the same reason.

Is it only in childhood that we are capable of taking in the whole world?

What does it do to us that we briefly have that privilege? And then, what harm, when the fund of novelty in human experience runs dry?

Dirk didn't know how long it would take to get to Bregenz at the eastern edge of the Bodensee. The city had once been under Bavarian rule and was now part of the Austrian empire. From there to Vienna, and on to the east. He would work it out.

He leaned on the rail at the stern of the squat vessel humping its way under summer sunlight, veering toward shore for occasional stops. Somewhere between docking stations, in a sudden fury of anger at Moritz, and maybe a sense of responsibility, Dirk fumbled in his satchel for the Nutcracker. If the Nutcracker could offer no comfort to Moritz, then Dirk had no use for him.

Something stilled his hand. It was as if the Nutcracker had shivered, trembled. A shudder of life from the corpse of a dead walking stick. Am I only less dead, thought Dirk, or readier to live? He pulled his hand away empty, flaring his fingers open at the water, flinging nothing to its depths.

Then on he went, to Vienna, to Bucharest, to Constantinople, to Isfahan, and beyond. The Nutcracker, in his satchel, never complained.

65.

Baghdad, Samarkand, western Cathay.

He discovered in himself a talent at languages. It was as if his ears had at last grown keener to compensate for the Cyclopean single eye.

He almost married a Chinese woman over the objections of her parents, until he realized just in time he had his own objections, too, even if they were hard to name. It wouldn't be fair to sacrifice the happiness of Wu Min on the mausoleum altar of the memory of Nastaran.

Though that wasn't the only reason. Once Wu Min had gotten over a pretty shyness and taciturnity, he'd asked her about her family. She'd gone on for nearly three weeks, roping in the complete histories of such bewildering strands of ancestors, seeming to recall with an ardent and clinical precision every moment of *their* lives, that he found her close to monstrous. Either she was from an entirely different species or he was. He escaped just in time.

Central Russia, northern Russia. Saint Petersburg. Copenhagen. Stockholm. London.

He honored the German disdain of France and a fear of their bloody revolutionary fervor, so he bypassed petty Paris.

Returned to Germany close to fifteen years after he had left. It had been a diverting exercise.

His satchel was now several trunks. He was getting older and they were too heavy to lug around anymore. He set himself up in business, a small shop behind cheery mullions that looked out over a seedy square east of the center of Munich. Despite the out-of-the-way location, he began to do a brisk business for his carved figurines. Parents called them toys, and bought them for their children. Drosselmeier never contradicted them.

The Nutcracker was travel-weary, chipped and bashed and showing his age. Dirk had made a sword for him out of the old broken knife blade, and fixed it with a leather thong slung around his hips. The Nutcracker presided over the toy shop. His eyes bulged while overlooking his domain. Superior to it, protective while faintly irritated all the time at matters of unknown complication. The only fresh part of him was the thrush feather, which Dirk tried to replace once a year.

Then one snowy evening, as Dirk was about to close up shop and retire his awl and knives to their wallet, and tidy the wood shavings up to feed to the stove, the little bell on the front door tinkled. A late customer pushed through, brushing snow off his lapels. He wore a ginger beard in the Prussian style and his eye was guarded and acute.

"They say you've become the best toy maker in town," he said. "How did I miss you all these years?"

"Well, well," said Dirk. "Good evening, Felix."

66.

So it *is* you," said Felix Stahlbaum. He clenched both palms upon the head of his walking stick as if he might pick it up and thrash Drosselmeier with it. His hands were angry but his face seemed wry. The smile was tentative, perhaps slightly acidulous. But what did Dirk Drosselmeier comprehend, now or ever, about what the expressions of people meant? He knew himself to be a simple-minded person. Or perhaps not—but in any case, he communicated as a simple-minded person. It was safer.

Speak in short sentences.

Avoid the abstract.

Beware the extremes of feeling. Enough of Goethe's poor miserable Werther—let him get on with it and kill himself over that fool Charlotte. Spare us the bombast and the breast-beating.

Admire the little, the low. What lies unnoticed by the steadying gaze of educated citizens of one nation or the next.

Trying to divert Wu Min from the subject of ancestry, he had made the mistake once of asking her about her own early memories. A month later when she had paused for breath, he went for a stroll, hoping to find a way to sever his cranium from his shoulders. The world of delights and advancements, slights and misapprehensions that constituted her young life! She was a savant. She was normal. He was the idiot.

When in turn she had asked him about his childhood memories, he had only answered something about a mother mouse and

HIDDENSEE

six babies. She had taken that as a metaphor and assumed he had
five dead siblings, and wept on their behalf. His protestations that
he didn't speak with Oriental theatricality were useless. She loved
him the more for his apparent deficits and losses.

Wu Min had asked the names of his original carers. He
couldn't supply them. In fact, all he could really say was that, as
he'd grown older himself, he'd realized that they hadn't been quite
as ancient as they'd seemed when he was a boy. The old woman
had had shapely legs; the old man's beard had been brown, not grey.
They were simply peasants, untutored in the ways of the world and
therefore frightened of it.

The less he could answer about his parents, the more Wu Min
cradled him, until finally he fled.

The silence in his own head wasn't the sound of loneliness, he
discovered. There was nothing to be lonely for.

Yet here was Felix Stahlbaum. His chin elevated by slow degrees
as if he was letting his eyes take their time to accustom themselves
to the gloom of the toy shop.

"Some people you expect to see again, and some you never do,"
said Felix.

"I expect nothing," said Dirk. Perhaps he had become a little
Buddhist in his travels—it had never occurred to him before. But
he stood as he spoke, the work desk between them.

Felix: "Are you closing up shop?"

"That depends. Are you in the market to buy some toys?"

"Are you free to join me at dinner?"

Dirk thought about that. What did *free* mean? Once the question had been placed in the room, was there any freedom left about
the matter? The question really could be stated as this: Was Dirk
free to decline the invitation? And he didn't know if he was that
free. On what basis?

Yet on what basis might he be free to accept?

"Join me for dinner," said Felix cunningly, as if realizing that a command was more effective than a request. He rapped the iron head of his walking stick upon the workbench.

"Let me put away the figurines I've been repairing." To buy himself some time, to be able to turn away, Dirk picked up the wooden Zouave in his turban, and the Hussar in his green and gilt jacket, and he put them on the shelf above the stove. In the waves of heat the two figures seemed to buckle at the knees and then straighten up.

"Is this all your handiwork? You have considerable skill," said Felix. "I shall have to buy something."

"I am at your service," said Dirk.

67.

Later, in Dirk's memory, all the conversations ran together. By tiny adjustments the world shocks itself and becomes bored again at almost the same instant.

But he didn't forget the first time that they sat over a glass of golden schnapps in the firelight of a small salon behind Peters-kirche, where Felix was apparently a regular customer.

Dirk looked at Felix more closely now that Felix wasn't looming over him. A level edge to Felix's brow that Dirk didn't remember. Perhaps a strengthening of certain facial muscles, the ones exercised by wincing. Hard to particularize how a face grows older. Eyes, perhaps, become less romantic and more capable of scrutiny. At least Felix's eyes—in this light, hazel with a cast of moss. Of the character of his own eye Dirk had no idea beyond its color—cloud blue—for looking-glasses only show the masks we employ, those masks needed in considering ourselves.

"Tell me where you went," said Dirk, before Felix could pose a question.

The man relaxed a little. "Isn't what happened to you more interesting?"

"Not to me; I've been in my own life too long already. You disappeared."

"I didn't disappear. I went back to university."

"You never came to find me."

"Well, once I learned what had happened to that woman—Frau Pfeiffer—I wasn't sure if you'd forgive me."

"What had I to forgive you for?"

"Distracting you, maybe, from your duties?"

"My duties were my own, and any dereliction of them is a matter I take up with myself, not with you. Not that you gave me the chance after that."

Felix sipped the schnapps. "I did come by once, you know. The following summer. I was back in Überlingen, to stay with the von Koenig family again. One market day the family bundled itself to Meersburg, and I stopped by the Pfeiffer home. You weren't there, nor the small boys. Only the husband and another person, a woman of some proportion."

"Ach. Gerwig with Cordula, the second Frau Pfeiffer."

"I asked after you. Did they tell you?" Felix furrowed his brow in mock indignity.

"They didn't. But what if they had? I had no social standing to storm the von Koenig parlors to see you."

"Well, I wanted to know how you were."

"I suppose they told you how I was."

"I suppose they didn't. Does anyone know much about you?"

Dirk laughed. "You were always public! That music. I have never forgotten it."

"You're not going to speak about yourself? Again." Felix toyed with a spoon. "Well. As to the 'cello. Enjoy whatever tissue of memories you have about that. I don't play an instrument anymore."

"Oh, no. Don't tell me that. Why ever not?"

"I accepted at last that I have a better ear than I could ever have fingers or—or musical—. I don't know the word. Adroitness. Musical wit, if you will. So it was a punishment for me to listen to my own inept attempts at transcendence. Have you ever heard a person who is mostly deaf try to speak? The garble of it? I played like that, all garble. In the end, I wasn't willing to offend the music or its composers by treating it so shabbily."

"You had much to offer."

"You don't listen to enough music if you think that."

They ate from the *table d'hôte*, a veal dish with lemons and carrots and a portion of thin shaven potato slices in vinegar. "I am going to pay for this meal," said Felix. "So you owe me entertainment."

"I should have brought my most recent friend: an oaken Mandarin from Old Cathay with a wooden moustache that reaches on two sides of his chin right down to his curly-toed slippers. I'd have made him dance for you."

"Once, I'd rather you offered to dance for me."

"Oh, Felix," said Dirk. What a confusion, to feel flat and alert at the same time. Of that notion of Felix's about the possession of musical wit—it seemed to Dirk that Felix had had a capacity, while Dirk could feel in himself an absence of wit nearly as firmly as he imagined he might have felt its presence. He struggled for words. "You only needed to ask me."

"*L'esprit de l'escalier.* I did try to ask you."

"This is a fine portion of veal."

"You were too besotted with Nastaran to hear me out."

"I don't like to talk about her."

"I was crude, I admit it. I played with you, that time we spent a night in the farmer's barn. In the snow-storm. Do you remember that night? You couldn't know, but I found out."

Dirk looked at his fork, laid like a little hand upon the scallop of meat, its silver fingers bowed open, upward, to receive.

"I murmured to you while you were sleeping—"

"Felix, stop."

"I talked to you about her—"

"Really, I don't want you—"

"I was trying to find out for sure. If it was Nastaran who excited you."

Dirk shook his head. He wasn't one for tears, and had never been; this was about as close as he came. "And you—" He harrumphed. "And you—"

"Well, and I found out. When I whispered of her in the dark, you responded as any lover would when considering his beloved."

"Felix."

"You couldn't know, you were asleep, but I learned what I had to learn."

"Felix."

"Yes."

Dirk said, "I was responding to you, I think."

It was Felix's turn to put his fork down. He laid it upside down, in a closed position, its tines in the viscous sauce, a few bread crumbs stuck to the arched hip.

Dirk's voice was low. "I wasn't asleep yet. I heard you. I can't tell you what happened fully—who knows anything about that sort of thing? But it was your voice I was responding to. At least in part. The music in your voice."

The *maître d'* approached to supply a bottle of sweet wine before they began to talk again, a few moments later.

"So you see," Dirk finally said, "I was ready to dance."

"You're the one with the eye-patch. But how blind of me."

"Ah well. You need only have asked."

"You could have asked, too, you know."

"Me?" Dirk snorted. "I don't have that kind of language in me."

"If you need to speak, you learn a language."

"*Touché*. Someday I will learn."

"And all along," said Felix, "I thought you hadn't been back in touch with me because of Nastaran. I thought you felt guilty about her death."

"There wasn't much to feel guilty about. I didn't invent the snow-storm that kept us from returning that night."

"I've always wondered, Dirk."

"What have you wondered?"

"Whether you knew when we left that she wouldn't be there when you returned."

"Felix!"

"It isn't that improbable. You knew how unhappy she was. I wondered if she had talked you into taking the boys away, clearing a moment in which to end her own life."

"That would have made me culpable."

"Well. In a fashion, perhaps."

"How dare you!" Dirk couldn't speak of her. She had left a lambent stain that sometimes wicked itself forward into his nightly dreams from some casket locked during the daylight.

Felix shrugged. "I don't mean it as an offense."

"Anyone who might help someone take her own life is committing murder. I'm outraged."

"You needn't see it that way. Death might be the only way forward for someone. Or it might seem so at the time. The Werther solution. I wondered if you were plunged into regret for your complicity."

"*Complicity!*"

"Oh, you're capable of agitation. I oughtn't be surprised. I'm wrong in this matter, too? So I'm wrong. You needn't fuss so. Even the scope of your umbrage gives one pause, though." He began to eat again. "They have a fine torte mit schlag here, I can't recommend it highly enough."

Dirk pushed his plate away. "I've had enough. I can't eat any more. Let's go."

"Where do you propose?" Felix signaled the staff and withdrew a purse from a string around his neck. "Will you come home with me?"

He was ready for that. "Yes."

"Very well." Felix laid out the coin on the tabletop and from a standing position took a last forkful of veal. "Everyone will be thrilled to meet you."

"Everyone?"

"Ethelinda and the children."

Dirk jostled the table pushing back his chair. The plate rocked; the fork jumped to the floor. It landed like a thrown tool, its tines down in a seam between old floorboards.

68.

Felix Stahlbaum led Dirk Drosselmeier to a prosperous residential neighborhood of Munich, a boulevard that, somehow, Dirk had never before come across. Linden trees flanked both sides of the road and also stood in single file along a narrow strip of garden in the middle, which ran from one end of the road to the other. Snow began to fall with a sound like small claws— brittle pellets rasping against a few dried leaves clinging still. Felix stopped before a house at the bottom of the road and fished for a key in his greatcoat. The establishment was tall and warm-looking, its stucco the color of the flesh of pale Oriental peaches. White tinged with cream and blood. Lamps glowed behind windows that were shuttered on the ground level and draped in the upper stories.

"You've rooms here?"

"This is my home." Felix bounded up the stone steps, gesturing. He turned as he was bending to insert the key, and winked. "Marriage confers considerable privileges, as perhaps you know. The boys are Günther and Sebastian."

Dirk didn't answer, but allowed himself to be swept into the vestibule and then the atrium.

A sort of banner ran above the lintels of the broad doors marking a margin between the ground-floor level and the gallery above. A frieze. It was colored like blancmange and animated with plaster bas-reliefs of Graeco-Roman figures cavorting in procession. The atrium rose two stories, a central well of chillier air within that cheery home. It was bright at the entry level and upon the stairs, and dark up at the ceiling; a canopy of glass upon black iron struts. Grey glass upon which snow had fallen.

Sounds of domestic mayhem sputtered behind closed doors. Unalloyed odors of tar soap and caramelized carrots gently offended. Someone was performing upon a clavichord with stupendous lack of aptitude. A door slammed, a child shrieked, a woman's voice gave firm command, something fell and smashed. "Papi!" cried a child, and a figure—several figures actually—ran along the upstairs gallery, behind a balustrade with wrought iron teased into flour-ishes, spears, and sheaves. The noisy *arrivants* tumbled down the arched stone staircase at the back of the hall.

A manservant, meanwhile, had come to take Felix's coat and brush the snow away. Dirk was handing his hat to the aide when a flaxen-haired child, a boy most likely, leapt into Felix's arms. Just behind the lad capered a King Charles spaniel with tangerine markings. The dog, elegant enough, appeared confused and con-sequently frantic. It skidded to a halt before Felix and Dirk, and ran circles around them, leaping up and nipping at Dirk's heels and calves.

"Otto! Otto von Blotto!" cried the child. "Stop that!"

But Otto von Blotto was aggravated, and his bark had the curve of the scimitar in it. The sound rang like steel against the marble noses of the busts of eighteenth-century unknowns. "God in heaven, an intruder at last!" called a woman's voice from above. "So our meek Otto has the menace of the Cavalier in him after all!"

"What's gotten into him?" asked Felix, laughing. "He's never like this. Clearly he thinks you are somebody else."

"I *am* somebody else," said Dirk.

"Take Otto away and then come back and give our guest a proper good evening, Günther liebchen," said Felix. "Oh, the sur-prise of it." The child, Günther, picked up the agitated animal and turned away. The dog scrabbled to the boy's shoulder, fixing Dirk with an accusatory eye, yapping with increased alarm at being exiled. Günther, in green velveteen, seemed all done up for an occasion of some sort. He couldn't be more than seven, thought Dirk.

The woman descended. "Unexpected society, Felix."

"Ethelinda, let me present an old friend—Herr Drosselmeier. Perhaps you remember him . . . ? Dirk, this is Frau Stahlbaum."

Dirk took her measure. She had a slender belly and hips, with a high-waisted gown clasped by a cincture in the Empire style, though under her burgundy sleeves her shoulders were robust and thrown back in a military fashion. She wore a high stiff cap of uncompromising severity. Ethelinda's eyes were kind and guarded, her skin powdered to bleakness, her chin retracted into her jaw like a turtle's head into its shell.

"I couldn't have had the pleasure," she said. Dirk heard in her sentence a clever ambiguity. She was wary.

"Yes, of course, you might have, at least I think so?" replied Felix, grabbing at her hand and pulling it forward to place it in Dirk's extended palm. "One summer at your father's home. On the lake? Surely?"

Dirk raised an eyebrow. Felix had married— yes, he had. A von Koenig daughter. The sister of that university friend, what was his name. Kurt von Koenig.

Ethelinda Stahlbaum, née von Koenig, shook her head. "No matter. How pleasant to make your acquaintance, Herr Drosselmeier. But, Felix, you have forgotten our engagement with the Foersters. I have sent the man over to say you were detained and not to hold the meal. But really, we mustn't delay."

"Forgive me, my dove. But isn't it too late to go out now? It is snowing."

"This is Munich. In December. It always snows," said Ethelinda. Her pleasant tone was dismissive and imperious. "I should think they could find a chair for Herr—"

"Drosselmeier," supplied Dirk. "Madame, it's all my fault. I hadn't seen my old friend in many years, and we lost track of the time. I shall take my leave, asking your apologies for the disturbance."

Günther came back into the hall. The dog was still yapping in some distant closet. "I think it was your eye-patch that frightened him," said the boy, as his younger brother, a sprite in blue satin, came trudging forward with his thumb in his mouth. "Why do you wear it?"

"Yes, why?" asked the one who must be Sebastian.

To see these lads, Dirk was filled with a horror of loss for Franz and Moritz Pfeiffer. Those kids had been lumpy and ordinary, Persian anomalies, nothing like these elegant male sylphs. But the way the smoky Pfeiffer children had just evaporated into the husks of their sorry, leaden lives—the loss rose in him. He had to turn.

"Boys, such a personal question!" said Felix. "Shame on you."

"But he's a person, so of course the question is personal," replied Günther, covering his own eye with a patch of fingers.

More or less leaving the matter open to discussion, Dirk made a gesture to request his coat again. How foolish, allowing himself to be beached here in a very wrong place.

Ethelinda addressed her husband. "The Foersters, they've been preparing for the feast-day with an ornamented tree in the lobby. It shall be divine. Sebastian, Günther, put on your cloaks and you'd better use your hoods, too. It's snowing. Surely you'll join us, Herr Drosselmeier?"

But Dirk made his swift good-byes and fled out into the night. Flakes seethed with pulmonary hiss along the boulevard. The family hung about at the street door, amused and slack-jawed at the flight of their guest. Deep in the bowels of the house, that infernal dog continued to publish his opinions with force and anger.

69.

At some later time, when Dirk had recovered from the sense of being an intruder upon their family hearth, he found himself in the small yellow salon with the Dutch tiled stove in the corner. Felix was poking ineptly at tobacco in a meerschaum. Dirk nursed a beaker of Lyonnais cognac. The boys roughhoused on the carpet behind the settee, sometimes pretending fisticuffs, sometimes settling down to act out scenes with their new toys. Dirk had brought them an Abyssinian and a Sultan. The boys didn't quite know what the figures signified, but the Sultan seemed dominant because of his starry blue turban, so Günther made the Sultan attack with his head, like a bull with lowered horns, knocking the Abyssinian onto his back over and over. Sebastian was partly laughing and partly crying, being unable to launch a winning feint on behalf of the Abyssinian. When it got too much they threw the toys aside and pummeled each other.

"What I don't understand, even now," Felix was saying, "is why you haven't married, Dirk."

"Please, is this suitable—?"

"They don't listen to adults. Why should they? Did you listen to your parents when you were their age?"

Dirk didn't answer questions about his parents.

"I suppose what I mean," said Felix, succeeding in getting the pipe to draw at last, "is whether your sympathies are so large as to make your choice difficult. I don't pretend that everyone would be happy with a wife, but you adored your beloved Nastaran. And you were pestered by friendship with me. Is it that the two energies compete for your attention, and thus make it hard for you to settle?"

"The things you talk about! Why don't you take up a musical instrument again? Channel some of that curiosity into melodic enquiry, which would irritate a little less."

"Don't count on that. I was quite an irritating musician. Am I offending?"

Dirk was happy to have become an acceptable guest in the Stahlbaum household. But he trod carefully. "The person who asks questions like yours always gets to choose the terms," he said, and shrugged.

"What terms would you choose, were you to turn the question around to me?"

"That's something I wouldn't do. Is Ethelinda joining us?"

"In the smoking parlor? The cognac is going to your head. She says she is taking Otto von Blotto out for a stroll up and down the street. But really she's showing off her new Parisian bonnet. Isn't she fetching?"

She gave you these grand boys, this comfortable home, thought Dirk. She's serene and secure and nearly lovely. You might have done a great deal worse.

"Or instead, perhaps you have no—appetites—at all," continued Felix.

"That's preposterous," said Dirk. "I should like right now to knock your head off your shoulders, that's the appetite I have." The boys paused their own skirmishes at the sound of Dirk's raised voice. He had surprised himself and tried to turn it into a bit of theatre. But Felix heard the note in his retort, and put his hand on Dirk's knee, and poured an inch more cognac. The conversation turned to the possibilities for increased commercial wealth in the revived confederation of German states promised by the March revolution. Felix had every intention to play strategically with the liberal elements and shore up his investments. "My hope is to take possession of a home for the summer in the north—it has come down to me from my grandfather because his wife has died long ago and my miserly father doesn't want to take it on. A place to which we can repair, as Kurt and Ethelinda have fallen out some time ago, and so we no longer can go to the schloss on the Bodensee."

"About what did they fall out?" asked Dirk, glad for the change of subject. But it was Felix's turn to indicate the presence of the boys, who had quietly been amassing a contingent of earlier gifts from Dirk—the two Cathay scholars, the Ukrainian milkmaid, the wide-hipped Mother Ginger with all her little babies that hid in her skirts. The world of toy was lined up along a curl in the Turkey carpet, listening to the grown-ups. The boys' hands hovered.

At this moment Ethelinda came through and lost control of Otto von Blotto, who raced in and, this once, forgot to abuse Dirk and instead grabbed the new Sultan in his teeth and ran around the sofa, growling.

70.

Felix:

"We do eventually grow up."

Felix:

"Are you—all—or nothing? More . . . or less?"

Felix:

"Sebastian, get down off Herr Drosselmeier's lap; you're too big for that kind of thing."

Felix:

"I don't know where childhood goes. Sometimes I remember . . . something. I wonder if you do."

Felix:

"You so seldom answer me. Am I to be offended?"

Felix:

"Will no one shut that damn dog up?"

Felix:

"Someday it will be too late, Dirk."

71.

One day, when it *was* too late, Dirk had found himself in a powder-blue and gilded salon, at a concert to honor the late Frederik Chopin. Though the sinewy, exhaustive explorations called the Nocturnes were still relatively new to the general public, the room was full. The selections were presented by an aesthete with expressive locks, a vampire who played with a violent agitation of his arms. Despite the melodrama of performance, the music itself could muscle up, oh yes, a power to shock.

To avoid losing the Chopin in the service of mere and selfish memory, Dirk struggled to follow the architecture of the piece. If Bach was music for the court and the church, Chopin was music for the bedchamber. Or the moonlit copse. If Bach had been Euclidean, as Felix once asserted, Chopin relied on a different rhetoric. Dirk had no reference for it. Dionysian? An opiated Dionysus.

A recurring spiral in the melodic line, first up but then corkscrewing back to lower registers, with turns and hesitations as languorous as the drip of rainwater from branch to leaf to upraised lips.

In listening to music Dirk usually tried to empty his mind of vapors and images. Tonight, however, the first three nocturnes returned Felix to him in ways it was hard to fathom. Dirk struggled to escape such particularities—how Felix had sometimes looked at him, quizzical, with a half-smile, the way a dog turns its head on its neck as if waiting the answer of an unasked question. What next?

He let the music unfold in his mind a certain apprehension that it took a little while to recognize. There is Felix, dropping out of the sky, tumbling from the basket of a hot-air balloon. (Do people come to us any other way, really?) I am on the ground, knocked out by the contact. Felix is on hands and knees, leaning over me, slapping me awake. What am I trying to say about this? This happened to me, it truly happened. Preposterous as it seems—it's no more preposterous than anything else. And I remember it here, under the influence of Chopin. Life has made this experience a memory.

Without a memory, what does experience mean—or matter?

He thought of those poor invalids who had been dead and then somehow revived, and how often it had been said they were severed from their true nature. Maybe they had had their memories broken off, and so they weren't truly alive, not the way others were.

But then memory could kill one—as it had done Nastaran.

At the height of outrageous curiosity Felix had once asked him about the eye-patch. "Behind that black circle, is your bad eye actually still there? You say you lost your eye—do you mean that actually? If you lost it, where is it?"

Of course Dirk hadn't answered. The truth is, he didn't know for sure. Maybe the falling tree in the woods had prodded his eye out the way a spoon dislodges a stone from an overripe cherry. Maybe the eye was rolling about in the Black Forest someplace, minding its own business, having experiences without memory.

Oh, the nonsense music could liberate from the wretched mind.

The otherness of it—the wordless significance.

The 'cello music assaulting him with beauty in the decommissioned chapel at the von Koenig schloss. The unplayed *dotar* in Nastaran's bedchamber.

Chopin's theme, a simple descending descant the first time round, articulated itself in the repeat with nuanced embellishment. It was music remembering itself. It meant something different, something more, to hear those simple phrases repeated so soon, qualified by chromatic variations. Clarifications.

Not redundancy, but a hypothesis about how consolation works. A second chance at getting it. A second chance at life.

72.

While Felix was still alive, Dirk visited the house known as Meritor only once. He remembered the circumstances the rest of his life, though, as a kind of coming home. If that sort of comparison wasn't baseless at its heart.

The Stahlbaum family—its guests and assigns and lackeys—had packed themselves into three carriages. They'd spent the better part of a week on the road from Munich. They'd stopped at Nuremberg. Another night at Leipzig with its publishers, for all Dirk knew, still buying their paper stock from Herr Pfeiffer & Sons back in Meersburg. Then, alighting for several days in grandiose Berlin, they'd heard two terrific concerts.

The boys were bored at the long carriage hours but thrilled with the idea of travel. They were frantic to get to meet the sea. Ethelinda was equally enthusiastic. She had never been farther north than Berlin. Still, only Felix had yet seen the property. Had he promised them too much?

They came upon it toward the end of the sixth day. It sat at the knuckle of a high spit of land on the island of Rügen. At first, all closed up against the sun and winds, the three-story outpost looked as if it must have been built as a fortress against the Danes—or maybe, when the Danes held this region, by themselves as a fortress against others.

The proportion of window glass to stone façade was ungenerous to light. And the grey granite was hewn in larger blocks than a house usually required. The place had something of the air of a temple, or perhaps a banking establishment. But the channel beyond it was glistening, and all agreed the sobriety of the house counterpoised sensibly against the dash and impudence of the sea.

The parlors, with one broad door and a lot of small windows with shutters, looked out to the west toward the smaller island of Hiddensjö, in the Danish, or Hiddensee as the locals called it. If Sebastian and Günther climbed on the desk in the corner of the parlor and peered through the high window, they could spy the small stretch of open Baltic Sea that divided Hiddensee from a northerly hangnail of a promontory that curled around from Rügen.

Dirk chose a room at the top of the house, facing the north. Though he had misgivings about the force of the wind through the casements—misgivings that proved well founded on the first cold night—he concluded that the view of islands in light was worth the bother of shivering. Instantly he fell in love with one break, where water met sky. No intervening land to disturb the sense of everness. The pale dash of horizon between homeland and Hiddensee. Such, perhaps, is to be expected of one born in the steeps of Alpine vales. Claustrophobia becomes a characteristic of childhood.

Dirk would come to adore Meritor—the name that young Sebastian concocted out of *meer* and *tor*—sea-gate. The vivid broom bucking in the wind was lively and silly. And even on stormy days, the countryside near the ocean possessed more light than the brightest Munich days. Only when the fog bellied in, as it liked to do of a summer morning, did the house hunch to its stone knees and seem to be thwarted.

That first visit, Dirk found his way down the cliffs with Felix and the boys and the wretched Otto von Blotto. They meandered along the shore. The dog growled at every strand of seaweed he came across. The boys collected rocks and shells, and threw them seaward, trying, they said, to build a bridge of stone between Hiddensee and Rügen.

"Meritor was repurposed as a hotel, a sort of seehotel, I think," said Felix. "But it failed. Until the roads are improved, it remains too far for the summer traveler."

"It is lovely, but is it sensible to fall in love with a place so far from Munich?"

"*Au contraire*, I find it usefully distant from Munich concerns, all those eyes and opinions. My hope is that by next year we might live here all summer. People are starting to do this sort of thing, you know."

"I should be sorry to see so little of you and your family for such a length of time."

"You'd come, of course. That's the idea."

Dirk laughed. They linked arms against the wind. "You're mad. I have a small shop. I can't afford to close it for a season."

"You can bring your tools and paints and grommets, your adzes and awls, and work here all summer. I'll arrange a workbench for you. The boys will promise not to pester you."

"The boys are never a bother. But it's out of the question. I shall come to visit from time to time. Let that be enough between us."

Sebastian had found a stone shaped like a butter roll. With ferocious noise Otto von Blotto was trying to scare a dead fish back to life. Günther was paying no attention to either of them, dashing toward the teasing waves, dancing away before getting his toes soaked. Gulls came in from Sweden with all the Scandinavian news. The light seemed to have a long up-swung curl to it at horizon level, some trick of atmospherics.

They sat to admire the view. It was blindingly blue today. Then Felix shifted his seat to a rock behind Dirk, and clamped his knees about Dirk's shoulders. As if Dirk were a 'cello. "I'll change your mind," said Felix. "Give me time."

"Take all the time you need. My mind is a capricious beast, and you may not find it where you expect."

"Haven't I already learned that."

They sat without speaking. The boys waved, and their father waved back. Dirk's hands were clenched tightly, one packed into the other.

When they stood and prepared to turn back, they clung closer together. "Boys," shouted Felix. "The wind is a monster. Keep back from those tidal pools or the North Wind will push you in, and your mother will have my head on a salver."

"You're right to worry," said Dirk before he could stop himself. Nastaran at the edge of the jetty at midnight. He pushed past this. "What good boys. Do they always obey you so well?"

"Rarely. As soon as this new situation becomes commonplace to them, they will begin to break the rules. The nature of boys. I hope you will look after them, Dirk."

"I—?"

"I mean, should anything ever happen to me."

"Like what? Your getting abducted by a sea monster?" Dirk gave Felix a sudden shove with his shoulder, knocking Felix off balance. His knee went out and he sat down in the wet, pebbly sand. "Yes, the world is a treacherous place, Felix."

"You reprobate. I'll get you." And they chased each other as far as the boys, and a little ahead. Meritor came into view around the curve of the bluff. From here they could see the castellated roofline facing the sea. Perhaps the place had housed cannon at some point.

"This is a perfect place for you to work," said Felix as they began to scale the bluff. Otto von Blotto was in his arms, as the incline was too steep for stumpy legs. "Look at the lovely openness of it. It just calls . . . to be filled with invention. No?"

Dirk paused for breath at a turn in the path. Felix was right about that. A row of narrow trees, too slender to serve as a real breakfront, made an open lattice against the shimmery spangle. But the shoreline was otherwise spare of flora—only tall needle-y grasses, low shrubs contorted into the shapes of flame by the ceaseless wind.

"You could move in your Little Lost Forest. There's plenty of room . . ."

Dirk didn't answer. So much caprice and nonsense spent in negotiating the sorrier and grander realities. "The forest would get blown out to sea," he said at last, as neutrally as he could.

That night, after the family had retired, Dirk noticed a door at the back of the clothes cupboard that proved to be the way to the parapet. His greatcoat hung on a peg; he pulled a sleeve forward into the doorjamb to make sure he wouldn't get locked out by accident. He had the impression he was climbing the dark sleeve of his own coat. Up a narrow set of stone steps he ventured, and lifted a trap to arrive, shivering, onto a flat part of the roof.

A middling moon emerged, a sore that was soaking the raveled sheets of cloud with white blood. It shed enough light that Dirk could make out the brow of Hiddensee to his left, and the low sweep of north Rügen to his right. The cleft of sea between them, that narrow verge of horizon that led his eye to no land . . . He stared at it, as if expecting a ship to round the promontory of Hiddensee, to come and rescue him. Until the wind finally got the better of him, he stared. In love, and in fear. The ocean, however milder in this channel than it would be on the far side of Hiddensee, was still rough and active, and the noise was thousands of drowning 'cellos.

73.

For four days Ethelinda struggled to establish some kind of routine in the household. The local staff proved sullen, the Munich staff styled themselves as superior. A stalemate from the start.

Unless the sky was spitting rain, Felix kept the boys out of the house, and most of the time Dirk joined them. They walked north to where the headland of the Rügen promontory turned east. All the time the low brow of Hiddensee winked in and out of view, depending on the strength of the fog and the warmth of the melting sun. It was too early in the season to bathe in the sea, though the boys tried. Their father stripped as well and got in as far as his calves. Dirk watched from the shore, shivering. "Take us in a boat to Hiddensee," the boys wailed.

"Too rough today," said Felix, lovely when he was being lazy.

"One day I will," said Dirk, but they weren't listening to him.

By the fifth day in Meritor, the Stahlbaum family and retinue had concluded, regretfully, that the house needed to be made more comfortable before they could truly enjoy it. The old plaster walls were buckled with hidden damp. The woodwormed chestnut wainscoting in the parlor required oiling at best and perhaps replacement. The well would have to be rebuilt, as the water had proven brackish enough to make their tea somewhat tidal. Next summer would be better.

The boys were disappointed in the change of plans. They expressed themselves, backstairs, in vital attempts at blasphemy that were almost charming. Ethelinda and Felix pretended not to hear them. "We never said we would stay the full two weeks, only that we would investigate," their father told them. "On the way home we shall visit the carousel in the Berlin zoo in the Tiergarten, I pledge you this."

"We were going to do that anyway!" shouted Sebastian.

"We'll be back next year. I'll take you by boat to Hiddensee. I'll row you myself."

Felix didn't keep his promise, though, as he died suddenly a few months later. Word about this from Ethelinda arrived at Drosselmeier's shop in the form of a scribbled message. She needed him at once. Dirk glanced at the figures upon their wooden stands, but he couldn't find one that warranted bringing as a consolation. He locked up and hurried to the Stahlbaum home.

Ethelinda met him at the door. The boys were upstairs in the nursery, weeping. Dirk took both her hands in his and said, "But why?"

"That's not the right question," she told him through her tears. He didn't know what other question might work, but maybe it wasn't a time for questions.

"You are Felix's—you were Felix's dearest friend," she said to him. "The boys need you now. I need you now. Please accompany me to the services as if you were my brother."

"But your own family—"

"It is too late for them to make amends."

He needed to know how Felix had died. His heart was engorged, said Ethelinda. His grandmother had died young from a similar condition.

She adorned herself in bombazine. With an admirable steeliness she saw her way through the services and the timid meals meant to appeal to a woman with a failed appetite. Dirk's ductless eye, behind its patch, leaked for the only time in its blind life. He wiped away the tears with a scrap of small colored scarf he had taken from Nastaran's cupboard after she died.

He'd been surprised to sit in the crowded nave and glance around at the choir in their robes. They did not sing. "He wanted no music," murmured Ethelinda. "Silence is loud enough."

For quite a while Sebastian and Günther wouldn't acknowledge Dirk with a hello, good-bye, or please jump off the railroad trestle. It was as if he had disappeared from their lives as completely as their father. Curious, then, that the most significant change of heart in the household seemed to belong to Otto von Blotto. The filthy fawning thing nuzzled at Dirk's arches and toes when he was sitting and kept to Dirk's heel when he stood or walked about.

74.

Ethelinda pulled back into herself as she became more used to being a widow. "You have your own life," she insisted to Dirk. But did he really? This was a question he could frame, but he couldn't come to an answer. He kept his distance.

After a few months, though, Ethelinda relented and showed up at Drosselmeier's Toy Shop. The boys were in tow. They became engaged in small racks of tin soldiers Dirk imported from Great Britain and France and set up on a tabletop to fight the Prussians and a certain militant strain of giraffe.

Ethelinda: "I need you to bring a packet to Meersburg. I don't trust it by the usual couriers."

"What's in Meersburg?"

"Have you forgotten? My family home? My parents have passed on to their reward, but my brother is still there. The lake place is too big and cold for year-round, and Munich won't do, but the Meersburg house is all right for him."

"Why don't you bring it yourself when you visit him?"

"We're not in touch. Surely Felix told you all about that?"

"He never did."

She explained. It turned out that, long ago, Kurt had sired a bastard with a member of the household staff. This had only come to light some years later when the mother showed up with the child in tow. He was something of a dullard, the boy, but his resemblance to the von Koenig line was unmistakable. The mother had once been a kitchen maid in the family's lakeside schloss. It caused a great ruckus in the whole family.

He fumbled. "And you—how were you inconvenienced?"

"I took Felix's side, of course. I was his wife."

"I don't understand. Why should Felix have any opinion about this?"

"Don't you remember? I thought you were around that summer. At the time, Felix was believed to have gotten the girl in trouble. He had admitted as such. My parents didn't want me to marry Felix because of that. Felix's presumed licentiousness was the cause of their estrangement from me because, you see, I'd already become enamored of Felix. I learned far too late that the bastard was actually Kurt's child, and that my own brother, so cowardly, had allowed his friend Felix to accept that stain upon his own reputation. And Kurt stood idly by as my forbidden romance with Felix caused a rift between me and my family—you see? Ach, Kurt betrayed both his friend and his sister. And this paupered my boys of their grandparents. So I can have nothing to do with Kurt. Though he's my brother, he's a selfish brute. No fit model for his nephews. You'd be a better godfather to them than he is an uncle."

So Dirk agreed to convey the packet of documents to Ethelinda's family home. Before the von Koenigs departed his shop, he tried to give the boys the pair of wheeled elephants he had carved from some cherrywood, but Ethelinda insisted on buying some soldiers instead. The boys had turned their noses up at the pachyderms anyway—girls' toys. They both accepted, however, a small sack of boiled sweets—acid drops in citron yellow and pear green. The Stahlbaum sons didn't thank him exactly, he noted, but at least they nodded acknowledgment at the thump of sacks in their open palms.

He left when they did. Closing up, he watched Ethelinda's passive face float up in the darkening shop windows, like the visage of a marble statue tipped over backward into shallow water. Her expression was full of purse strings, he thought; variously tightening and loosening. When her eyes were welcoming her mouth was snapped tight. When her lips softened and she bit her lower lip, her eyes went mechanical.

Dirk had little feeling for her of any variety, but even a sensation of curiosity was something of a novelty. She was keeping her grief to herself as a private treat to enjoy in her own boudoir, not to share among her friends. Ach, as if he were a friend of hers. He didn't know if he might qualify for such a position. Nor whether he desired to do so.

75.

He had felt queer all morning. By the time Dirk went to the Stahlbaum house to pick up the parcel of documents, the setting sun seemed to be etching lines of gold-foil in the damp gutters. Dirk cringed at the shouting and screaming and the throwing of toys upstairs. When Ethelinda came downstairs long enough to thrust him a packet of papers, she said, "And take this—as long as you're traveling." Felix's walking stick from the stand in the corner of the vestibule. "I always meant you to have something of his." Dirk knew the thing. He'd never noticed that the dark metal knob at the tip, the grasp, was the old iron knife-head of that wizened, crouching folk figure. Felix must have had this stick bespoke.

Tucking the papers into his vest, gripping the cane, Dirk escaped the household as quickly as he could. He paused at the bottom of the stone steps and looked along the boulevard. The trees were half unleaved and the ground was littered. He turned his collar up against a pebbling of rain. The door of the house behind him opened, the noise increased. He didn't turn to see who was looking after him—he had had enough of them. Felix wasn't there anymore. Dirk wasn't sure why he allowed himself to be involved.

He walked briskly as the rain steadied. The plashing of drops were like stains—he heard them fall on the cobbles before him. They registered to him as a splash of annihilation. As if a painter, rejecting everything on the canvas, were daubing out the view in blotches of angry nothingness. The patterns of blankness began to meet up, and he slowed his step for fear of losing his way. He was becoming blinded in his single eye. He'd never felt the like before.

He'd stopped cold for fear of walking into a carriage. He held one hand over his face. The other hand steadied the whole tottering stack of himself upon the walking stick. Horrifyingly melodramatic, but he couldn't help it. His body shuddered, from the backs of his ankles to the sensitive indentations in his temples. This was, perhaps, a cousin to the swollen heart that had felled Felix—*simpatico*. Dirk would leave now, he would go at last, after much too much waiting.

Until he became tethered to the world once more, this time by the furry yoke that wreathed around his feet, barking to alert him of the danger.

"You're a damn fool to come out in the rain," snarled Dirk to Otto von Blotto. He picked him up to return him to the household. Resentment at being importuned was a slender reason to live, but it was better than nothing.

76.

As he headed for Meersburg for the first time since he'd left, he began to think about those siblings, Kurt and Ethelinda von Koenig as they had once been, way back then. During his summer at the von Koenig lakeside estate, all those years ago, Dirk remembered seeing Kurt at a distance, because Kurt had been joined at the hip with Felix. But Dirk couldn't recall if Ethelinda, *née* von Koenig, had even been in residence at the family home during that bright season of youth. Perhaps she'd been visiting friends or cousins elsewhere. He wasn't aware of her existence until he met her as a married woman in Munich.

He had no desire to run into the kitchen miss over whom he'd made such a spectacular romantic failure. He doubted he'd recognize her, and indeed it took him a while to recall her name. Hannelore, it came to him, with the feeling of a scarf being knotted too tightly around his neck. Hannelore. She would be a matron now. A matron with an adult child.

His route from Munich to Meersburg took him through Memmingen and then Lindau, toasted golden towns set in the rolling nap of the Alpenvorland. When it stretched itself out in languor, Bavaria seemed to Dirk, somehow, tamed. Well, he'd traveled half the world since he was stupid enough to be young. The wild forests of his youth—perhaps they no longer existed. The world was too strictly regulated now. The idea of ever being able to find his way back to that waldhütte where he had been raised—to the extent he had been raised—was as impossible as Nastaran's need to return to her lost childhood in Persia. It couldn't happen.

Idle thoughts for a tedious journey. No value could attach to revisiting his youth, even if he could manage it somehow.

Still, the notion returned, and he had to throw it down repeatedly, like bread crumbs in some old tale—hoping the wild thrushes would eat them up. Despite those romantic stories that had become so popular—even Felix's little boys adored the sweetened renditions of Grimm as served up by stern Frau *Gouvernante*—sometimes one wandered into the woods because the ominous woods were safer than home was.

In the intervening years, Meersburg had grown, yet it opened its familiar prospects to him with a grudging heart. It seemed busier than he recalled. A gloss of foreign tongues spoke of a strengthening economy. Naturally, he'd never been invited to the von Koenig Meersburg quarters during the time he had lived with the Pfeiffers, both during Nastaran's life and in those years afterward. But he was able to locate it easily enough. He stood looking through the iron gate at the shallow forecourt of the Kurt von Koenig manse. Maybe the brother would be in residence and maybe not, but either way, Dirk hoped to avoid Hannelore. Surely she'd been sent packing with a nice residual, but maybe she'd been taken in with her son. Lived here as a retainer of some sort.

Dirk was performing this duty for Ethelinda but really for Felix. Steady now. Some impulse Dirk hadn't felt in years prompted him to utter a silent prayer as he pulled the bell cord. The fact of a prayer made him think of Pfarrer Johannes. Dirk had left his village church with a message for the Bishop of Meersburg and had never returned . . . What a layabout he'd been! What a bad son.

A doorman powdered in the old manner ushered Dirk into a chamber crowded with pots of straggly geraniums brought in from the early frost. A glass of beer was offered; Herr von Koenig was at home but occupied. But before long the head of the family arrived, stout as any Bavarian burgher, his thinning hair the color of melted marzipan.

"I served briefly at your family estate one summer," said Dirk, wanting only to be honorable and not to engage beyond what was necessary. "As I've come recently to befriend your sister in Munich, I've been deputized to deliver a packet of documents to you following the death of her husband."

"My old friend Felix," said Kurt. "My former friend. Former in both senses, as there is no hope of reconciliation now."

"I wasn't asked to await a reply," said Dirk, standing. "I'll confirm to Frau Stahlbaum that you have received the parcel. Thank you for receiving me."

"Sit down. Wait. A reply may be in order, whether one was requested or not." Kurt waved a fat hand distractedly, unfolding handwritten documents. He flipped pages, humming to himself. Some were letters. "If you were thinking of marrying the Widow Stahlbaum, you'll get neither support nor protest from me about it. We aren't much involved in each other's lives now."

"I understand that." Dirk managed to sound sniffy and also to avoid addressing the issue.

"She thinks I wronged Felix somehow."

"I don't enjoy such personal standing with the family that I could comment."

"I'm not pushing my life story upon you, sir. Just explaining the circumstances. This is an interesting letter. Have you looked at it?"

"Certainly not. May I be excused now?"

"You've come all the way from Munich on family business. It would be improper of me not to offer a meal."

"Thank you; it would be improper of me to accept. I'm an incidental messenger."

"Not according to this, you're not," he said, gesturing to the paper. "You did say you are Herr Drosselmeier?"

Dirk looked as officious as he knew how.

"I see that some of these are letters my brother-in-law sent my sister while he was away in London one year. Explaining to her why he had stepped in and named himself as the father of my child. It seems he had thought he was protecting *you*, and didn't learn I was the guilty father for some years. Until it was too late."

Dirk, not skilled at lying, made a stab at it. "I know that story and, truly, it doesn't concern me, or even much interest me."

"You were close to Felix, though. How droll, for him to be shielding a peasant boy from scandal—how could a reputation for scandal have hurt the likes of you? And all along it was my good name he was accidentally saving—at least until the wretched woman, I mean of course my *lovely* wife, showed up with my *genius* son."

"I counted him as a friend," said Dirk. The only friend, actually.

"And what are you, really, to my sister, from whom I will remain estranged for the rest of my days, it seems?"

Dirk stood again, this time clasping his coat in business-like fashion. "I am a neighbor and a well-wisher of your nephews, Sebastian and Günther."

"I see she has named you godfather to the boys, and that should she die, you will be the one to raise them up."

Dirk said nothing. He hadn't heard that item.

"Godfather, is that what it's called now. Frankly, I was surprised that Felix could claim to have fathered them. I took him for something of a washout with the gentler sex—indeed, initially I thought his false claim of foisting a child upon a country maiden was intended to bolster for him an unlikely reputation as a ladies' man. That much I was happy to give to him. As a friend—of course." Now Kurt von Koenig stood, too. "There's no written reply to my sister. But I should be in your debt if you could carry my condolences to her on the death of her husband."

"I'm unequal to that task."

"I loved him, too, you understand."

"I shall tell your nephews you send appropriate greetings. They oughtn't be tainted by the mistakes of their parents' generation."

"Whom are they more like? Felix or Ethelinda?"

"I never know how to answer a notion of impossible comparisons."

"I don't imagine you want to meet my son, so you can tell Ethelinda what *he* is like? His name is Adolphus Wolfgang."

Dirk didn't answer, just achieved the door before he turned around. "You might do me one favor. Do you know the whereabouts of an old doctor named Mesmer?"

"If you mean the hypnotist, that tendentious human hypnagogue, he died years ago. Disgraced and made much fun of. Few speak of him any longer."

77.

Dirk wasn't surprised to learn from the second Frau Pfeiffer that Gerwig Pfeiffer had passed away. "But the boy still lives here, and he takes care of me as if I had give birth to him myself," said Cordula, now a thickened old woman. "He'll be along presently. Come in if you like, or stay out in the garden if the house gives you a case of jelly-stomach. But it's too cold for me to sit here with you. I'll send out a mug of hot cider. You're certain you won't come in?"

He wouldn't. The outside air, enough.

No ghost of Nastaran had arisen here in the walled garden to welcome him or to affright. Such a terrible, sad absence. The Pfeiffer house was a tombstone standing on an old road that wanted to get somewhere else, but couldn't—it petered out into fields. Behind it, the twin structure, the barn. Invisible from the street, Dirk realized now, but just as large. Just as real.

Sheets of appearance hung to distract, to conceal.

In this garden, once, walnuts had been strung on strings.

Now the small orchard was falling apart through neglect. Large limbs lay on the ground. It was a battleground. No Florence Nightingale had been through to clear up the corpses. He couldn't think what this might remind him of.

He felt like a tall old ledger, an accounting book open to a page in midlife, but the sum of knowledge registered herein was slim, and the pages behind were scrawled over illegible, and those ahead empty.

Someone arrived with a cup of cider, aromatic and steamy. It wasn't Frau Pfeiffer the Next, but a solid tall woman about Dirk's age, with good skin and grey hair.

"So it *is* you," she said. "I thought the old woman was floating in her mind."

"Frau—?" said Dirk, confused.

She winced. "You don't recognize me. I'm Berthilde."

He took the cup.

"Tilda, the boys called me. Tillie."

He nodded, chagrined.

"The laundress," she prodded. "I was here the first year you arrived, and I stayed four or five years until my marriage. My husband has died."

"Condolences, of course…"

"Don't strain yourself, you. Not worth it. You never knew I was here. You had your eye on the first Frau Pfeiffer, and when she died you went blind. Did you really never know I was waiting all those years for you to look at me?"

He took a sip, unable to confirm her suspicion or to lie.

She shrugged. "Ah well. It's not as if I want to be married again, so don't act so terrified."

"This is a very excellent cider."

She had the good grace to laugh over her shoulder at that as she returned to the house.

Nearly dozing in the chill, he started, and the cup dashed to the ground but didn't break. A man was coming in the gate.

"Only one person I know wears an eye-patch, but he is much younger than you are," said Franz. "He doesn't have grey at his temples."

"He does now."

"It's shaking with cold at this hour."

"I wanted to wait here. I don't want to come in."

"Well, we're not going to bring supper into the garden at this time of year."

"I won't stay. I just wanted to see you and your brother, and find out how you are."

"Doing all right. The trade is brisk. Increasing unity among the German nations is good for business. I've four stout men under my eye now, can you believe that? When once my father and you did the whole thing by yourselves?"

"I did next to nothing, but you were too young to see that."

"A fine-grained crap of the family bull was I. Maybe you started out incompetent, but after Mutter died, you were indispensable. We remember. Gerwig couldn't have kept the business together without your help. He really ought to have given you an interest in the trade." Franz grinned, an old look from boyhood. "But as he didn't do it in his day, I'm not about to break with family tradition. Look, let me put down my wares and relieve myself, and I'll be back with two portions of ale. I won't loiter here for long, I never could tolerate the wind off the lake at this time of year. My balls retract so fast they thump my kidneys. But I'll stand with you over a stein."

Dirk watched Franz hump away. The current Pfeiffer trades-man was already thick in the middle. Where really did boyhood go, or childhood?

He tried to grip the invisible thread that slipped by—

Some sense of the parables, the loaves and the fishes, the con-soling spirit of the dead mother in the ash tree—

But it was like sifting a stream for its shadows. The sieve comes up wet and empty.

Franz was back, carrying two portions of a tawny ale with a sour, gingerbready aroma. He stood against a stone wall and Dirk rested an elbow on the wooden gate. At their knees, the abandoned childhoods of young Franz and young Moritz still thrived. Ghosts with random twigs and bird feathers invisibly acted out the history of the world once again. Franz didn't seem to mind, or perhaps notice.

"Are you here on business?" asked Franz, after quaffing half his share.

"Business done. Such as it was. Of no significance." Dirk wasn't sure if this was true, but in any case it was none of Franz's affair. Franz made no claim on Dirk's affections. He was more like the grown child of a long-dead friend than an actual intimate. Dirk couldn't entirely recall why he had come.

Franz was Nastaran's grown son. That was why. Dirk tried to keep this impossible notion central in his thoughts (it was a blur of incandescence), but it kept winging away and alighting elsewhere. Franz the grown man looked so much more Teutonic than Persian. Nastaran, having left the world, perhaps had taken her half of Franz with her.

"Our stepmother is still here. She'll want to see you," said Franz. "Won't you come in and give her a thrill? A little vague now but she'll recognize your grimace, and accept a rigid embrace for old time's sake."

"I've already greeted her. Her grip still seemed steady to me."

"Well, it comes and goes. Have you married, have you a family?"

"Have you?"

"I've a maiden in mind. She's just coming of age this year. If she'll have me, we'll wed in the spring."

Dirk finished his ale. He set the tankard upon the stone wall and said, "What about Moritz?"

"Ach, Moritz," said Franz. "Well, that's not so happy a tale, is it."

"I wouldn't know."

"He couldn't stay here, you know. It was too much for him. In the end we have put him in an asylum out the road toward Lindau. We visit him two or three times a year. You could go there if you liked."

"Oh, no, I could not," said Dirk. His hand shook as he dropped it in his leather satchel. "Look, Franz, here. Take this to him, though. A present for me, from the past." He brought out the old Nutcracker.

Franz wouldn't touch it. "He doesn't need to go backward, Dirk. He isn't made happy by memory. This thing cannot save him."

"You have it, then. A gift from me."

"You sound distressed," said Franz. "A weaker man than I am would take this just to get rid of you, Dirk, and toss it in the fire as soon as you were gone. But I am better than that. I won't take it either. All these years on, I don't blame you for our mother's death. All these years later. So many years later." He finished his ale. "But I don't credit you with saving her life, either."

78.

He spent the night in Meersburg, in a cold room above a quiet stable. He thought about the lost childhoods of Franz and Moritz and then, inevitably, about his own.

His clawed scraps of memory hardly seemed to signify a real life. Yet the more that the structures of his adult life failed, the stronger seemed the deep past. A life in the deep forest, that old man and old woman.

Some story that they used to tell about a little lost forest, and its cantankerous pair of ambassadors—a lovely goddess in a green kirtle, an untrustworthy hunchbacked gnome of some sort with long sharp teeth. Dirk couldn't remember how the story went.

Though as he slipped into sleep, he came near to dreaming—an unusual experience, dreams for him being a rare abrasion against cold reality. Branches of great trees came raking down over him like the collapse of an entire hillside. A sense of urgency—not for his own safety, but for that of the woods. The rescue of the numinous world. It made no sense at all.

The beer made him belch, and that woke him up. He arranged his thoughts a little more clearly for a moment. Mesmer and some folderol about an ancient forest of Delphi, severed from its sacred home by a tremor of the earth. Migrating for two or three thousand years to the north. Mesmer, thought Dirk, must have become enamored of those tales the Brothers Grimm had collected and published, with all their adventures carried out in the tremulous Bavarian woods. What a charlatan, foisting such a romantic tale upon a lost and sensitive young man such as himself.

Having someone of whom to disapprove made Dirk calmer. He slept in steep shafts of dreamlessness.

79.

Before leaving Meersburg the next day Dirk Drosselmeier went to the doors of the Roman Catholic mother church and looked in. A stout older man in a mis-buttoned waistcoat, whose hair corkscrewed above his ears and jowls, was singing an astoundingly powerfully sweet melody, while seven musicians plunged their bows back and forth across the strings. The tears stood in Dirk's eye in an automatic way, as without invitation tears will start from onions. He had no clear sense of sentiment, but he was wiping his face anyway.

When they had paused to refer to their scores over some accident of atonality, the first violinist saw Dirk. "*Ave Maria,*" he said. "It does that to you, doesn't it? But this rehearsal is closed. What are you doing here?"

"I want to find the episcopal offices. I need to make an enquiry about a Protestant church in the region. I figured Rome keeps tabs on renegades and apostates."

The violinist pointed Dirk on his way, while the portly tenor mopped his brow and swore unbecomingly about pains in his knees and his back.

Was music beautiful because it was full of mystery, Dirk wondered, or was it full of mystery because it was beautiful?

A smug-looking cleric at a stand-up desk checked the registry of vicars. "Why, you are indeed in luck," he said. "We are all less tendentious as we veer toward unification. A Reich eventually, no? Let me look. Well, it seems a certain Pfarrer Johannes is still installed at his position in the village of Achberg. If you are going that way, perhaps you could take him a message for us?"

"Depends on the message," said Dirk. "I don't recall your parties were on speaking terms."

"These days, it's all 'God bless you and keep you, if you're still alive,'" said the cleric, who was young. "Apparently, Pfarrer Johannes is poorly. But our Bishop would probably like to grace him with a greeting. It's only good form. Have a seat and I'll be back. Or would you rather make your devotions in the chapel?"

"No."

The packet was eventually delivered with an ecclesiastical wax seal. I've become an adjunct of the House of Thurn und Taxis, thought Dirk; I'll do nothing more with my life but carry messages back and forth. But just think: after all this time, a reply from the Roman Catholic Bishop. At last.

He spent an hour or so finding out how he might hire space in a carriage heading northeast from Meersburg. A day later, for roads were better now, he had made it to the village last seen in his childhood.

It had changed less than Meersburg or Munich. Indeed, he remembered his first approach to it, that pregnant maiden at the well early in the morning. Today, no one recognized him. He recognized no one, either. He'd never had a good eye for a resemblance.

The old vicarage leaning up against the edge of the chapel was in need of repointing. A kitchen chimney seemed to have scattered bricks and stone into the herb yard. Otherwise the place looked much the same. A young man and woman were leaving the small porch, calling their good-byes. Betrotheds, perhaps, making arrangements for their nuptials. Dirk stood aside, glancing at the ground, as they came through the gate. Certain sorts of happiness made him feel aloof if not skeptical. They were too young to know how love went.

They were too young, and he was too old. Or too—something.

A housekeeper answered the door. "Rather late in the day for the old fellow to be receiving guests, and strangers at that," she said reprovingly, but when she saw the seal of the Roman Catholic Bishop's chancery upon the envelope she relented. "I'll tell the Pfarrer you are come," she said. "What's the name, then?"

"He knows me as Drosselmeier."

He was ushered into the room that, as he recalled, had been a sort of study. A bed was set up near the fireplace, floating like an island away from all the walls. Pfarrer Johannes was propped up upon pillows of swan's down. Yellow his cheek, and pale his once ruddy lips, but his eyes were wide above the pince-nez.

"It never is, it never could be you, and yet it is, and could be after all," said Pfarrer Johannes Albrecht. "Come lean down and give me a kiss, dear boy. What took you so long?"

"I got lost."

"I should say so. Let me look at you. Stand back. No, that's too far back. My eyes are tyrants—they like the middle spot in the carpet. Yes, perfect. Oh, my. Dirk! Am I dying even faster than I thought, that you should answer one of my last prayers?"

"I am no answer to a wish." He pulled up a stool to the side of the bed. "What is wrong with you?"

"I am eight thousand years old, give or take, and the Lord is tired of waiting for me. Saint Peter has parked his celestial *char à bancs* in the courtyard. Can't you hear the horses snorting and pounding their hoofs in impatience?"

So Pfarrer Johannes had, in old age, gone fantastical.

Or perhaps he could hear the horses nickering there, after all.

"I haven't got long," said the old man. "I don't mean I am departing for heaven tonight—at least, I don't feel that I am. But my strength doesn't last, and you will find me nodding off just as you are about to tell me how you kidnapped Napoleon and conquered Malta and made love to some pretty young wife of a hoighty family. Very von und zu. So speak quickly. What have you made of your life?"

How to answer such a question.

"A long road toward a retreating horizon," he ventured. "Like everyone else's."

"No horizon but heaven."

"That must be true for you, good father. But the rest of us aren't so sure of our itineraries."

"Then you become your own destination, Dirk. That is what happens. As long as you are a person of conscience—of merit—one who makes the attempt—you head ever toward the geography of yourself. But I want the real map! Your own map in time, in days and years. Why did you never return? I was worried fair to desperation."

Brandishing the sealed greeting: "Here is a reply, after a fashion. The delivery of post is very slow in these parts." They both laughed, and Dirk continued. "I was taken in as a houseboy of sorts. For a while. One thing led to another."

"Industry? Marriage? Family? Education?"

"Well . . . none of that. Travel, though. I did travel widely. And now I live in Munich, and make toys."

"Toys!" Pfarrer Johannes wrinkled his lip. "I'd have thought you'd obey the injunction of Saint Paul and put away the things of a child."

"One does that when one has stopped being a child, as I recall the verse. So perhaps I've never stopped."

"Or you never started," mused the old man. "You were sober as a little magistrate when you arrived. No wreathing smiles. No easy games and jokes like other boys."

"Forgive me for disappearing. I never had a good sense of direction of any sort."

"I was worried. You worried me. You should be whipped for causing an old man worry." He relented. "Though I wasn't as old then, was I? I did look for you. Did you know that?"

"Of course not. How could I?"

"I hired a fellow from the precinct to go out the road toward Meersburg and see if anyone had word of a lost boy. Someone had seen you, but no one knew which path you might have taken."

Dirk shrugged. "It was a long time ago."

"You were my responsibility. The good Lord had deemed it so. I had failed you by sending you out into the snares of the world. How happy I am that you were not eaten by more bears!" He began to cry, and then suddenly slept for a moment or two. With closed eyelids, the brightness in the old fellow's face faded. He looked like a toy Dirk might make out of starch-stiffened old linen.

Shaking himself awake after a bit, the old man seemed surprised to see Dirk still there. "The boy. You. I also sent someone to go to look for your folk. The woodcutter. Have I told you that yet?"

"The woodcutter."

"Right. Those people you used to call the old man and the old woman. In the forest. I thought you might've gone back there."

"The old man and the old woman. But not my parents. I was a foundling."

"They weren't old as all that, according to report. If they were the right people. The man was still alive. He walked with a limp and a stout cane of sorts. His sister was dead."

"His sister?"

"One of the sins of Leviticus, I fear. Perhaps. 'Neither should any man approach a close relative to uncover nakedness; I am the LORD.' I rarely preached on that verse. I thought it was self-evident. Anyway, the sister died of consumption apparently. The woodcutter showed my agent a grave with a stone in which the woodcutter had crudely carved her name."

"I didn't know them by name."

"If I knew his name, I've forgotten it. It's amazing what leaks out of my memory and what stays put. I can't figure out the method in it. But I remember her name. Gretel, she was. His sister."

"Perhaps they weren't the same people," said Dirk, standing.

The old man was awake enough, alive enough still to hear the tonal change in Dirk's voice. The cleric stopped speaking for a moment. His eyes closed. Maybe he was praying. Dampness on his cheek. "Perhaps not. One woodcutter is much like the next. Anyway it doesn't matter now. You've come home."

"I'm not home. I've never really been home. And I'm leaving, Pfarrer Johannes." He had to get out of the place. He leaned down and embraced the old man as gently as he could. "Don't save me a place in heaven, Pfarrer. There isn't enough room there for someone like me."

"I reserve the right to petition for anyone I want. I can be persuasive. Just ask my flock. But Dirk? My blessing." He raised a hand about an inch off his chest and muttered under his breath, concluding, "My blessing, and also my advice. Spend what you have, give it away, Dirk. All, all away. The only chance to replenish yourself is to use up what you are given. It's called redemption in some circles."

Dirk took this to heart, though he thought better of offering the old cleric the battered Nutcracker as a memento. Pfarrer Johannes had fallen asleep again, and the housekeeper was at the doorway, tutting and beckoning. "You won't stay for a bite," she whispered declaratively.

"No."

"Ach. I thought not."

And then he was on his way back to Munich, a smaller person once again, though perhaps a slightly truer one.

Part Three

The Story of the Nutcracker
and the Mouse King

80.

Ethelinda survived her husband by nearly two decades. In those years, Drosselmeier became her closest companion and support. He spent every summer with her and the boys at Meritor on the Baltic. The boys were devoted to him until they grew too old to find his games diverting.

Sometimes he wondered if he'd ever given them the kind of organized attention they deserved. After they were grown, he conceded that he'd often muddled up Günther and Sebastian Stahlbaum, those doughty bürgerlichs, with Franz and Moritz Pfeiffer, the mixed-blood sons of a small-town merchant. None of the boys were alike at all, if he admitted the testing of his memories. On the sidelines of the tiresome business of his life, they'd seemed little more than interchangeable pairs of boys.

That fairy godmother of Cinderella must have learned her trade at a better establishment than Drosselmeier did. He'd been blind to the boys in more than one eye. In short, he'd failed them all, godfather or no.

To make up the loss of income from summer months and to oc-cupy himself during long afternoons, he took up clock repair. He developed a touch and, when back in Munich, began to build clock-work into a line of increasingly complicated toys—though simple anonymous dolls and armies of perfectly matched soldiers made up the better part of his income.

In all those years with the widow, never any question of marriage. During his more rueful moments he imagined that Ethelinda kept him around in order to boast of ownership of her Felix even after his death. But Drosselmeier learned to avoid that path to desolation. Ethe-linda did have superior claim, after all. And, though perhaps clueless, Drosselmeier wasn't absent from the boys even when they'd grown from lumpy kids playing games of mermaid and Poseidon and sea snake at the tidal pools—fashioned from driftwood just so!—into sleek male princes, attracting the gazes of fräuleins. He stood up for young Sebastian when he married a sober *mademoiselle* from Lyon. Her name was Clothilde. She had a high forehead and a tendency to be confident. She tolerated Drosselmeier with a philosophical neutrality.

In time, Ethelinda followed her husband to the grave. Neither her brother, Kurt, nor anyone from that side of the family both-ered to attend the services. The son, Sebastian, found their absence something of a mercy. The other Stahlbaum boy, Günther, couldn't contribute to the obsequies either, as he had moved to someplace across the ocean known as Ohio.

Sebastian brought his bride to Meritor. The spare, windblown terrain reminded her of summers spent on the Frisian coast. Clothilde had not enjoyed those summers, and Meritor was not a great success with her. When she became pregnant with her first child, she claimed the prerogative to cancel the annual trip. She wanted to christen the first child Alphonse, but Sebastian demanded a more Teutonic name, so he became Fritz. Four years later, when a daughter was born, Clothilde thought she had prevailed by insisting on Marie-Claire. Yes, Marie-Claire at the baptismal font—Drosselmeier weaseled into the role of actual godfather in both instances by dint not of faith but of his provenance with Pfarrer Johannes Albrecht—as the water rippled over the child's pale pink brow. As she grew, German custom won through, and the child became popularly known as Klara.

81.

Drosselmeier found, as he aged and stiffened, that he was becoming more interested in Hellenic matters. To the extent that he remembered the bizarre imaginings of his youth, they became entwined with what he was reading about the pan-Athenian festival. Evidence of which had been carved into eternity in the stones of the Parthenon, long ago removed to London and now displayed free of charge in the British Museum. The fuss those marbles had engendered had only grown these fifty years since. Wealthier Germans were traveling to Athens to see for themselves.

Drosselmeier read Homer in translation. He remembered something that Felix had said once about Athena being the model for the fairy godmother who had become, by now, not only a stock figure in tales popularized by Grimm, but also a personage abducted and pressed into service, in one form or another, by the Danish fabulist Hans Christian Andersen. The Athena/godmother seemed to be everywhere in stories. Wasn't that godlike of her? Always in disguise, like Christ in the urine-stained beggar beyond the newsstand. Like Elijah at the supper table, usually figured as a stranger with a hood over his brooding eyes.

In certain hours of the dawn Drosselmeier might remember clearly the woman in a green kirtle, her auburn hair bound only lightly with a band of hammered copper leaves. Try as he might, he couldn't conflate her with any Renaissance Madonna he'd ever seen, nor with the wasp-eyed or vinegary portraits of intelligent northern women by Memling and Dürer and the like. The sylph was more quicksilver, harder to interpret. Whether she might be virginal or a harlot, Drosselmeier had no idea. As the morning gloom dissipated through his drapes, which fell in volutes like those carved into columns of the neoclassical architecture of Munich, the revenant occasionally fixed him with a plaintive glare. Or accusatory. He was glad when she began to dissolve. A morning coffee rudely finished her off.

The other one, which he had finally come around to calling Pan, that stumpy little grinning demon—he thought of Pan more often. Pan seemed to gleam through the eyes of the old Nutcracker, which by now Drosselmeier wouldn't sell even if he were asked. Though that had never happened. The Nutcracker stood by himself on a shelf behind the counter, in pride of place. Sometimes he seemed to leer, or mock; other times his look suggestive of wisdom, even charity.

How many times Drosselmeier had tried to give away the Nutcracker, and none would have it. It might as well be Drosselmeier's doppelgänger, a toy weight around his neck. He felt he would have to get rid of it before he died. He wasn't sure why. In an Andersen tale, the old toy would be thrown on the fire, and the smoke from its immolation would wreathe the brow of the green goddess. Whoever she was. But though Drosselmeier believed in stories—in their power, that is—he couldn't place himself at the center of any of them. He had no standing.

Finally deciding the time had come to go to Athens, and perhaps even dare an overland trip to Delphi, for—for reasons he couldn't name—Drosselmeier made his way to an establishment in the arcade where tickets could be booked. Trains from Munich to Vienna to Trieste. Passage on a steamer from Trieste down the Illyrian coast, or Dalmatia, and around the Peloponnese into the fabled Aegean. Alighting at Piraeus. Waiting for the clerk to copy the details in a ledger, Drosselmeier dreamed of resinous light and recited lines to himself. By now he could read enough in English to appreciate something of Keats. "Of thee I hear and of the Cyclades . . ." and "Aye on the shores of darkness there is light, / And precipices show untrodden green."

Then, feeling a levity of being he hadn't imagined possible, he lifted off the top step of the firm's threshold and misplaced his foot coming down. He told the doctor a bird had flown in his face. Was it a bird, or the shadow of a hesitation? Its wings had made a protesting wind. He fell and broke a bone or two, and had to cancel his ticket. He took to relying on the imp-headed cane for balance. Travel to Greece was impossible. Indeed, getting back to Meritor this summer—for Clothilde had finally been bullied into returning—was itself going to propose a problem. In the end, he had to do without both the sunny Aegean and the cloudy Baltic.

Through this period of waiting—waiting for what, he didn't know—the question of green returned to him. Perhaps he was going mad in the way the elderly sometimes did. The Bavarian custom of garlanding the household with balsam, of sawing down a pine tree and erecting it in a parlor with candles and ornaments of all sorts—it thrilled him every Christmastide with increasing fervor. Once, when grief for his misspent youth had been washed down with too much Riesling at the table of the current generation of Stahlbaums, he remembered the Little Lost Forest. Sebastian hadn't allowed Drosselmeier to walk home in this condition, and had sent for the carriage. Drosselmeier's head was operating on a set of fulcrums at odds with his spine and hips. He tried to settle his mind and his stomach by watching the street lamps. They seemed lost in arms of greenery. What did the sacred grove want? What did it need? What was he to do about it?

By the time he was home and had surrendered his dinner to the water closet, the burning question once again retired. He could think only this: how frightful that visions so rarely come intact and coherent. Their nature is to be obscure. Fragmented, mad-deningly contradictory. It provides the work of a lifetime, at least for those poor souls afflicted with such sight, to puzzle out their meaning. No wonder the Saint Ambroses and Saint Jeromes of the world went off to their caves and steles.

What the sacred grove was missing was a population. Not of gods, but of the ambassadors of gods. Those who, through need, call the deities into being. The Odysseuses returning home to Ithaka, the Cinderellas in the ashes. The Persian poet naming the Divine as his lover. If Drosselmeier knew this, he knew it only in his deepest sleep, that sleep closest to death itself. He remembered nothing of this in the mornings, even on lightless mornings when the goddess implored him wordlessly.

He spent his life making toys. There is that. But what of it?

82.

But it is true that once or twice, when he saw the sloe-eyed damsel in the corners of his waking mind, he began to wonder why she so often recurred to him. He had had interest in women once upon a time, or thought he had, but then that had seemed to evaporate. Nothing much had replaced it. Felix had been, oh, an ideal of a friend, perhaps. The longer he insisted on remaining dead, the more a mystery Felix became.

Sebastian and Clothilde and their children stood in as Drosselmeier's family. They weren't replacing anyone—there was no one to replace. Nastaran Pfeiffer as once was—Drosselmeier found thoughts of her more fleeting, and less welcome, than those of the evanescent dryad. The Pythia as he'd sometimes called her.

Of all the figures he carved for a new generation of Stahlbaum children, Fritz and Klara, he avoided Persians. Young Fritz paid little attention these days to anything but the military, which now could be bought in sets of ten or a dozen. Identical blunt-faced orderlies born industrially, in pressed metal molds. Drosselmeier's more delicate and individualized figures were reserved as gifts for Klara. A Russian princess in a painted wooden cloak. A Cleopatra in Egyptian blue. A charming family of pigs in graduated heights that stood on hind legs and wore nothing but pince-nezs, all of them, except the very smallest, who with a potbelly and a sour expression stood looking down and sucking her cloven hoof.

Klara: "How do toys think?"

Drosselmeier waited for her to answer her own question. She usually did if he kept silent. She concluded:

"They listen to us and learn to make guesses."

Then, using his clockwork prowess, he came up with a new Mother Ginger. This variant possessed a real cloth skirt hemmed with a tight lead hoop that, when a button shaped like a bow was pressed in the small of her back, sprang open, not an indecent amount, to reveal a few human children huddled therein. They were thick, dwarflike. Drosselmeier found it interesting that though the overall effect was among his best, it was compromised because he was so poor at doing children. Barbarians, animals, imaginary creatures—all came to life under his set of knives more easily than that most exotic of beings, the local child.

83.

Klara, though, adored Mother Ginger and didn't seem to mind that her children looked like trolls. "She is my favorite," said Klara, climbing up on Drosselmeier's lap the better to handle the bow and open the skirt. She moved the lumpy children in and out, and pulled off the petals of a rose in a nearby vase so the children could have sheets to cover them. Under their crimson snugs they resembled chunks of beetroot. "Does Mother Ginger look much like your mother?"

"I have no mother," said Drosselmeier.

"Everyone has a mother or they can't be alive. It's not allowed."

"I never claimed to obey the rules. Do you think Mother Ginger looks too old to have these children?"

"She looks old enough to have some more. I wish our Mutter would have a child. I want a baby to rock to sleep and to boss around."

"You'll have your own baby soon enough." For Drosselmeier, time seemed to be moving more swiftly now. "Don't hurry it."

"Would it be too rude if the pig family could live in Mother Ginger's skirt, too?"

"The children might pull the tails of the pigs. The pigs would squeal, and Mother Ginger, what would she do then?"

"She would open her skirt and send them all out to play and scream until they could learn to mind their manners. She would be used to that."

"What would Mother Ginger do while her children and pigs were out playing?"

"Take off her skirt and lie down. It looks very heavy and tiresome."

"Ach, stop that, Klara. The dress doesn't come off. It's fastened at the waist, see? You'll tear it."

"But I mustn't ever lie down in *my* good outfit."

"Mother Ginger is a strong woman. She doesn't need to lie down. She just goes for long healthful walks."

"Perhaps she picks up stray dogs and cats under her skirts. Or like that seal we saw once at Meritor, remember?"

"A seal might make an unpleasant mess of Mother Ginger's costume. Not to mention the smell."

But smells meant nothing to children, and Klara seemed delighted by the idea, so the next time Drosselmeier came for dinner he brought a set of infantry with bayonets for Fritz, crudely painted, and a seal with a dropsical moustache to join Mother Ginger's family. Drosselmeier found Klara to be formal and grateful, but he suspected she really didn't care for the seal after all, for it got lost in short order and was never seen again.

84.

When Fritz and Klara played together, Fritz took the lead and Klara was quiet. If her brother happened to be out of the room, however, Klara spoke to her Godfather Drosselmeier as if in a language only the two of them understood.

Once when she was lying on the carpet with a wooden cat in one hand and a wooden dog in the other, she got tired making them chase each other or dance with each other or stand one upon the other. She rolled onto her back and held them both up and looked at them through a squint-eye.

"They are getting tired," she said, yawning.

"What should they do?"

"They sleep in an eggshell," she countered, "when the egg has gone out to take the air."

He waited.

"When a dog falls asleep, he dreams he is a cat," she said.

A coal shifted in the grate.

"When a cat falls asleep," she said, "she dreams she is a fox. *And she is.*"

A statement like that, for reasons Drosselmeier couldn't name, made his hair stand on end and the inside of his eye-patch damp. It wasn't because of a sense of identification with the child, he thought. Not any unseemly intimacy, but the opposite. She lay there only a yard or two away, but so incredibly distant, so fully, ethereally other that it nearly took his breath away. In her six-years-and-some she was already more herself than he had ever managed to become himself in the same number of decades.

Once when Drosselmeier was taking his godchildren for a walk, Klara felt suddenly tired and turned pale, so Drosselmeier decided to turn around for home. Fritz was cross and threw stones at a squirrel, which looked venomously back at the lad, as if contemplating the purchase of a delicate though powerful jäger rifle to return fire.

At home, Fritz disappeared into the nursery and began to toss toys about, breaking them. Klara drew her godfather into the small yellow parlor and sat him on the settee. She then proceeded to tell him he had come to the café and she would serve him. It was the best café in Prussia.

"What is it called?" he asked.

"You should know, you came in the door," she replied.

"But I forget. I am old and my memory is poor."

She puzzled over this. "I think it is called the Boys and Adders Café."

"Not Kaffeehaus?"

"I am part French. I am the owner and the chef. I also take the money and give you the spoons and stuff. What would you like to eat?"

"What do you recommend?"

"Some food, perhaps."

"That's a good start. I enjoy food. Do you have anything special you like to make?"

She climbed under the desk as if it were a kitchen belowstairs, and then emerged with a scrap of paper she must have pulled from a drawer. She looked at it. "This is the menu."

"May I see?"

"You can't read it. It is written in a strange language. I shall tell you about it. We have a chicken and olive soup. Also some pears on toast. And, what else. Some biscuits with honey icing."

"I'll have the soup."

"There's none left. I had the last bowl. It was very good indeed."

"Bring me what you like."

She disappeared to the kitchen and returned with an invisible plate. "Here is your food."

"What is it?"

"I don't know, but I wouldn't eat it if I were you. It looks nasty."

He took an imaginary bite. "I think it is a squirrel soufflé."

She wrinkled her nose. "It would be, wouldn't it? I wondered where that squirrel went. It was supposed to be peeling the potatoes."

It took Drosselmeier a while to wonder whether, in fact, there was something strange about Klara Stahlbaum. Different, that is, from the other children he had known in his life. He hadn't known many. Engorged with greed, children who came into the showroom didn't count. In any case, German burghers and their wives were more inclined to steal into the shop to make selections without their children in tow.

Of the children he'd befriended, after a fashion, little very accurate could be said. Children were a set of broken puzzles. Sloppy puddings. Throwaway woodcut proofs, blurred outside their margins. And how many children did these examples add up to, in his life? Not many. Not many at all. Franz and Moritz Pfeiffer, back in those horrible days of Nastaran's breakdown and death. Sebastian and Günther Stahlbaum, when they were glowing golden shadows of golden Felix. These days, yet another generation of Stahlbaums: Fritz and Marie-Claire—Klara as everyone called her.

Klara, alone of them, was a girl.

Maybe that was part of it, Drosselmeier thought. But also, Klara had something of Felix's glittery openness. A recklessness of heart, you might say. And from her mother, a Gallic hesitancy and tact.

When he turned up at the Stahlbaum home—the fine Munich place that Felix and Ethelinda had left to their older son—something ached in his chest. It was like a muscle tear that couldn't quite heal because he kept twisting it, wrenching it beyond the range of play. Klara was a cipher, something as much flame as charcoal. The boys he'd known before, he'd liked them and played with them, and even been surprised that he could amuse them so. But they'd stayed in the portable cages of their own characters, just the way he stayed in his, and always had. Klara seemed, on the contrary, frequently to be emerging. Not from silence into sociability—something other than that. From herself into herself—as if she had been born bearing multiple veils of Klara, and they were all legitimate. Echt.

He raised the matter only once, with Sebastian, and was sorry that he had.

"Is she entirely all right?" he had asked.

"Klara?" Sebastian stabbed the bowl of his pipe with hard jerking motions. Flecks of tobacco peppered the table. "Whatever are you talking about, Drosselmeier? Why shouldn't she be?"

"I only mean…there's a quality."

"She's young, she's gullible. She believes in fairy tales. Also in the saints of the Church. Give her time, she'll firm up. Christ, man, you're hard on her."

"I've offended and I have no idea how. I don't mean that she's young. I'm old enough to be able to recognize the young for what they are. I mean that she is . . . fickle. Capable. Capricious. Attached."

Sebastian Stahlbaum drew on his pipe for several long drafts, which gave Drosselmeier time to formulate a peace offering. "I am trying to find a way to say how charming she is. She hardly seems of this world."

At this Sebastian threw the pipe into the hearth, where it cracked, and the man burst into sobs. Raw eyes, angry mouth, distended nostrils like a frightened horse. Drosselmeier scrabbled to his feet and went to stand by the door, his hand at his mouth. He had no strategy for such insanity. He couldn't stop it. Sebastian might have gone on like this for hours but young Fritz came wandering by looking for something to smash. That cleared up his father's face as quickly as a wet cloth will blank a chalked slate. Sebastian was protecting his son from the sight of distress, Drosselmeier saw. So the godfather found some coins in his pocket and flung them at the older Stahlbaum child, and that diverted him from the room.

"What has taken *hold* of you?" Drosselmeier demanded of Sebastian.

The man blew his nose upon his sleeve. "Too much to go into. You cut into a nerve, Drosselmeier. My apologies. Unseemly. The doctors don't know if she will make it to adulthood. She has an excitable heart."

"You're deranged. She's perfectly normal."

"I mean the heart muscle. It may be like what my father— Felix—died of. And his grandmother before him. All too suddenly. We don't know. I don't want to talk about it. I don't know how you wrestled it out of me." He glared at the older man, bested.

Drosselmeier was aghast at every part of this. "They're wrong, whoever they are, those doctors. They always are. I knew a doctor who spoke balderdash to me and distracted me from my life. Don't let them do that to you. She has more life in her two tulip-petal palms than you and I have in our whole frames. She won't leave life in childhood. She won't."

"Don't bring this up with Clothilde," warned Sebastian. "She worries so about the girl."

"She won't leave this life in childhood," said Drosselmeier. "She can't. I won't let her."

"We'll give her a good Christmas, and see if she strengthens in the spring."

"All this is *nonsense!*" shouted Drosselmeier. "I won't have it."

85.

But Drosselmeier did raise the matter with Clothilde. The next morning he closed up his shop and went by the house when he knew Sebastian would be out at the exchange. The wife was less frail than her husband had led Drosselmeier to believe, or she was better at prevarication. She poured the older man a coffee—in these days, coffee was just starting to be made at home—and they sat in the smaller parlor that looked over the snowy garden.

"Perhaps an infection, it's hard to say," said Clothilde. "The good doctors know so little about us, after all, don't you agree?"

"But what are the symptoms, Frau Stahlbaum?"

"After all this time, you may address me as Clothilde."

He lifted the cup to his mouth, burning his lips in preference to revising his question.

She relented. She was a steady sort of person, rather hale, with a frame more of oak than aspen. For a strong stork like Clothilde to have given birth to such a frail daughter seemed a wicked taunt. "A fever mounts and subsides, dear Godfather Drosselmeier. They think it's related to her heart, which sometimes races. There is not much we can do but apply the cold compress and change her nightgown when it becomes too damp. I'm sorry Sebastian worried you about it."

Perhaps, thought Drosselmeier, she doesn't perceive the level of threat that Sebastian had indicated. A mother can be so blind. Blindness a skill for survival. He said, "Would you consider taking her for a cure to the thermal springs in Salzuflen, the mineral caves of Berchtesgaden? Something of that order?"

"We wouldn't rule it out. Though at the moment she isn't up for travel. And of course we would have to wait for the warmer weather. Perhaps she will improve by then."

That child was so full of curious observations. "What does Klara *say* about how she feels?"

This was the only moment when Clothilde seemed distressed. "We are often alerted to the spike in her fever when she begins to spout nonsense. For instance, she sometimes complains that the walls are running with mice. She says that she can hear them talking after we have all gone to sleep."

"Oh indeed." He tried not to look either alarmed or relieved. "Does she report their gossip?"

"She says it is very rude indeed and we should be shocked and think she was making it up, and she'd be punished for repeating what she heard."

"That doesn't sound ill to me. It sounds rather adult."

"You profess concern and then you mock me."

"Please." He put his hand on hers, truly. "What I mean is that she sounds quite like herself, so how could you tell it is a fever? She is a fanciful child."

"I was never so *fanciful*." She made it sound like a barnyard insult.

He began to think that Clothilde was not a very motherly mother, but then he caught himself. On what basis of comparison could he propose such a scandalous notion?

Yet he looked at Clothilde in her brocaded shoulders, garnets looping around her bust-of-Europa marble neck. Her eye was stern and her wrist trembled slightly as she stirred her coffee. She was a Frenchwoman being maternal in a German setting. How pomp-ous to presume that an old peasant man such as himself, however well traveled, could winkle out the degree of Clothilde's affection or wisdom about her own daughter.

Neither, though, would he abandon Klara. Just in case.

86.

Drosselmeier's material needs were few, as he lived quite simply in a pair of rooms over his shop. Still, he wasn't sorry for the annual coin he earned in the weeks leading up to the holiday. He needed that income. And so the feast-day of the nativity of the Christ Child approached with its usual panic, uproar, and greed.

Sitting at his bench and carving his figurines by what light there was, he watched carts pass. They were trundling in from the countryside with fir trees bound in ropes, intended for sale in the squares and alleys of Munich. In the evenings, if he wasn't visiting the Stahlbaum household or, once in a while, taking in a string quartet or an organ recital in a chilly church, he lowered the oil lamp on its cord so that it hovered nearer the workbench. He labored with his brushes and lacquers until the midnight bells rang in the church towers. Sometimes later even than that.

Where are those elves who are said to come help old palsied shoemakers? Why don't they bother with toy makers? I should make my own assistants out of clockwork, he thought. But he didn't have enough years left for that. Klara might have her concerns with her heart, if her parents were to be trusted, but Drosselmeier had his own thoughts about mortality.

He tried to think what he could give Klara for a present this year. He felt it needed to be something correct—something instrumental. His whittling knives teased figures out of contorted segments of birch or balsam. They came out of the wood as menaces, though. Always leering eyes, a faint, lewd sneer.

The world isn't that horrible. *It's a sin to tell a lie.*

But Klara may be in trouble. *It's another sin to conceal the truth.*

A pair of apothegms, where had they come from, maybe Pfarrer Johannes Albrecht, may he rest in peace. Wherever that might be.

But wherever *might* that be? For Albrecht, for Drosselmeier himself?

A place where one might feel at home. The old minister.

Drosselmeier himself. Klara. But it wasn't just the population, it was the map that was needed, the coordinates. Dante had done it. John Bunyan, and Sir John Mandeville. Milton, in his time. Prester John and Marco Polo. Even Homer, charting the world by sea. The vagabond human spirit requires a chart of possibilities in order to keep putting one foot in front of another, keep licensing the next heartbeat after the previous.

It was so late that the mice stole out, looking for the crumbs he sometimes left for them on the floorboards. One bold fellow came right up to the edge of Drosselmeier's workbench and sat with his tail in his front paws, a look of subservience in the gesture. "Well, in lieu of the elves I requested, are you going to help?" asked Drosselmeier. The creature waited a moment before running up the edge of the broom handle, whose top leaned against the wall behind Drosselmeier. Amused, thinking it was probably time to turn in, the old man revolved in his chair to watch the ambassador. The mouse dashed halfway along the shelf and then peered over the edge, as if he really intended to deliver a Periclean peroration to all the toys in the shop. He didn't speak, of course—or if he did, Drosselmeier could neither hear nor understand.

He thought, then, of a mother mouse cowering at the base of a tree, and small blind mouse babies rippling around her fundament. A vaguely distressing picture in his mind.

"If you're a descendant of that family, send them my best wishes," he muttered, dunking his brushes in linseed oil to keep them supple till the morning. In the viscous gritty amber, ribbons of bloody red unfurled from the hairs of the brush.

The mouse then scurried back and cowered for a moment behind the shabby old Nutcracker. Back to its own palace of possibilities somewhere in the walls.

Well, maybe, thought Drosselmeier.

87.

He visited the night before Christmas Eve. Klara lay on the settee in the yellow parlor, weighed down under a scratchy coverlet of blue and silver Rhenish tapestry-work. Drosselmeier had the sense she was growing a bristled skin, generating a cocoon. "Let me pull that back, it's smothering you."

"I'm cold. Let it be. It's my kingdom."

"Your what?"

"See?" Her fingers dallied along the stitchery. "I'm the world, and these are my mountains, and over here is my waterfall, and a temple."

A huge ungainly doll in a beige pinafore was kicked upside down into the corner of the settee. From underneath the lace of her petticoat, which nearly covered her whole face, she peered glassily at the cornice of the door. Drosselmeier: "Is she some sort of deposed goddess or wretched fairy godmother?"

"You're a godfather, you should know." Her voice was smaller than usual. "I hate her. She's no good. All broken and useless."

Fritz came through with an armful of Drosselmeier's figures and set them out on the edge of the sofa. He wasn't always a thoughtful brother, so Drosselmeier sat up to observe. "I think we should have a war," said Fritz. "I'm going to bring in the cavalry and line them up on the carpet. Don't step on them."

Klara fingered the Ottoman princess, a recent favorite, but then stuck her headfirst into the seam between the back of the sofa and its seat. The child was too old to suck her thumb, but Drosselmeier had the feeling she was about to start. He took her hands in his and leaned forward on his footstool.

"Your brother is being nice to you. Isn't it strange?"

"It's Christmastime. He knows that if he is good, the Christkindl will bring gifts."

Such a little realist.

"Why is your doll so very ugly?" he asked her.

At the notion of ugliness, she rallied a little. "I think a mouse bit her and made her that way."

Again with the mice. *Was* the house overridden? He would have to ask Sebastian or Clothilde. Why was it bothering her so?

She got to the question ahead of him. "I saw a seven-headed mouse in my bedroom last night. It came to my pillow and spoke to me."

"My, that's distinguished. It must have been the Mouse King. What did it say?"

"I don't know. I don't speak Mouse."

"Ach! You remind me of a mouse I used to know. She was out on a constitutional with her six young ones and a cat came along with a hiss and that look in the eye that says *Yum, seven fresh mice for tea.* The mother mouse was afraid but stood up in front of her babies and said in a firm voice, *'Bow wow.'* The cat ran away in fright, and the mother mouse turned and said to her children, 'Now, my dears, let this be a lesson to you all in the value of learning a second language.'"

"But I don't have time to learn Mouse. What if the Mouse King comes back tonight? He was very cruel."

"You must ask him what he wants."

She was almost in tears. "I *told* you! I can't talk to mice!"

He felt her forehead. Warm. "Are you sure you need this blanket so snugly pulled up, my dear, you're quite hot."

"I'm chilled. I want to know why the mice are here."

"Are they here in this room? Now?"

"You know if they are."

He kept his eyes trained on her, didn't turn left or right so as to avoid confirming or denying her apprehensions. "Shall I get you a glass of milk?"

"Did you ever meet a mouse? What do they want?"

He began to arrange a few of the figurines into a procession. "I knew a Nutcracker once who was the sworn enemy of the king of the mice."

"Why?"

"The Nutcracker wanted to chop down a tree to get a golden walnut, but the king wouldn't let him."

"Why not?"

"Because the mice wanted the walnut for themselves. They were waiting for it to be ripe, so they could crack the shell open and eat the nut inside. They didn't want to share. They're quite greedy."

"Why did the Nutcracker want the golden walnut?"

"I think it held a secret, but I don't know which one. Do you?"

She closed her eyes to think about this and he began to hope she had fallen asleep. He tiptoed to the door, shushing Fritz, who was just back with another armload of tin grenadiers and Hussars. "Fritz, where is your father?"

"Mutter and Vater are in the yellow parlor with the tannenbaum. We aren't allowed to go in until late tomorrow night. It's Christmas Eve tomorrow, you know."

"Oh, is it? And the Christ Child may bring you some gifts?"

"It's possible."

Drosselmeier found coyness in a young boy repellent. He excused himself and knocked on the door of the yellow parlor.

Sebastian and Clothilde and the downstairs maid were dressing a voluptuous balsam tree with laces, baubles, and candles. A few wrapped presents were laid below. Marzipan and gingerbread figures hung on silvered string, keeping company with small toys like drums, bells, other musical instruments. Drosselmeier cradled a small 'cello in his palm, then let it free. The tree wanted at least one golden walnut on a string. Well, tomorrow, soon enough.

"You'll join us for the grand unveiling tomorrow evening?" pressed Clothilde.

"Are you having a serious problem with mice in the house?"

"No more this winter than any other," said Sebastian.

"What an insult to a tree, don't you think?" asked Drosselmeier. "I mean, to be severed at the ankle and dragged in and mocked like this."

"This tree grew for a decade so it could be honored in death and give joy to the children. At least that's how I like to think of it," replied Clothilde. "We would not think of inviting forests into the house in Lyon when I was young, but I have come to admire the barbaric German custom."

"It is so beautiful it makes me ill," said Drosselmeier.

"Are you becoming sentimental, old godfather?" asked Sebastian. "We have enough of that between the two of us, under the circumstances. We rely on you to lend a certain crankiness to the proceedings. It's not too early for a glass of Tokay, if you're thirsty."

"I have some work to finish up in the shop," said Drosselmeier, and left the house. Only on the street, steeped in the cold clarity of snow-odor, could he identify the aromas he had left behind: the sap of a fir tree, its pungent slow blood; the lavender of soaps and camphor of blankets; the gingerbread; the dusty wood-mold smell that comes up from the floorboards in the winter; the reek of a cabbage being boiled senseless, with caraway and perhaps a touch of fennel seed.

He worked with wood and glue, a brush and a pot of gilt, on through most of the night, paying no attention to the mice. He'd long ago used up the blue of the sky—he'd called it Nastaran blue—from the pot he had once opened for her with a knife. But the very same wide-mouthed jug had made a good home for his brushes all these years.

88.

Christmas Eve. Drosselmeier closed down the workroom and drew fast the shutters. He fixed his cloak with fingers stiffened by labor, and he picked up his parcels. Most were smaller gifts, but one was large, so he hired a carriage to make his way through streets masked with snow grit.

He descended the carriage and paid the fare. When the wind dropped suddenly, he felt encased in invisible ice. He turned to the swept stairs of the Stahlbaum manse. Lamplight from between the swagged drapes at the front windows, like the limelights of theatre, turned the snow on windowsills to gold.

Entering, he shucked off his coat and sidled with the packages into the servants' passage. He made his way to the yellow parlor, where Sebastian was lighting the candles on the tree with tapers.

"Clothilde is upstairs with them, keeping them calm until the clock strikes. Drosselmeier, you've outdone yourself. You'll make them sick with glut."

"I'm the godfather. I'm allowed. How is the little invalid?"

Sebastian didn't answer.

Drosselmeier put his packages about. Holly decked the mantel. A fire hissed and ticked. "Is Fritz behaving, at least?"

"He's worn out with trying to be decent. It's too wearing on a boy. I shall be glad when the holidays are over."

"Only children love the arresting weirdness of these days."

Again, Sebastian kept his silence.

Drosselmeier pushed. He wanted to tire Sebastian into giving a different sort of answer. "Has she had more dreams about the mice?"

"Dear Godfather. I'm doing what I can to keep her comfortable. I don't have the wherewithal to investigate the nonsense of her dreams."

"Oh, well, then." But now Drosselmeier was chastened. The poor father was sorely tried.

"Are we ready?" Having lit the last of the tapers, Sebastian trimmed the wicks of the oil lamps on the credenza. "Shall I call them in?" The sounds of the impatient children, now in the antechamber, were building.

"One last thing." Drosselmeier finished arranging his great gift on a low table. He had built it in four pieces for easier transport, and affixed it with tabs, small bolts, braces. A broad assemblage of a fairy-tale palace, with turrets and a drawbridge and a central courtyard. Drosselmeier had painted it in shades of buttercream with blue shadows and red tile roofs, and he'd hidden a music box in the empty space of the chapel. A key for winding the music fit into a slot in the back of the chapel. He'd made a hiding place for the key in a walnut that he'd parted with a small-toothed saw. Pried its halves apart with an awl, and then reattached them with a small brass hinge with tiny screws. The whole thing was painted with gold leaf and fitted with string.

Drosselmeier wound the music box. It made a few hesitant plinks, then settled into a merry tune not unfit for dancing. If tin soldiers and wooden figurines might be so moved as to dance. Satisfied, Drosselmeier tucked the little key into the hollowed-out golden walnut shell. He hung the secret among the other marvels and baubles festooning the tannenbaum, including a dozen other golden walnuts on strings. Decoys.

"I think you've outdone yourself, Drosselmeier," said Sebastian with just a hint of disapproval.

"Let them enter while the music is playing; it runs down in just a few moments."

Beginning to warm to the drama of it, Sebastian slid open the doors. Fritz came tiptoeing forward, eyes wide with greed and adoration. Clothilde was behind him, carrying Klara. The girl's head was too heavy to lift off her mother's shoulder, so Clothilde rotated, giving Klara access to the view. The child smiled before putting her thumb back in her mouth.

"Oh, a castle!" cried Fritz, finally letting the clue of music distract him from the balm and seduction of candlelight. At this Klara tried to straighten up. Her mother supported her back. "It has little figures in the windows, and they're moving!" cried Klara.

"They're at their own Christmas feast. They don't know about ours. They don't know we are watching. Luckily they are very polite and they cannot be embarrassed. They are moved by music," said Drosselmeier.

"Do they fight?" asked Fritz. "You may not know this, but we're in desperate need of reinforcements."

"I doubt they fight, but I do think they dance extremely well," commented the godfather, though as the music slowed down, the dancers began to flag, too. Fritz tried to poke the residents through the unglassed windows. "Don't, you'll dislodge them from their tracks, and it'll be nearly impossible to reestablish them. They'll spend their lives lying on the floor, unable to see out the windows."

"Stupid peasants if all they can do is dance."

"It's a holiday, not a military call to arms."

"How do we get them to dance again?"

"Ah, there is magic in this music, but you must find the key.

It's not far. Be patient. It will not stay hidden for long. Magic never does."

Fritz lost interest at once and began to root among the other gifts. Clothilde settled her daughter on the settee. They began to ferry small wrapped presents to her. Klara was too listless to work the wrappings, so her mother helped her but let Klara finger out the little treasures one by one.

A small wooden cat bought from some toy maker other than her godfather. "I think that creature has little personality," observed Drosselmeier coolly. Despite being under the weather, Klara had the good sense to drop it on the floor.

A bear wearing a bishop's mitre.

A fisherwoman with a net. Under her shawl she had a fish face.

"A person from Spain?" asked Klara of a small carved señora featuring a real scrap of lace as her mantilla.

"Only one, I didn't have time to make her a lover. I hope she won't be lonely."

"She looks nice. She will like everyone else."

"But can a Spanish lady talk to the Russian men and the Chinese rice farmers? I am never sure if they can talk together."

"Of course they do, Godfather. They speak the same language."

"Not Spanish or Russian? Or Mandarin?"

"No—it's the language of Toy."

"Oh."

"Children speak it, too, so that is convenient," said Klara.

"Don't get excited," said her mother. "It'll wear you out. Fritz, have you something to share?"

Fritz had made some drawings as presents for his parents and sister and godfather. His gift to Drosselmeier showed a regiment of sclerotic soldiers with raised bayonets, each one apparently ready to drive his weapon into the skull of the man standing in line in front of him, except the lead soldier, who was bravely facing down a monster of imprecise species. "There's about to be a bloodbath," said Drosselmeier. "I admire the courage of the league of men and also their uncanny resemblance. Identical quadruplets, perhaps? But tell me, dear Fritz, is this enemy a lion shorn of its mane, or perhaps a wild horse having a difficult day? Having left its eye-patch at home? That one eye is immense. Compelling."

"It's a spy for the King of the Mice." Fritz was offended, but not very. "Can't you see his mouse tail?"

"Beg pardon. A magnificent specimen."

"I did a better one for Klara," he admitted. "This one was a little messy. You see the last soldier's feet are on backward. I forgot by the time I got to the knees and there was no room to make them go forward."

"All the better for running back to camp and calling for rein-forcements," said his godfather.

"Mine has a *very* good King Mouse." Klara spoke more vividly than she'd done so far. She leaned forward to show her godfather.

"Really, you're making quite much of nonsense," murmured Clothilde to all of them, but Drosselmeier arranged the paper at a distance where viewing could be clearest.

"Now, this is quite a success, I agree," said Drosselmeier. "Why seven heads?"

"Because he's the King," said Klara. "Everybody knows that."

"I was practicing heads, but they look pretty good all together, no?" whispered Fritz to Drosselmeier.

"That's what the King looks like," insisted Klara.

"And mine is . . . a lovely flower," said Clothilde, with motherly insincerity.

"You explain mine," said Sebastian, holding up a muddle for all to see.

"I didn't get to finish," said his son.

"I see. A fine study of procrastination, and I shall treasure it."

"What is going to happen in the battle?" asked Drosselmeier, "or has it already happened?"

"It's happening tonight," said Klara.

"What are they fighting over?"

"Dirk, please. It's Christmas Eve," said Clothilde, but her daughter was looking around the room, trying to make sense of the question.

"It must be the tree," she said. Dirk felt the wind from outside come up through the sleeves of his coat somehow, as if he were catching Klara's fever.

"The tree is very beautiful, I agree," he said, "but mice don't live in a tree. Why do they want it?"

"The tree is hung with walnuts," she said. "Walnuts are good for eating—and the mice are hungry during the wintertime. Snow on the ground. They have to come indoors."

"I suppose so. And the King of the Mice has seven mouths to feed, all his own."

"But you need walnuts to plant other trees, too. Walnuts are seeds, aren't they? They grow in trees."

"We need seeds to grow trees; that's true."

"The toys live in the tannenbaum, because it's Christmas and the tree is magic now. If the mice win and swarm the tree, over-run it—how horrible, it will become brown and die. But the toys need it. So they will fight to the death to save their own home. Look at so many of them hanging on strings there! It's their home."

"I insist," said Clothilde at last in a voice that could not be gainsaid. But she needn't have worried as far as Drosselmeier was concerned. He was standing, suddenly feeling frail, and he shambled from the room, knocking against the doorsill as he went.

89.

Drosselmeier knew that at the far end of the long black-and-white-tiled atrium, toward the back of the Stahlbaum house, a set of steps descended to a pair of double doors opening into the garden. Sometimes in the early summer, before the family left for Meritor, Clothilde would invite friends over and serve hock and strawberries under the lindens. It was a bit of a French garden, the way the linden trees were planted in a box formation, all sixteen slim trunks pruned to rise like pillars, branches joining overhead. Drosselmeier was fond of linden. When he did carvings of figurines, linden wood proved supple, accommodating. He knew that no less than Grinling Gibbons had formed linden wood into all sorts of delicacies, as the wood could mimic the details of genuine botany.

Tonight, however, Drosselmeier was more aware of the balsams beyond the stately center of the garden, those that grew up against the stone walls that edged the property. Shaggier than those firs whose limbs lifted upward like the arms of a candelabra or menorah. The snow, which had kept falling since Drosselmeier had arrived with his presents, weighed down the branches of these balsam trees like thatch, turning them into the heaped, furred folds of somnolent woodland animals sleeping on their massive feet.

Breasting the margin on the right side of the garden, being overtaken by growing trees, stood a stone pedestal. Upon it capered a satyr or Caliban of some sort, his leer less erotic than furrowed with worry. Opposite him, through the formal grove on the other side of the garden, a twin pediment featured something like a dryad. At this hour, the stone was black and her filmy garments a sort of nubbly white, but Drosselmeier knew she was usually greened with a light moss, hers being a north-facing prospect.

For the first time, Drosselmeier wondered if poor lost Felix had installed these statues out of some vague homage to the silly story Drosselmeier could now barely remember. At any rate, the stone characters had been here forever, looking out season after season at Sebastian and Günther as they grew, and now at Klara and Fritz. The eternal lusty youth, the eternal maiden. Keats again: "For ever panting and for ever young."

Without his coat, no hat on his thinning pate, in his dainty dancing shoes, Drosselmeier left footprints on the shallow stone steps and descended to enter, and pass through, the chamber of lindens. He reached the margin of fir trees beyond. There was no doubt that the Stahlbaum house was behind him where he'd left it, rising its shoulders to the equal of its neighbors. But the sense of the house was gone. The trees in front of him shrouded the world. It was as if they met behind him as water does when you wade drunkenly into the sea.

One day he would finish the job of dying he'd begun in child-hood.

He put his hands over his face and leaned into the arms of the trees, trying to push among them as if there was someplace to arrive beyond—someplace other than the stone wall of the garden. In this nighttime, the trees in their white lace looked less umber and forest green than they did black, as if they were inked approximations of trees. But they wouldn't let him in. They linked their limbs against him. He lost the balance of his feet and leaned into them. Their arms wouldn't let him fall to the ground, but they wouldn't enfold him either.

Perhaps he murmured *Felix?* or maybe he just thought it. So Godfather Drosselmeier has finally grown old enough to learn how to be lonely.

It wasn't Clothilde or Sebastian who brought him around, but little Fritz, who had dampened his own stockings to come tug on Drosselmeier's sleeve. "You've missed the best surprise," he said in an aggrieved way. "Klara has found a box with a Nutcracker in it."

90.

B ut where did he come from?" asked Klara.

"He was once a handsome young boy," said Drossel-meier, "but he didn't find love in time, and this is what happens to some of us."

"Can he really crack nuts?" asked Fritz, and dove around the room to various crystal dishes. But they were filled with softly yielding marzipan fruits.

"Why is he so ugly?" asked Klara.

Drosselmeier thought about that. "He was going to marry your doll, Pirlipat, when he was a very young and handsome prince."

"Even though the Mouse Queen bit her and her head went limp?"

"Oh, is that what happened? Ach: But even the ugly deserve rescue. He was going to rescue her. He was a handsome young prince and he searched the wide world until he found a tree with a magic walnut hanging on it, called Krakatuk, which would restore her to her health and vigor. But before he could give it to her, he tripped over backward and dropped it, and a curse caused him to turn old and wooden. So then Pirlipat wouldn't marry him, and sent him away."

"I never liked her very much. She's upstairs under the bed. She can't come down tonight. Is the Nutcracker really old or does he only look old?"

"Nobody is ever *really* old," said Drosselmeier.

"Aha!" cried Fritz. "I found it! Krakatuk! Among the other walnuts!"

He was turning from the tannenbaum. His clever eyes had scissored their glance more quickly than fever-sullen Klara could do. The golden walnut with the minuscule gold hinges and clasp mechanism sat in his palm like a glowing lump of coal, a deified strawberry.

"Ah, you're ahead of yourself." Drosselmeier tried not to sound cross. Klara became so excited she began to cough. Both her godfather and her parents turned to her in worry, Clothilde lifting a cloth to Klara's mouth. While their attention was diverted, Fritz lunged for the old Nutcracker and shoved the golden walnut in his mouth. Drosselmeier pivoted in horror at the sound of the crack. The beautiful walnut was spoiled, its halves rolling away on the floor. The secret key hung on its red thread from a splinter of wood of the Nutcracker's jaw, which dragged at a dreadful angle, as if he had suffered a fit. The latest thrush feather, its rachis broken, had fallen out to the carpet.

Klara's coughing was now fueled by anger and panic. She couldn't stop herself. Drosselmeier stood at once and led Fritz by the hand out of the room, mastering an impulse to give the boy a swift slap. The sound of coughing followed them and could be heard behind the closed doors.

91.

Clothilde bundled Klara upstairs and organized a mustard-plaster for her chest while Sebastian ushered Drosselmeier, Fritz, and a few elderly neighbors and business associates into the dining chamber. The family had outdone itself with festivity. The food was ornate in the French style, and some of the adornments to the table were edible. The elderly ladies cooed over Fritz and lowered their lorgnettes to regard Drosselmeier behind his eye-patch. As they roped him into conversation he realized that they weren't his seniors but his peers. One of them had hairs upon her chin and another wore a shade of puce so revolting that it put Drosselmeier off his meal.

Without Klara at the table, time taken for a holiday meal seemed pointless.

Fritz was allowed to march new soldiers up and down the napery until, wreathed in apologies, Clothilde finally arrived and took her seat. She waved the soup away and plunged into the fish. "But how is she feeling?" asked Drosselmeier when, for a blessed moment, all the other table guests were involved in chatter.

"She will be better for a good night's sleep. Too much excitement, I fear," said Clothilde with a faint air of censure.

"I'll offer my good evenings to the guests after the main course, and forgo the pudding, and I'll slip upstairs," he said.

"I cannot sanction that."

"I am her godfather. It is my place."

To this Clothilde had no reply, and she turned to the guest at her right.

The snow fell upon the lindens, upon the Pan and the Pythia, or the Bacchus and the Athena, or the gnome and the goddess, whoever in heaven or hell they might be. The dark forest beyond the arithmetic of garden leaned in like an army circling the house at night, waiting for all the lights to be extinguished. It came down, merely, to this: Can a child be saved?

"I shall come back in the morning with a small pot of glue, and set up the Nutcracker's jaw. He shall be right as rain by this time tomorrow," said Drosselmeier to Fritz. "But for tonight, I'll bind it with one of Klara's ribbons to keep the wood from splitting further. That was a silly thing for you to do, you know."

"What is the key for?" asked the boy with shocking lack of penitence.

"There are two keyholes in the back of the fairy castle. The key fits in both. Inserted in the top keyhole, the key winds up the music. But if you put it in the bottom keyhole, the key unlocks the castle itself. Like the golden walnut in which it was hidden, the castle itself is hinged. The buildings around its courtyard can open their arms to make a large platz. A whole kingdom making a hug."

"For soldiers to march in!"

"Yes, I suppose, and also all the figures I have made for you over the years. The animals, and Mother Ginger, and the capering Arabian nomads and the Kings of Sheba and the merchants of Cathay and the Ukrainian peasants. They all have a home in the fairy castle." He looked about. "It is like this dining table at a holiday. Everyone is welcome."

"Even the boring old ladies," murmured Fritz.

"No one is left out. Where is the key now?"

"Papi locked it in the glass-fronted cupboard. He was angry at me for ruining your gift. Nothing is going right tonight. Klara is sick, and the mice are frightening her. I think they are planning an attack."

"A good thing you have so many new soldiers to help defend the castle."

"But the key is locked up, and I can't get it. And so we can't open the castle to let the others rush in for protection during the battle."

"The toys can help in the battle."

"Mother Ginger? I doubt it!"

"Never underestimate the value of a mother in wartime. She has the most to fight for."

Fritz thrust his lower lip forward, unconvinced. "What do *you* have to fight for?"

"I can't sit here and have stupid conversations like this," he replied, and pushed back his chair. The old woman sitting across from Drosselmeier thought he was talking to her, and she stuck out her tongue at him.

92.

Though he knew Clothilde would be vexed, Drosselmeier made his way across the black-and-white tiles and mounted the steps at the back of the atrium. He paused for breath at the first landing. The housekeeper or perhaps Clothilde had drawn the drapes across the broad window there, so if there were armies massing in the night, anything at all happening in the back garden below, he couldn't see it. He stifled his urge to inch the drapes apart.

The door to the nursery was open a little. A lamp trimmed low was burning upon the mantel. Drosselmeier put his hand on the doorknob and leaned in.

"I knew you'd come," said Klara. "It's not fair that I should be sick on Christmas Eve."

"It's nor fair you should be sick at all. May I come in?"

"Mama will scold." She beckoned. Her hair was fanned out across her pillow.

"I brought you a marzipan pig from the side table. You could adopt him or eat him, I don't mind which."

"*He* probably minds." She took a big bite so there was nothing left but his face. "But too bad." The snout and eyes in her palm looked up complacently at her. She gobbled them down. "You never told me why you have an eye-patch."

"You never asked me." He sat silently on the stool by her bed-side.

She pouted. "Are you going to make me ask?"

"Not at all."

Still he sat silently.

"All right," she said, cross with him, "why do you wear an eye-patch?"

"I lost my eye when I was a little boy."

"Oh." She licked marzipan pig crumbs off her forefinger and sighed. For a while she just lay there in the half-dark, closing one eye and then the other in turn, practicing what it might feel like. "I think," she concluded, "maybe a shark found it and ate it."

"It was in the woods."

"A very rare shark, then, a forest shark. Or a wolf."

"That's more like it. Are you feeling up for a story?"

"You're trying to distract me from the mice, aren't you." She pointed at Fräulein Pirlipat, whose head was now almost en-tirely severed from her body. She maintained a certain composure throughout her ordeals, managing to seem both acquainted with grief and philosophic about it. "That's what they'll do to me next."

"I'm going to leave the Nutcracker downstairs to defend you, my dear. That's why I brought him. You're in the finest hands. He's a very capable soldier."

"He is an old man with a white beard."

"He is a young man inside, and strong."

"Fritz broke his jaw." She began to cry a little. "The Nutcracker might have helped, but nothing can help."

"Nonsense. He merely needs to be bolstered. He needs a token to remind him what he is fighting for. That's why I came up. A soldier or a knight always likes to have a memento of his beloved when he goes into battle. I wanted to borrow a ribbon of yours. I will bind up his jaw with it, as we do when we have a bad tooth. Tomorrow morning I will come back with a pot of glue and make him all better. And you will be better, too. I insist."

Klara didn't say anything for a long time. Drosselmeier thought she might have fallen back to sleep. But then she said, "A pink tape came off one of my dancing slippers. If you think that would do, you will find it on the chest of drawers with a bobbin of thread. No one has had the time to fix it yet."

"This will do nicely," he said. It was cool and smooth, and in the half-light of the lowered gas lamp the pink ribbon took on the color of a French-German child's inner forearm. He coiled it in his palm. "Klara."

She didn't speak, but opened her eyes.

"I hope Fritz doesn't ever touch you."

"Of course he touches me. We fight all the time."

"But never more than that. Don't ever let him. Will you promise me that?"

"What are you asking her to promise?" asked Clothilde, appearing at the doorway. "I thought you'd be here. This won't do at all. You must leave at once."

93.

His workshop looked cold and abandoned. He passed through it without turning a Teutonic knight on his horse to face a different damsel, without rearranging a wood-and-plaster set of the Brementown musicians. It was as if all figures of play were frozen if there wasn't to be a child like Klara to inspire them to life.

The building was chillier than usual because he'd been out most of the afternoon and evening and let the fire die down. He dressed for sleeping and he piled extra blankets and an old coat on top of the bed. Sometimes at night he read by the light of a candle—he had the new tales of Andersen in translation, and something called *A Christmas Carol* by that Englishman everyone went on about. But he had set the book aside at the Ghost of Christmas Past. It wasn't the ghost that was improbable, but the possibility of a happy past.

He blew out the candle.

Klara has my childhood, he thought. She is my childhood brought forward, the one that died in me.

And he enjoyed at last a small spasm of something he'd rarely noticed in himself: understanding.

So that's why I've spent my life making toys.

He tossed and turned to keep warm. He thought of the girl's clever imagination, its readiness to receive a serving of story. It isn't only Klara, of course, but that fine-grained soil of childhood itself that can receive a seed of mystery and recognize when it starts to flower.

Midnight bells announcing the sacred day. Somewhere, a skirmish of mice and toys raged back and forth across a parlor floor.

If he did sleep, he didn't mark the passage by dreaming. Dream may be many other things besides, but at its heart it is the primary proof of sleep. In dreams, as he had heard people say over and over, the world is rearranged. Battles are fought, and refought; the terms of life are overturned, reinterpreted; the columns of figures add up to new answers.

Klara could walk along the coast at Meritor hand in hand with her godfather and with Fritz and chatter for twenty minutes about where she had been in her dreams the night before, until Fritz got bored and began to pitch stones at the seagulls, and Klara's recitation eventually trailed off. The dreams never seemed to crest to a finale, like an opera. They failed, perhaps for lack of energy or, perhaps, due to Klara's inability to remember.

Admittedly, Drosselmeier had rarely had a dream in his life worth remembering upon waking. All his visions, were they visions, had visited him on some flooring other than ordinary sleep. Yet across that floor rolled a walnut, containing a secret vision sacred to some child or other.

94.

As invited, Godfather Drosselmeier arrived at the Stahlbaum residence shortly before luncheon on Christmas Day.

"Ach, things went from bad to worse in the middle of the night, but they've stabilized this morning," said Sebastian, pouring a cup of whipped eggnog for the old man. "Fritz is glazed with greed and pleasure, and Klara's fever seems to have broken overnight, despite her misadventures."

"Oh?" Drosselmeier tried not to bolt from the parlor and head up the stairs. Though in any case he wasn't much for bolting these ways. The word would have to be *creak* or *toddle*.

He turned, studying Sebastian to distract himself from the curiosity about Klara's evening. He noted the way Sebastian's chin and lower lip seemed newly segmented—in fact, just the way the jaw of a wooden Nutcracker slips into the casing of its cheeks. Those lines running from the corners of his nostrils along the sides of his mouth. Worry was aging Sebastian. And if he is aging, though Drosselmeier, remembering the first time he himself had been brought to this house by Felix, and met that galloping boy in these rooms, the same is true for me. Elderly, but not wise. An old fool.

A shaming tear stole from his eye, though whether this was about the lost boy Sebastian once had been, or the lost boy Drosselmeier had never himself managed to be, the old man didn't know. But he thought of Nastaran suddenly, and her hunger for the locked and forbidden garden of her childhood.

"Klara is on the mend, perhaps, though it's probably too soon to be certain," said Sebastian. "Each crisis seems like the final one, but thank God . . . But have you caught a germ from her, my dear Godfather Drosselmeier? You're looking peaky. Let me add a tot of rum to your eggnog."

"Don't bother, you'll have me singing sad arias, and that would be a dreadful error, as I can't carry a tune." Drosselmeier set his cup in the saucer definitively. "And what happened over there?" He had noticed the glass-fronted curio cabinet.

"Ah, evidence of the mishaps of the young," said Sebastian. "Fritz slept through it, but both Clothilde and I were awakened at the crash. It happened in the middle of the night."

"A burglar?"

"It was an inside job." Sebastian's eyes twinkled tiredly. "You may interview the miscreant in her cell if you choose."

Liberty granted, Drosselmeier mounted the stairs. The drapes were flung open, and the garden was domestic. Its evening mysteries, had there been any, were erased by the smudges of snow that blandished all.

Heading around the corner to the first-floor landing, he thought, I didn't even notice what the faun and the dryad looked like today. Perhaps they weren't even there—they'd stepped off their pedestals in some sort of miracle of the Nativity. Gone out to take a meal together in the Odeonsplatz. Or left to examine *Eros and the Painter*, the latest work of Nikolaus Gysis, or some other artist prominent in the the Munich School. Or a concert of sacred cantatas by Bach.

What a pair of guardian angels to be dogging me my whole life, he thought. The only way to be free of them is to die, so there is nothing left for them to guard.

Or to die again, perhaps.

The door to Klara's room was wide open this morning. Clothilde was sitting in an upholstered rocking chair diligently stitching that pink tape from Klara's dancing shoe—the one Drosselmeier had used as a poultice for the Nutcracker—around the neck of Fräulein Pirlipat. "I think more than one inhabitant of the nursery deserves therapeutic tending," Clothilde said to Drosselmeier. She made as if to rise, but he stilled her and leaned down to graze her cheek with his whiskers. "Klara's doll seemed to have slipped dangerously near some guillotine, but I'm resolved to tend to her wounds." How flush and relaxed, Clothilde, to enter into the spirit of it like that.

He looked at Klara, who was just waking again. Her arm was done up in a sling of some sort. "What in heaven's name?" he cried.

"Godfather Drosselmeier," she replied, and smiled a great lopsided grin. "Did you hear we won?"

"I see you are better," he observed. "So something was won. Whatever happened?"

"I woke up in the middle of the night. Ach, I was worried about the poor Nutcracker! He was left all alone in the downstairs parlor. I thought his jaw must be hurting, having cracked itself on that golden walnut. So I dragged my coverlet down the stairs and lay on the settee and looked at the tree. Even thought the candles had all been whuffed out, the snow-light through the windows made the tree seem to sparkle. Then about midnight? When the clocks all struck? The King of the Mice came out to bite my head off, like Pirlipat's. Despite his broken jaw, the Nutcracker roused Fritz's armies into battle. All the toys from around the world joined in.

Back and forth across the carpet they fought, and I thought the Nutcracker and his regiment was winning until guess who came to join the enemy's side!"

"Who?"

Klara pointed at the doll. "This traitor! Bad doll! She must have been poisoned by that bite. It was very unrespectable of her. I think she's sorry this morning, but last night she was an Amazon, and her help turned the tide against the Nutcracker. They began to take him prisoner and drag him into the underground. Then they would come back for me. I was so frightened that I knelt up on the sofa and I took my dancing slipper—the one without the tape, you know—and I threw it at the King of the Mice. I accidentally broke the glass in the curio cabinet, and the panes of broken glass fell everywhere. A piece of glass fell like a sharp knife and cut off the tail of the King of the Mice. And you know what that means."

"I don't know what that means."

"You can't be King without a tail. Not if you are a mouse. So all the mice fled in disarray and confusion. And then, since the glass was gone, I climbed up and reached in and got the key. And we opened the music and we opened the fairy castle and we all went to that land."

Drosselmeier glanced furtively at Clothilde. She was not protesting. Under her capable hands, Pirlipat was almost fixed. The rebellious doll looked abashed as well as reconstructed.

"The land you have always told me about," Klara said. "You know. The place where magic things happen."

"I think it was the jagged glass in the door of the cabinet that scraped your arm," observed Klara's mother.

"No, it was the sword of the King of the Mice. I was there, too. In the battle. Please, did you bring the pot of glue?"

"Of course. Would you like to eat it with a spoon?"

"Godfather Drosselmeier!" She almost snorted.

"I'll fix the Nutcracker. You have to fix yourself," he said.

"I'm very much almost all better already," she replied. "Aren't I, Maman?"

"You have a way to go. And I am going to sleep in here with you tonight to make sure you don't go wandering about again." She put down her needle and reached out to feel Klara's forehead. Her own face was softened in a way Drosselmeier hadn't seen in years. "You're not out of the woods yet."

95.

When Klara had nodded off again, cradling the Nutcracker in the crook of her sling, Clothilde motioned to Drosselmeier. They stood outside the door and spoke in hushed voices.

"We had to send for the doctor in the middle of the night, did you hear?" she said. "Her fever was raving. She'd been throwing toys around the parlor as far as we could tell. She was right about the key though; she did extract it from the curio cabinet and open the fairy castle to its fullest extent. We must have been sleeping deeply, as we didn't hear the crash—instead it was the melody from the music box that slowly and gently woke us. When we stole downstairs we found her in the dark, sweating through a dream that made her moan."

"She's made a great recovery. I'm so relieved."

"The doctor said she is still in danger. She must rest quietly. That is hard for her. If you can help in the next few days . . ."

"How can I help?"

"You will make me beg you?" But she knew she didn't have to beg. "Your fancifulness occupies her in a way her father and I can't possibly match. She must be kept to bed for a few days, perhaps a week. Last night may have been the turning point of the current crisis, but she mustn't be allowed to slip backward. Recovery is a long process. We'd be broken if we lost her, Dirk. Quite, quite broken."

"Of course, you know I should be honored to be of assistance."

"And forgive me if I was ill-tempered last night," she finished.

"You were worried. We all were worried."

"We must remain worried."

Later that day, when Drosselmeier was allowed to have a plate of his Christmas supper upstairs while Klara had hers in bed, he said to her, "I know your parents want you to get better for their own selfish reasons. I mean, they love you and all that."

"Why do you sound sad when you say that?"

He didn't answer. "More to the point, my dear goddaughter, is that you have to get better because I need you."

"Can we get married when I grow up?"

"What a lovely idea. But I'm afraid I shall be too old by then. So you'll have to find your own prince somewhere else. Or someone. Maybe not a prince. It's hard to tell this early. No, I need you for something other than a wife."

She pouted, but said, "What can I do for you? You're so old."

"That is exactly it. I have a problem I have never been able to solve."

"I'm not good at sums."

"It is not addition or subtraction. My problem has to do with the Little Lost Forest."

"What is that?"

"Haven't I told you before?" He told her again. He didn't mention the faun and the dryad, the Pan and the Pythia, whoever they

— 274 —

were; let those creatures stay in stone, frozen in a northern garden. They had frightened him as a boy, and he wouldn't pass that on to Klara. He simply said, "I know of a sacred forest that needs to have a home. It needs someplace to grow. But I don't know where it should be."

"Is this real," she asked, "or is this a story?"

"Well," he said, "that I don't know, either. But I'm afraid I'm getting too old to find out. If I haven't located a home for the sacred forest yet, I shall have to leave the job to someone else. Will you take on that chore?"

"Where is the sacred forest?"

"I'm not certain," he said. "I suppose it may be all around, disguised as the garden. Or perhaps it is hiding in the depths of the Black Forest. I think it's been wandering for a very long time looking for a place it can root, and grow, and make itself at home. If you could go to the fairy-tale land last night, perhaps you can find a way to send the forest there, too. It might be willing to grow and thrive in a place like that."

"Godfather," she said, "but you *made* the fairy-tale land."

"I only built it," he said. "You visited. I gave you the key. You opened the lock."

96.

Clothilde said, "I always sensed that he liked Klara better than he liked us."

Sebastian took her elbow. "He had a way with children. An appeal that worked upon me, too, until I grew up. I felt it was my fault, a little."

"Growing up?"

"Well—not quite. But—losing track of something he wanted to give to me. Losing the way to hear him."

"Nonsense. That's sentimental. You were always kind to him, don't forget."

"It's odd, isn't it, that there isn't more—more fuss over his death."

"Who mourns a toy maker? Toys get broken, and so do their makers."

Sebastian was silent. They sat alone in the chapel. "I'm not quite sure a Protestant burial is the right thing," he said finally. "But I never heard him profess any sort of faith, really."

"He was raised by a minister somewhere south of here, wasn't he? That's evidence enough. Besides, he was godfather to our children."

"Yes. But what god or gods did he represent to them?"

Clothilde had no answer for that. "Klara will be distraught to hear about this when she is back from her honeymoon."

"I'm glad there's no way to reach her for another week. Let us see the old man to his grave. It is something we can do for our young bride."

As the minister entered for the service, the side door opened and Fritz slipped in, too. He knelt upon the stone floor for a moment and his shoulders shook with a wretched sort of abandon. Then he took a seat next to his mother. The stone walls of the chapel closed them all in, a prelude to mausoleum finality, though the eternal sky through colorless panes appeared to make an argument otherwise. Exalting, if ultimately unpersuasive.

Coda

Hiddensee

All her life Klara was gifted with dreams and pestered by them, too.

She enjoyed a full-throated if perhaps innocuous life. She outlived her own children and lost several of her grandsons in the Great War, by which point her daytime memory failed her completely. She used to sit and look out at the few remaining linden trees next to the third-hand Daimler that belonged to the upstairs tenants. She was too deaf to hear the occasional ruckus of brownshirts in the streets.

When she was failing and needed removal to an asylum for the elderly, her surviving grandchildren cleared out the several ground-floor rooms in the old family house in Munich to which she had been reduced.

There were too many copies of her stories, printed in German journals and also translated into English. Those of Klara's tales that had been collected and published in fine gift editions at the turn of the century were set aside for younger generations of the family. They were children's stuff. Sweet gingery old pfeffernusse that she was, Klara had had a life, after all, and someday someone might want to read through the nicer volumes of what remained of Großmutter

Klara's work and see if there was anything worth remembering. The rest was tinder.

If you were standing on the landing of the stairs, you could see the grandchildren—Felix's great-great-grandchildren!—bringing the literature to the flame. The stacks of old *St. Nicholas* magazines made a glorious bloom in the bonfire. That bookburning was also going on that season in the Konigsplatz was a coincidence upon which no one remarked.

The night before she died, her last night on earth, Klara had a particularly vivid dream. It was like a dream she'd had before, though maybe in different form. It seemed familiar. It began in the yellow parlor of her childhood. Mice, and a grotesque huge ugly doll-child, and small carved figurines, Citizens from Around the World, some set or other. The dream included toy soldiers, and a rampage of wild mice that were more like wolves, really. And a nutcracker. The battle was joined and won, and Klara went on to visit a serenely peculiar and fitting land in which food and drink, music and dance, love and laughter were cunningly made all of a single piece, somehow.

This part of the dream Klara had had before, but the next part was new.

She understood this much, that she would have no words to tell anyone about it when she woke up. She'd been beyond words for some time now. She didn't know that, in fact, she would never entirely wake up after this.

Still, the dream.

She was a child at her grandfather's house up at the sea. Meritor. In actuality she hadn't been there in over half a century, and who knew if it even still stood or if it had fallen down the battered bluffs. In her dream she wasn't tall enough to reach the handle to the front door. She couldn't get out. The house was growing spooky, dark as a tomb, and she needed to go out into the open, but she couldn't get out.

Then she realized she had the Nutcracker crooked in her arm. She held him up as high as she could, and he reached up and worked the latch and turned the knob. The door swung open, and they both stepped over the sill.

A stiff wind was howling around the corner of the house. The sky was bright and cloudless but not quite blue—rather more like mother-of-pearl. She could stand and look one way and then the other, to see if anyone was coming along the strand. No one was.

She saw the spit of Rügen descending from the north, on the right-hand side of the horizon. After a stretch of open water, she saw the island of Hiddensee on her left. She had always meant to go there, but it had never yet happened.

She walked to the edge of the water. The Nutcracker looked up at her with a quizzical expression. She took out a key and inserted it into a buttonhole on his fancy red coat, and his breast-plate opened in two halves like a severed walnut falling apart at the seam. It was empty as a drawer at the end of summer when she was all packed to return from Meritor and go to school.

She took Godfather Drosselmeier out of her apron pocket and said, I guess this is where you go. He was very small, like the toys she used to have when she was little. Only three or four inches. She could tell it was her godfather because of his eye-patch. But the visible eye was closed.

She laid him into the breast of the Nutcracker and closed the two halves of the red coat. She didn't lock the coat closed in case he ever wanted to come out.

The waves pressed into the shore in long rocking motions— gentle swipes against the world.

She set the Nutcracker on his back to float in the foam by her feet. One of her feet was clad in a pink dancing slipper and the other was bare. With her bare foot she nudged the Nutcracker away from the shore, as if he were a little boat like the kind Fritz used to play with in tidal pools.

Fritz would be coming soon. She missed him and wanted to see him but she didn't want him to wreck everything as usual, so she pushed the Nutcracker a little harder. She wanted it to float beyond easy reach.

She thought she heard Fritz shout for her. She did hear him. She turned to see. He must be beyond the bluff, he was calling her, he would be here soon, around that barrage of stranded rocks, but she couldn't see him yet. She turned back to watch the Nutcracker float away.

He had moved out onto the busy foam as if on another military campaign—this one naval. Who knew he would be so clever at sea?

Of course he would be that clever.

She expected to lose sight of him as more and more ranks of waves drew their white parallel lines from left to right between the Nutcracker out to sea and Klara left on shore. But his red coat remained visible, a dot on the blue-black steel of the waves and the glass-green of the waves and the white lips of the waves.

Then he was beyond the pounding of the tide and going farther out, and still through the spray she could see him on his back, that old Nutcracker. His head was facing one way and his feet the other, so he was long and low like the spit of Rügen, like Hiddensee.

She realized with a glad clasp of her heart in her chest that he wasn't drowning, he wasn't sinking. He wasn't even diminishing. He broke the laws of perspective, holding his own shape and size the farther out to sea he went.

He was on the horizon now. A broad swath of red on the horizon like a sunset, only he was as large as Hiddensee. He was a bridge between Rügen Island and Hiddensee. He was an island, he was a land unto himself, he was a whole place. He *was* that other place, the Nutcracker: It was he, himself, a sovereign kingdom built of himself.

She rubbed her eyes against the grit of the wind and the smudge of atmosphere, for finally the mists that always collect around horizons at sea were blurring the edges of the Nutcracker. She peered again. He had separated from Rügen and begun to drift behind Hiddensee. She might never see him again. She rubbed and rubbed, and it seemed to her that the red of his coat and the black of his hat and the white furze of his beard had gone green and black and bristled like a forested nation, a refuge out on its own on the high water.

Over the sound of the waves and despite that distance, some sounds rose that made Klara's heart feel bright and yearning, itself rising in accord. She heard some music, pipes perhaps, a stringed instrument, a tambour, and the sound of children at play— not the high shrieking of school-yard mayhem, but the quieter murmur of children in small groups, working, reading, thinking, laughing. With the kind of sobriety, so often forgotten, that children possess. The trees hid the children from view—maybe toys were playing there, maybe even mice. In any case, above that ground-level murmur of children in the sacred grove, she could make out the threaded notes of a thrush's song. Perhaps all the sweeter for being so long delayed.

Das Ende

Acknowledgments

- Marc Platt at Universal Studios, for asking the question about the Nutcracker.
- Betty Levin, for inspiration and friendship these forty years and counting.
- Barbara Harrison and the team of *The Examined Life: Greek Studies in the Schools,* and also that of its sister organization, *Children's Literature New England,* for welcoming me back to Greece—especially Olympia, where this novel was seeded.
- Bob Piller and Beatrice von Mach, for dearly valued friendship and for travel assistance and companionship from Zürich to Meersburg and beyond.
- Jill Paton Walsh, whose Hellenophilia has been constant and contagious.
- Vivien Rameau, of München, for advice on Bavaria and on the German language (any mistakes are mine, for failing to ask the right questions).
- Christine Johner, M.A., Abteilungsleitung, Kultur & Museum, Stadt Meersburg am Bodensee, for answering

questions about Meersburg in the nineteenth century and especially about Mesmer.

- Moses Cardona, of John Hawkins and Associates, literary agents.

- Cassie Jones, Liate Stehlik, and the rest of the great team at William Morrow and HarperCollins US.

- Scott McKowen, for the arresting cover artwork on the U.S. edition.

- Ann Fitch, Rafique Keshavjee, and Andy Newman, for comments upon the manuscript, read in parts or entire.

- Nikos Trivoulidis and Christos Lygas, at whose Athens home—a home in the Plaka once owned by Irene Papas!— sections of *Hiddensee* were first read aloud. On a rooftop terrace, just below the Acropolis and the temple called the Erechtheion, as the April evening fell. Elysium.

- Mara Kanari, ambassador-goddess of Greece to the scholars and fellows of the Examined Life: Greek Studies in the Schools, for embodying the ideals of Greece, which yet survive, stamped on living generations.

- Eva Varellas Kanellis and Panos Kanellis of the American Farm School in Thessaloniki (site of the GM Writing Center), for steady friendship.

- The stalwarts of IBBY/Greece, who nominated GM for the Astrid Lindgren Memorial Prize: Vagelis Iliopolous, Eva Kaliskami, and Vassiliki Nika; and the staff of the I. M. Panagiotopoulos School in Pallini, Athens, for their continuing welcome.

- Zacharias and Ana Tarpagos, flautists of Rafina, Athens, for heightening readings of *Hiddensee* with melodies of Greece and of Tchaikovsky.

ACKNOWLEDGMENTS

- The Gregory family of Albany, New York, and the far-flung Yiannapolous family, especially cousins from Kato Toumba, Thessaloniki, for keeping lit the flame of family feeling.
- The Prabhaker family of Northampton, especially L.L.P., for serving me at the Boys and Adders Café. We all get to come home sometimes.